Wildflowers and Kisses

By

Jaclyn M. Hawkes

Spirit Dance Books™

What readers are saying about Jaclyn's books:

"Was so excited for this book's debut that I forked over $8 for in-flight WiFi just to be able to download it. Jaclyn has a gift for giving her characters a fullness of personality, spirit and intellect that make them come to life. Her dialogue is quick, real and witty. I can only imagine what her life is like to have spawned the ideas, wisdom and humor she brings to her books."
                                    Ms. Janie

"Extremely well written. Hard to put down and do other things."
                                    Margaret Morrison

"Excellent book! Everything I have read from this author has been incredible. This book pulls on the heart strings and will wash out your eyes many times. I loved it!"   Jess Bybee

"This was another great Jaclyn M. Hawkes story. There was a damsel in distress. A knight in shining armor. A villain. Lots of angst and misunderstandings. The chemistry is always yummy and clean, the best kind!"   Cici J

"Oh man this book was awesome! I started this book by crying, and ended it the same way. Keep up the great work!"

                                    Erinzachjj

"I'm so grateful for this book. It's clearly a wonderful read! I couldn't put it down! Thank you." Michelle Reding

"Once again, Jaclyn has written a wonderful novel of love, redemption, suspense and family ties. I love each and every one of her books and look forward to the next."   Dahl

Dedication:

This book is dedicated to my beautiful youngest daughter. Like the heroine of this book, she is happy to the bone and always chooses to dance in the rain and laugh in the face of a storm. If life gave her lemons, she would probably sigh, and then smile and go on about how much she absolutely LOVES lemonade. Voted "Happyy Pants" of the fifth grade, she sings, she dances on her tippy toes, and she laughs. Her attitude is a precious gift, and I am so very grateful to have the honor of being her mother.

It is also dedicated to my best friend and husband, her daddy. He is the rock that keeps our family steady and strong, and I truly adore him. With him around, it's no wonder she stays happy!

Acknowledgements:

Thanks again to everyone on my Spirit Dance Books team who help my stories make it all the way into publication. I could never do this without you. Some of you help by encouraging me, and some of you help by being brutally honest about my mistakes, but it all works out in the end. (Sorry, Mand, that this one ended up with a mushy title.)

And thanks to my mom, who is always my best fan. She is the world's most enthusiastic book promoter, even if she's just slightly loopy from the anesthetic of a recent surgery. All those doctor's and nurses will buy books, I'm sure of it, Mom. How could they resist you in those compression socks?

Chapter One

The Medicare auditor pulled up yet another set of files and Dr. Gage Garrison glanced at his watch and sighed. They'd been at this for nine hours already today, just like they'd been at it for several days before this, and honestly, there didn't appear to be an end in sight.

Even though in all this time, they had unearthed three marginally questionable bills, the man across the desk from him was on a blood scent somewhere and seemed absolutely convinced he'd find some earth shaking misdeed if he just kept at it long enough. Either that or he took infinite pleasure in torturing his fellow law-abiding Americans because he could. At any rate, Gage felt years older than he had a mere week ago and any thought of accomplishing actual work with his time here in the office had become wishful thinking.

When his faithful secretary, Sandy, knocked and walked in carrying a long suit bag, Gage felt like he'd been saved by the bell. As much as he had tried to almost grovel to keep the auditor mollified, leaving a child hanging outranked even the federal government and he tossed his pen onto the desk as Sandy hung the bag inside the nearby closet and said, "The florist closes at six, and Sophie will be one heartbroken seven year old if you fail to show up, bouquet in hand."

She glanced pointedly at the auditor and continued, "Even Uncle Sam goes home by this time on Friday evening."

Gage glanced at his watch again, stood up and shoved his chair back. "Thank you, Sandy. I had no idea it was after five thirty already." He turned to the auditor. "I'm sorry, Donald, but I've suddenly become a surrogate parent and staying later isn't an option. We'll have to pick up where we left off on Monday."

Checking the time again, he realized there was no way that was going to make it home to dress and back to the florist and he shrugged out of his suit coat, draped it across the back of his desk chair and reached up and loosened his tie. He grabbed the suit bag out of the closet and headed for the door, speaking to his secretary over his shoulder, "Would you mind helping him pack up, Sandy? And do you have the address to that florist?"

She handed him a Post It with the directions written on it in her neat, concise handwriting and a disposable razor as he went past. "Fourteenth south and Crestview. She said you can't miss it. Look for the windows full of flowers. It's between a coffee shop and a dry cleaners in a little strip mall. Oh, and have the tux back by five tomorrow night. If you want you can bring it in with you in the morning and I'll drop it by on my way home. You are coming in tomorrow, aren't you?"

He looked at the auditor again, wondering if he said yes if he'd have to agree to meet with him over the weekend and then answered, "I have to, to try to catch up on everything I haven't gotten done this week, Sandy. Would you mind dropping the tux? That would really help."

"Not a problem. Just change and get out of here. I'll have Rich bring your car around to the front door."

"What would I do without you?"

"After the week you've had, you don't even want to think about that. Enjoy the ballet."

Gage grimaced as they stepped out and she laughed. "Oh, stop. A bunch of beautiful, athletic women in leotards can't be all that bad. At least they're not singing opera in some foreign language."

"It's not the dancing I'm concerned with. Russ's sister Candice is going to be there."

"That I can't help you with. You should have gotten a date."

He sighed again and pulled his tie off. "And just when would I have had time to have found a date?"

She pushed him down the hall. "Get used to it. Donald doesn't seem to be winding down at all. This might be a long month. Or six."

Gage groaned. "I think I feel a bout of clinical depression setting in just at the thought."

Sandy laughed again. "At least it'll keep your mind off of Candice."

He was worrying about Candice again forty minutes later as he pulled into the little strip mall parking lot and all but screeched to a halt in front of the shop that was indeed filled with huge pots and baskets of growing flowers of every shade and variety imaginable. In the deepening darkness, the well lighted shop fairly glowed through the huge windows in spite of the metal gate that had been pulled all the way across the front. The sight of that gate would have completely disgusted him if it hadn't been for the gorgeous blonde woman he could see inside tending to the myriad containers of living color. Crossing his fingers that she was an amiable gorgeous blonde, he got out of the car and smiled as he knocked on the door.

****

After waiting an extra fifteen minutes for some doctor who had requested a small bouquet, Skye Alexander put the flowers back into the big walk-in cooler and pulled the huge color pots that stood sentinel outside the flower shop door inside. Pulling the metal gate closed, she began to lock up, glancing out at the street festooned with red and green Christmas decorations as she did so. When nothing but Christmas decorations in this desert town appeared out of place, she took a deep breath and squared her shoulders, wishing the little Italian restaurant down the block delivered. Francesca's clam chowder would have been perfect on this December night.

With the click of the second deadbolt on the door, she spoke to the big brindle boxer that padded loyally beside her everywhere she went as she put her shop to bed for the night. "Well, Kitty, Kitty, another Friday come and gone. What do you say you and me spend a lovely, dynamic night beside the fire with a crossword puzzle?"

The dog simply looked at her with those wise brown eyes as if to say, "You and I both know that sounds miserably lonely, but whatever, Mistress."

Skye patted her and spoke to her in German and instantly her sleepy, mellow, waggy canine demeanor perked up as she clicked into guard mode. She didn't bark or growl or even stop padding around behind Skye, but there was no mistaking the alertness that signaled the change in responsibility from gentle companion animal to guard dog.

Skye finished locking up and had begun the sometimes overwhelming task of watering all of the containers and pots that needed to be cared for before she could retire to the tiny apartment at the back of the shop. She looked up as a sleek, forest green Jaguar darted into the lot outside and a striking dark haired man stepped out and approached the locked door. He would have been extraordinarily handsome even without the tuxedo and luxury car, but with them and especially with the smile he unleashed as she looked up, he was positively lethal.

She couldn't help but grin back as she began to unlock the door. She would have opened back up for most anyone, but it wasn't every day you got to rescue a dreamboat physician in a tux and a Jag from going wherever he was headed empty handed.

"You must be the doctor in desperate need of flowers. Come on in. I'll get them out of the cooler."

As he walked in, Kitty began to growl and Skye spoke to her in German before heading into the shop as he followed her saying, "And you must be the angel of mercy who will let me in twenty minutes after closing time. Thank you. I'm sorry I'm so late."

Skye returned with his flowers and smiled as she went to ring them up. "You're very welcome. I was just putting all the pots to bed anyway." Her smile widened as she took in his obvious haste in getting there. As gorgeous as he was, his collar was still turned up on a decidedly lopsided bowtie below a jaw line that sported a tiny piece of tissue he'd stuck on a nick from shaving. He was still straightening the satin cummerbund at his waist and his hair had a rebellious curl near his temple that had chosen to point down instead of back smoothly with the rest of its counterparts.

As he laid his money down, she picked up a spray bottle of water she used to mist flowers and walked around the counter with a grin. "You look like a million bucks, but this little guy . . . " She gave the rebel curl a spritz. "He's a bit out of control." She smoothed it back and laughed as he put up a hand to protect himself with a look of smiling disbelief.

"Please tell me that's water and that you're not fertilizing me."

"Pure H2O. You're absolutely safe." She grinned as she gave him another shot, smoothed the offending curl back into place again and then reached up and straightened his collar. With another laugh, she dampened a sheet of paper towel with a third shot and then gently smoothed the tissue off the shaving cut and tossed it into the garbage beside her before reaching up and untying the off-center bow.

He chuckled but then said, "Oh, man! What did you go and do that for? I spent days tying that thing. That was the reason I was late in the first place. My secretary ordered it and I forget to tell her I'm bowtie impaired and need the prefab tied kind you just clip on."

He went to tie it again and she playfully patted his hands away and began to repair the damage. "Oh, stop whining. I'm a florist. I'm definitely not bow impaired. Where are you going all dressed to kill? My goodness you hammered this thing. What did you do to it?"

"It was self defense. I swear." She gave the bowtie a shot of water this time as he continued, "The ballet. Where else but the Nutcracker would a perfectly respectable human being wear a get up like this in the burgeoning city of St. George, Utah?"

She paused in her tying for a moment and remembered wistfully, "Oh, the Nutcracker. My mother used to take me to the Nutcracker every year at this time when I was a little girl. We'd dress all up and go out to dinner and then to the ballet and I thought I was a princess. For years I aspired to be Clara and wanted my own tin soldier." She finished the tie and gave it a gentle pat and smiled up into devastatingly blue eyes. "There now. You look positively lethal. Your ballerina will probably swoon."

She made his change and handed it back to him as he was thoughtful for a second before he took it. Finally, he said, "So . . . I have an idea. Come to the ballet with me."

Laughing, she commented, "Oh, I'm sure the woman on the receiving end of these would love that."

"Sophie is seven. I'm sort of her uncle and her parents are out of the country so it's up to me to be the doting papa after her stellar performance. She is Clara by the way. C'mon. Wearing this is bad enough without showing up solo."

Skye grinned at him as she picked up her watering can again. "I'm sure it wasn't from the lack of willing female admirers. Sadly, I can't go to the ballet. I have to water my plants."

He laughed right out loud at that. "Oh, man! That is the all time most brutal brush off I've ever heard in my life. My ego will never recover."

She grinned again. "Yeah, I'm sure. I really do have to water everything. Then Kitty and I were going to have an appointment with a crossword puzzle in my little apartment back there." She walked around behind a behemoth flowering pot and said mildly, "And I never go out with men as devastatingly handsome as you. They can't be trusted."

He followed her, shaking his head and chuckling and said, "Talk about adding insult to injury." He pushed on. "There was a compliment in there somewhere and I refuse to accept being bested by a crossword puzzle and a dog. And I'm choosing to ignore that snatty little trailer because I'm sure a woman as astute as yourself can tell that I'm trustworthy. But in the interest of staying trusted, you should know that I'm fluent in German and know exactly what you told the dog. Besides, you chose to trust me before you ever decided to unlock your little fortress here and let me in. What's with all the security, anyway? This is a pretty quiet town. Have florists become the new hot spot for burglary all the sudden?"

As she continued to water she said almost breezily, "The last doctor I went out with turned out to be a stalker. That's another reason I can't go. I never date doctors anymore."

"I'm not a real doctor. I'm a chiropractor, not an MD. C'mon. Please say you'll come. Sophie's aunt Candice is going to be there and she tends to think I'm on the menu. Think of it as a mercy mission."

Skye turned to look him up and down and then glanced out at his car and laughed again. "Yeah. I'm sure you're in desperate need of a mercy mission. You definitely do look good enough to eat, though. You can't be serious. You're in a tux and I'm in a canvas apron, and you're already late."

"I was only late to reach your shop before you closed. The ballet doesn't start for another hour. And I have no doubt that you have a knock out little black dress tucked away somewhere that will look great with this tux. Go put it on. You love the ballet." He came to stand directly in front of her and looked into her eyes. "Remember?"

She studied him seriously for a minute and then said almost to herself, "I really do. I can't believe I'm letting you talk me into this. I don't even know your name."

Putting out a hand, he said, "Gage Garrison. Nice to meet you."

She reached around and untied her apron. "Throw in a bowl of Francesca's clam chowder and I'll rescue you from the cannibalistic Candice."

"Deal. That was a terrible pun."

"Hey, I didn't name her. Blame her mother. I'll hurry. Here." She handed him her watering can. "Give all the biggest pots one gallon. No more. I've already done this side." With that, she tossed her apron onto a nearby counter and walked into the back, wondering if she'd suddenly lost her mind.

****

Gage watched her walk through a door at the back of her shop and had to laugh. What a spunky, funny, beautiful little wildflower she was! If he had known he would meet someone this entertaining tonight he wouldn't have been dreading this evening so much. And it wasn't really that he was dreading the ballet and Sophie. It was Candice that had been such a downer and this girl had hopefully just solved that issue quite nicely. At least for tonight, anyway.

He walked from plant to plant, watering and musing about the beautiful girl who had given him a shot with her flower spray bottle the first moment he'd met her. Here he didn't even know her name and he was watering her plants and waiting to take her out. He could hardly even fathom it. It had been forever since he'd met someone he'd honestly wanted to go out with.

As he refilled the watering can, he looked around her shop. It was a unique mix of organized business and free form, unrestrained vibrant living color. This shop exactly fit the sunny, unfettered personality she exuded like her flowers exuded fragrance.

She'd left him out here with her cash register, but then she'd also left that dog that had gone from snarling beast to sweet old pooch with a couple of words in German. He'd heard of dogs that were trained that way, but he'd never seen one. He glanced at the huge boxer that was watching him across there. Yeah, no doubt the cash register was absolutely safe with Kitty on duty.

He'd made it through about half of the largest of the planters and stopped to study a photo taped to the door of the cooler. It was a stunning scene of an Irish countryside above the blue ocean and stark white sea foam of the wild coastline below it. The light on the green of the vegetation brightened it to the truest emerald, but in the distance a storm gathered glorious dark piling clouds with curtains of rain falling from them. The photo appeared to glow with brilliant color and it brought that same, soul deep longing he had ever had to go again to this Emerald Isle of his ancestry.

He reached out and touched the white line of the surf where it crashed up onto the lonely, beautiful beach. He was going back there someday. He'd been once. And it had been both wonderful and disappointing. The country had been incredibly beautiful, but the friend he'd been going with had canceled at the last minute and he'd gone alone. And while it had been glorious, he'd needed someone to share the glory with. Ireland alone had been lonely. He'd vowed then to go back, but with a friend that he could revel in the experience with.

Hearing a sound from her back room he glanced up, thinking she had excellent taste in photographs. Exactly nine minutes from the time she had disappeared, she reappeared, now as absolutely dressed to kill as she had intimated he was earlier. She was indeed in a breath-taking black dress, heels and sexy dangling earrings that changed her from the dynamic and teasing wildflower into a classy and alluring temptress. For just a moment the shocking difference held him speechless as he stared at her. *Holy Moses! Talk about smoking hot! Now that was a transformation! And he'd thought she was gorgeous in her apron and carrying a watering can!*

He didn't realize he was staring until she hesitantly waved a hand in front of his face and looked at him doubtfully. "Is something wrong? Do I not look okay? I can go change again."

Still a little astounded at the beauty before him, he assured her quickly, "No! No, you're perfect. Don't change. But okay is decidedly the wrong adjective. I'm going to need to stop and find something a little nicer to wear in order to accompany you is all."

She rolled her eyes and smiled as she began to turn out some of the lights. "Are you always this much of a Romeo? I don't believe I've ever met someone who can take being turned down several times and still blithely flatter like you."

He held the door for her. "I'm never a Romeo. In fact, I'm categorically opposed to all forms of Romeo-ing. That had nothing to do with flattery. I was being absolutely sincere. You look perfect." She looked at him skeptically, but he met her eyes and then helped her pull the heavy metal gate closed again over the entrance. As he held the car door for her, he asked, "You aren't really named Daisy, are you?" He nodded to the shop sign that read Miss Daisy's.

Sliding into the sleek car with the grace of a dancer, she didn't miss a beat as she replied, "No, Tulip. Tulip Von Snowdrop."

After walking around the car and getting in, he glanced sideways at her as he went to start up the ignition. "Yeah, and I'm Howdy Doody. Point me toward Francesca's, Ms. Von Snowdrop."

At that, she let out a peal of laughter as light-hearted as her personality appeared to be. "Two lights down on the left, Mr. Doody."

The cat was out of the bag as soon as they walked into the tiny elegant Italian restaurant and the hostess gave a low whistle and grinned at his Tulip as she said, "Look at you, Skye! That is you, isn't it?" The hostess took two menus and laughed up at Gage. "And here with Prince Charming! You go girl! Come on back." Gage raised his eyebrows at his date as he followed the two women to a private booth near the rear of the intimate little dining room. Skye fit her. Her eyes were the perfect blue for it and she seemed to provide her own style of pure oxygen.

Even though he was ravenous, he watched Skye for a few seconds before glancing down at his menu. That she was a regular was obvious as the two young women chatted and laughed together for a moment. When the hostess left, Skye got back up and came over to his side of the booth and slid in beside him and pointed a slender hand to the parchment in his. "I hope you like Italian. If you do, you'll love this place." She looked back up at him. "Or have you been here before?"

"I've never been here and I love Italian. I'm starving, but we should probably hurry. What do you recommend?"

"I recommend it all."

He set the menu down. "Perfect."

That made her laugh again as she picked it back up. "I thought you said we needed to hurry."

"How big is the clam chowder? Will it tide me over until after the ballet?"

She looked up at him and glanced him up and down and then shook her head. "No."

Feeling the phone in his breast pocket buzz, he pulled it out and glanced at it to make sure it wasn't Sophie having an emergency, grimaced when he saw the number and put it back in his pocket. "Sorry. I don't usually do that, but then I don't usually need to worry about a little girl either. How about a salad and some kind of bread with the soup? Will that work?"

"Add a dessert and you'll be fine." She set the menu down and got up and went back to her own side of the booth as she commented. "I thought medical professionals always had to take their calls."

He pushed the menu to the edge of the table to signal the server. "I used to think that too when I really was more of a medical professional. Now I've come full circle and have decided that most of the patients who call me after hours aren't desperately in need of adjustment. And honestly, I'm behind a desk now far more than I'm behind a patient. The lion's share of my time is spent managing the practices and the building."

"Practices? Plural?"

"My dad helped me build the clinic right out of school and I leased some of the other office space to doctors and then hired some to man the rest. We weren't sure at the time if that was the best way to go, but on paper it looked good. It turned out to be perfect for the boom St. George has been having. With all the retirees who come here, the clientele grew faster than I ever dreamed. I was able to pay my dad back for all the start up capital in less than two years. So yeah, now I'm basically several doctors' boss and their landlord."

A server brought a hot loaf of Italian bread that smelled like heaven and she sliced off a thick slab and handed it to him as she asked, "Are you just being matter-of-fact, or are you not happy with all of that lightning success?"

That made him think for a minute as he buttered the hot bread. He was happy, wasn't he? After all, he had it all, didn't he? He glanced back up at the blue eyes that were watching him so quietly.

Finally, he said, "That's probably not the best question for me tonight. I'm a week into a Medicare audit. You probably don't know what that means, but just trust me when I tell you that auditors from the federal government don't particularly care if you're honest or not. They just enjoy the power trip of trying to find anything they can pin on you and watching you struggle as they make you jump through their hoops. They know they're in complete control of your whole life and it's like a drug to them. At least the ones I've had to deal with. It's like he's just hoping he can fine me millions and millions of dollars for filling the forms out wrong. He's been camped out in my office so long I'm beginning to wonder if he plans to just stay until he can either find something or until he's ruined my business, whichever comes first."

She didn't say anything right away and he finally asked, "That sounded really negative, didn't it?"

Still looking at him quietly, she smiled and nodded. "Yes. But it's okay." The server brought their soup and then Skye continued, "Sometimes it's good just to have someone listen to you vent and then you feel better and can move on. Do you really stand the chance of being fined millions?"

He thought about that too as he watched her take a bite. "Anything is possible, I suppose. I know there hasn't been any criminal wrong-doing. But whether there have been honest mistakes that I'll be held accountable for remains to be seen. The government billing processes are hopelessly involved, so mistakes do happen from time to time. It's simply the nature of the beast. And it's me who has to ultimately take responsibility, even though it's the billing office staff who does the paperwork."

"But you're also the one who drives the Jag and has the houseboat on Powell, so it all evens out in the end." She grinned at him. "I'm Skye, by the way. Skye Alexander. Thanks for feeding me. I was dreaming of this chowder. Have you ever tried it with lemon? It's to die for." He smiled as he watched her squeeze a lemon wedge that had automatically been brought with her bowl into the creamy liquid and then offer him one.

He began to squeeze it into his own bowl as he shook his head and laughed. "How did you know I have a houseboat on Powell? You didn't go into your back room and do some sneaky background check on me in the hours you were gone, did you?"

She laughed. "What? And check out your portfolio before actually getting into the Jag? Please tell me you're not serious. I apparently didn't turn you down enough times. The houseboat thing was simply making a point. Are you joking? Do you really have one?"

"I never admit to a houseboat on a first date. I wouldn't even have brought the car if I'd known I was going to be tempted by the flower lady. I have an old compact I keep just for special occasions like first dates. It weeds out the mercenaries quite nicely."

She laughed again and shook her head. "I almost think you're being serious. You really do?" All he did was look up at her and she laughed that incredibly musical laugh one more time. "Oh, that is priceless! How many actually go out a second time?"

He smiled. "You're making the assumption that I have time for a social life with all of my various government oversight monopolizing me."

Her sky blue eyes sparkled as she said, "Now you're being negative again. If you don't like the hassle, sell the whole deal and go to Margueritaville, but don't whine about it. You're the one who built your empire. Most people would be forever grateful. It could certainly be worse. You could be stuck in an old compact."

"You have a point."

They ate quietly for a few minutes and then she said, "You know, there was a time when women actually expected men to be the breadwinners while they were the nurturers, and making sure the men they dated made a respectable living was not only appropriate but, necessary. Maybe those mercenary women were only being prudent."

He thought back to the last several women he'd dated since becoming relatively comfortably well off and shook his head. No, those women had anything but nurturing on their minds. They were definitely just mercenary. Somehow it had been a long time since he had even met anyone who seemed the slightest bit nurturing. The only women he came in contact with were usually career oriented types looking for not much more than a houseboat on Powell and a weekly nail touch up. He didn't tell Skye that though. "Maybe. Then again, maybe the prudent ones think an old compact *is* financially responsible. You know, use it up, wear it out. That old adage."

"There you have it then, Mr. Doody. You've got the women of this world all figured out and the next stop is a cure for cancer. Your management prowess is commendable. Did you like the lemon? Now there's the real enigma to a man in control like yourself."

"The lemon really is good. How did you figure that one out? I'd have never thought of lemon in clam chowder."

There came that magical laugh again. "Didn't you ever have those sleepover Friday nights when you were a kid and you made experimental food with your buddy? You know, avocado pancakes and maraschino cherry and butterscotch milkshakes?"

He laughed and shook his head again. "I must have missed that part of my upbringing. Usually on Friday nights as a kid I was honestly so tired from football practice or baseball that I fell asleep while everyone else must have been doing the avocado experiments. My sisters used to do terrible things like paint my toenails when I crashed so early. I was a terrible bore. Until I woke up and saw my toes. Then I got pretty lively."

She grinned. "Somehow, I can't picture the man in the tux with toenail polish."

"Which is a good thing." He glanced at his watch and pulled some cash from his pocket and tossed it on the table. "I think I'd better save the desert. We need to be going soon. How close are you to being finished, my little Petunia?"

"Ready when you are, Howdy." She picked up her clutch from the bench beside her and stood with a smile. "I don't believe I've ever been anyone's little Petunia before."

He put a hand to the small of her back as they made their way to the front of the restaurant. "It'll be a whole new experience for you. Maybe you'll finally get that tin soldier."

****

As Skye felt his hand gently on her back and then when he offered his hand to help her down the steps of the restaurant, she wondered if maybe he wasn't right. Maybe the tin soldier thing wasn't as much of a distant dream as it had seemed lately. It had been forever since she'd been on a date and she'd almost begun to succeed in telling herself that male companionship wasn't really all it was cracked up to be.

She hadn't been joking when she'd told him the last doctor had turned out to be a stalker. That experience had long ago turned dreams of any kind of a white knight into the cold harsh reality of a nightmare that had her much more concerned with personal security than any real or pretend prince charming. Still, tonight had been fun. Not once had she second guessed her decision to open the shop back up and let him in and then even consent to going out with him. He'd been right. Somehow, she had known she could trust him before she'd ever decided to unlock her little fortress as he called it.

The drive to the Cox Performing Arts Center didn't take long and she walked into the foyer at his side, excited for the ballet. It had been a long, long time since she'd done this. They had hardly made it in the door when a beautifully costumed little ballerina launched herself from a side hall where she'd apparently been watching for him. "Uncle Gage! Uncle Gage! You made it!" Obviously small for her age, she fairly jumped to hug him and Skye smiled to see him pick her right up as he asked.

"Sophie, shouldn't you be backstage waiting for this to start? You're the star. What are you doing out here?"

"I was worried you wouldn't find it. I've been watching for you."

A pretty brown haired woman Skye hadn't seen at first took the girl's hand and tried to calm her down. "I'm sorry, Gage. I told her you would never get lost, but you know how she is."

The woman seemed to suddenly notice Skye and her glance was obviously not pleased as Gage put a casual arm around Skye's waist and turned back to Sophie with a smile. "Yes, I know exactly how she is. Beautiful, talented, smart, fun and all those other wonderful things. You look very pretty in your costume, Sophie. Say hello to my friend Skye and then you need to go find whoever is probably looking frantically for you right now. I'll bet they're worried."

Sophie giggled. "I'll bet she is too. She's freaking out tonight already. She's been so grouchy for the last couple of days." She put out her hand to Skye. "It's nice to meet you. Uncle Gagey is right though. I gotta go. See ya."

Gage set her down and she fairly skipped back the way she had come and the woman who must have been Aunt Candice glanced after her and then back at Gage as if wondering what to do and then hesitantly followed the little girl. Skye smiled as she heard Gage release a sigh. He gently nudged her toward the concert hall as he leaned close and said, "I so owe you. Thank you for agreeing to come."

In the crush of the crowd, Skye barely had to lean in to whisper, "Anything for you, Mr. Doody."

The ballet had been everything she remembered and more. Skye was surprised at how emotional it made her and she was glad for the low lights. It was strange, because she was definitely not that kind of a girl usually. As it ended, and they watched the last curtain call of the dancers, Sophie was obvious looking for her Uncle Gage and her face lit up as she saw him in the crowd. Afterward, they found her again and Gage gave her the fateful bouquet that had netted Skye this invitation. It had been the best evening she'd had in a long time and she was so glad she'd finally let him talk her into coming.

Sophie was still fairly bursting with energy even though it was nearly ten o'clock at night and she was thrilled when Gage offered to take her and Candice for a celebration dessert with them. Skye could see that Candice seriously considered coming with them as she studied Skye before finally bowing out and arranging for Gage to drop Sophie back with her afterward.

Sophie opted for a hot fudge sundae from Cold Stone. An ice cream parlor actually worked in this desert town even at Christmas time and the three of them trooped into the packed establishment in spite of their black tie attire. Skye was content to watch the little girl interact with her "uncle" as she enjoyed a sundae of her own.

Seeing him with the pretty, diminutive child put him in a whole new light from the handsome and smooth businessman he had seemed earlier. They obviously adored each other and were completely comfortable as he lifted her in his arms so she could see into the ice cream cooler to choose her flavors. He was a strikingly handsome man and stood out even more dressed as he was in the casual crowd. Several women were quite obviously watching him as he and the animated ballerina talked about the evening's performance.

Sophie finally wound down and, in fact, fell asleep in the back seat before they got her back to Candice. Gage simply picked her up and carried her inside as Skye waited in the car. Skye knew he'd probably only be a minute and that they were in a safe neighborhood in a safe town, but still, when Gage was far enough from the car not to notice the click, Skye reached over and pushed the lock button. Then as he was walking back out, she unlocked it again. She knew it was a little paranoid, but she'd learned to be paranoid the hard way.

It was only about fifteen minutes back to her shop and she wondered the whole way what to expect from him at her door. After all, she hardly knew this man and she could hardly expect him to know that she wasn't the type to even kiss on a first date, but then she hadn't been the type to go out with someone she didn't know either. The stupid thing was, she had thoroughly enjoyed this man tonight and to say that she had been attracted to him would have been a huge understatement. If she were honest, she'd admit that she wanted him to kiss her.

Instead of having him drop her back at the front of the shop, she had him take her around to the alleyway behind the strip mall where she could let herself in without dragging the gate open and shut. There were still bars on the windows and doors, but it was much more simple to get in. She glanced up at the neighbor's house next door and was glad there was still a light on. Mrs. Woo was still up so she could go over and check and make sure she'd taken her medicine.

He pulled up next to the little porch with the vine covered trellis and more pots of herbs growing beside it, shut off the car and turned to look at her in the street light without saying anything for a minute. She met his gaze candidly and reached over and placed her hand on top of his where it sat on the seat beside her. "Thank you for talking me into going to the ballet with you, Dr. Garrison. I had a wonderful time and I'm glad I didn't miss it. Your niece is adorable, not to mention a gifted ballerina."

He turned his hand over so it was palm up against hers without intertwining their fingers. "She is pretty cute, isn't she? I'm glad you finally gave in. In fact, I'm not really happy about letting you go yet, although I have to work tomorrow and I imagine you do too, so I guess it's for the best."

"Probably. I do have to work and actually Christmas time is one of a florist's busiest seasons. But you can come and help me tuck my sweet little adopted Grandmother in if you'd like. She just lives next door here. She's buried three husbands and five children and is alone and we've sort of taken each in. Come in and meet her while I make sure she took her medicine."

"Five children? That's awful."

"She's actually a Laotian refugee and they were all killed in the civil war there. She's only told me a little of what happened. It's a gruesome tale I can tell you, but she has somehow overcome it and is the most happy, positive, sunny little old soul you've ever met. You'll love her. But she's getting up there. Sometimes she just needs a little reminder to take her pills, and rides to the grocery store. She's still awake. I'm sure she'd love to meet you. She'll be so happy for me to have gone to the ballet."

He came around and helped her out and followed her the few steps to the door next to hers as she explained, "She used to own the dry cleaners, but she sold it and just kept the little apartment here in the back." Skye knocked quietly and then took out a key and they let themselves in as she called out softly, "Knock, knock, Sulee. It's just me. I've come to tell you goodnight, Mama Woo."

Mama Woo's voice came from inside and Skye led Gage into a small living room where a miniature Asian woman sat in front of a little TV, watching an old Perry Mason rerun. Skye went over and laid an arm around the tiny woman's shoulders. "Has he figured out who did it yet, Mama Woo?" Skye nodded at the TV.

"Oh, heaven yes. He almost ready tell whole jury how he knows. You look mos' lovely, Missy."

"I brought a friend with me. Isn't he just absolutely handsome in those fancy duds? This is Dr. Gage Garrison. He took me to the ballet tonight."

"Oh, my. The ballet. You both very nice, Skye." Mama Woo struggled for a moment to get out of her chair and then continued, "Let me get camera, Missy. You look too nice not have little picture. You think?"

Skye handed her the camera that lay on the nearby table. "I do think so, Mama Woo. Did you eat dinner?"

"Yes, I ate chicken you bring me yesday. It so good. Now stand here in front of door with friend. Yes, jus' like that."

Skye stood next to Gage and smiled as the little woman clicked off several photos and then Skye stepped away from him and reached for the camera. "I'm sure that's great, Mama Woo. Where is your medicine? Did you take it tonight?"

"I take with dinner." She got a perplexed look on her face. "At least think I take. Oh, my. Maybe better check for me, Missy." She turned to Gage. "Skye keeps Sulee together, bless heart. I don't know how manage without her. She's angel."

Skye took a compartmented medicine box, opened Friday night's section and took out the two little pills and then checked to make sure none of the other later compartments had been emptied. "No, I think you must have forgotten tonight, Mama Woo. Here you go." She handed over the pills and the water glass that was on the end table beside her. "Have you got everything you need?"

Mama Woo put a tiny arm around Skye's waist. "I fine, Missy. Just finish this silly show and go to bed. You go on and tell friend goodnight." She turned to Gage. "You kiss girl goodnight, you hear me, young mister? Life too short pass up chance like that, you think?"

Skye was horrified. "Sulee! Stop that." She could feel herself color as she apologized to Gage. "Sorry."

Gage just grinned and winked at Mama Woo. "Life is pretty short, isn't it, Mrs. Woo? You think I should?"

Mama Woo nodded definitively. "Absorutely. No regret later I always say. Now off go, you two."

Skye put her hands on her hips. "Since when do you always say that, Mama Woo?"

Clicking her tongue, Mama Woo nudged them toward the door. "Kissing to be done and here she sits ready argue. Docto' Garrison, I don't know what become of this new young missies. In my young, never passed up goodbye kiss from dreamboat. You talk sense with her. Or maybe no. Backwards isn't? Forget talk and get straight to good stuff." Patting his arm reassuringly, Mrs. Woo opened the door and pulled Skye toward it. "It lovely to meet you, Docto' Garrison. Don't forget advice now. I getting old, but I wise, you know." She fairly pushed them out the door and Skye had to laugh as they both stood there on the minimal porch and looked at each other.

Finally, Skye said, "Sorry. I had no idea she'd pull that on you. Forgive me. She's quite a character."

"That she is. So your story is she and you don't have this thing all pre-arranged that you take your dates in to tell her goodnight and she orders them to kiss you, huh?"

Skye laughed again at him. "Okay, I admit. It's all a ploy. I hired this slightly demented tiny Asian woman to help me get enough lip action. Most men find it absolutely alluring. How did you figure it out so quickly?"

"Oh, was she supposed to be being subtle? Or am I just very intuitive?"

"You're very something. I think it was you two who had this whole thing all pre-arranged."

They made it to Skye's tiny porch and she turned to look up at him, unsure of whether to laugh or worry as he smiled down at her and said, "I'm good, but I'm not good enough to orchestrate anything that perfect. I should hire her though. She's very persuasive."

"Is that the word?"

"I can't answer that. I've been ordered not to talk, remember?"

At that Skye did laugh and put a hand on his chest. "I wouldn't have pegged you as someone who obeys many orders."

He put his hands on her waist. "Well, there are orders and then there are orders."

She glanced at his mouth and then looked back up into his eyes. "I really shouldn't kiss you. I hardly know you."

"I know. I never kiss anyone on a first date. Especially ones I've just discovered. But what am I supposed to do about these orders? I'm sure the next time I see her she'll want a full report. You want me to face her and tell her I have regrets? Anyway, she's right. Life is short. I'm sure a woman who has buried three husbands and five children knows that brutally well."

"No. Don't kiss me because of Mrs. Woo. If you're going to kiss me, kiss me because you want to."

"I am definitely not doing anything because of Mrs. Woo. Trust me." He bent his head and watched her eyes for a long moment and then gently rubbed his cheek against hers and cupped her other cheek with his hand. "Yeah. I regret not kissing you, but I'd probably regret doing it more. Goodnight, Skye Alexander. Sleep tight and dream of tin soldiers."

Chapter 2

It was Wednesday. It had been five days since the ballet and she hadn't heard word one from him. Skye was so disappointed she was a little embarrassed. Even though she was inundated with orders on this week before Christmas, three times she had gotten online to find a phone number for him and then had decided against it. He knew where to find her if he wanted to see her again. Anyway, the last thing she needed was a male entanglement in her life right now. Her business was booming and she needed to milk that for all it was worth before Shane found out where she was and she had to pull up stakes and start over again somewhere.

This was the fourth time she'd moved to hide from Shane and started a business, and the start up was slow and costly every time. Before she had designed water gardens and then done landscaping, but she'd had to find something different each time she started over. She'd been here for almost a year now and even though she tried to be careful, she knew that eventually Shane would find her again. The only reason he hadn't already was that the narcotic addiction that had seemed to start all of this mess had also damaged his brain enough that he couldn't focus very well anymore. That and the money troubles it brought on were the only things that had saved her, she supposed.

The first time it had only taken him six months to find her, but she'd learned a lot about hiding her tracks since then and his addiction had gotten worse. Still, the longest she'd gone before he showed up before had only been eleven months. She knew that was the reason for the constant strain she could feel in the muscles of her neck and back lately. It was only a matter of time.

Knowing all of that didn't lessen the disappointment that had steadily grown over the last several days when she hadn't heard from the incredibly attractive Dr. Garrison. They'd hit it off so well that night that she had been sure he'd ask her out again. As the days stretched out, she felt more and more foolish for offering to let him kiss her that night. Kissing someone wasn't something she took very lightly and obviously he hadn't thought as much of her as she had of him.

She pulled a new bunch of roses toward her and began to strip the extra leaves and take off the thorns, then drew in a fast breath as she stabbed herself hard enough to draw blood. Darn that chiropractor. She hadn't been able to focus all week. Putting the bunch of roses back into the water, she glanced at her watch and went in search of a Band-Aid that she knew would stay put for maybe half an hour in this line of work. She decided it was time for lunch. The girl who helped her and made deliveries would be here soon and could watch the shop for a few minutes.

Kitty didn't even get up to follow her to the first aid kit. Somehow the dog seemed to know her mistress was a hint out of sorts this morning and had simply watched her typically sunny tempermanted owner go from task to task without even turning the radio on, which definitely wasn't like her. Skye stooped to pat the loyal canine's head. "I'm sorry, Kitty Kitty. I'm all kinds of a fool to let this bother me, aren't I? I'll do better this afternoon, I promise. Come on. We'll eat together. I'll even give you a bite of mine to make up for being a grump. What do you say?" The dog hopped up as Skye spoke to her and the stub of her tail wagging made her whole back end sway back and forth as if she was doing all she could to encourage this first sign of enthusiasm she'd seen all day. "I could learn from you, Kitty. We girls should all be as steady and dependable as you are. The world would be a better place for it."

Skye puttered for a few minutes until Hailee came in the front door and she greeted her, "Hey, Hai! How's it going?"

"Good thanks. Are we still busy?" The cheerful seventeen year old with the long red ponytail gave her a high five and then leaned down to pet the dog.

"Yes, thank goodness. I have a whole load of deliveries. Let me grab a bite of lunch and then I'll help you load the van. How was school? Are you ready for the break?"

Hailee grimaced and then laughed. "I'm ready. My geography project isn't. It's so hard to focus at Christmas, isn't it?"

You're telling me. Skye wasn't going to admit to this carefree teenager that her lack of focus involved a handsome doctor who drove a dark green Jag. "Just two more days, girl and then you're home free. What have you got planned for the break? Anything terribly exciting? Is Devon still going to be in Hawaii the whole time?"

Hailee's green eyes sparkled as she said, "Yeah. He's heading out the second school gets out, but there's this darling guy in my third hour who has kindly offered to keep me entertained while he's gone."

Skye laughed and shook her head. "It's too bad you'll have to spend the holidays pining away, huh? Devon will learn to hate warm, sunny beaches."

"Yeah, guys usually can't stand all those bikinis. Not. Nah, it's actually good. My mother has been worrying that I've liked him too long anyway. She's always reminding me about the prophet's counsel not to get serious at my age. I don't know what's up with her. It's only been, what? Two months. She knows I'm hopelessly fickle."

Skye put a hand on her shoulder and gave it a squeeze. "What's up with your mother is that she has this marvelously pretty and talented child who she knows has unlimited potential and she wants the best for her. She knows getting too serious with a guy right now could throw a major kink in this wonderful season of your life. These next few years are going to be so much fun and yet so vital to the eternities if you stay the course. She just loves you, Hai."

"You're right and I know it." Hailee grinned. "That's why I'm kind of looking forward to Devon being gone. It might be really fun!"

"Good. Be honest with them both, but that's the way seventeen is supposed to be. You need to get a taste of all the flavors so you'll know which one you really want to be with forever and ever." Skye turned toward her apartment. "I'll just be a few minutes."

She went back and warmed up leftovers from the night before and thumbed through a travel brochure as she ate. Giving the dog the promised tidbit, she rinsed her dishes, put them in the dishwasher and headed back into the shop, determined to focus and put thoughts of Gage Garrison completely out of her mind for the duration of the day.

As she was tying her apron back on, Hailee came over and handed her a beautifully wrapped long slender box with a card tucked under the gold metallic bow. "This incredibly hot man just brought this in and asked me to see that you got it, just before he got back into this sweet green Jag convertible. Is there something I should know? That I don't know? 'Cause I would love to know all the details."

Skye laughed as she took the package and felt all the frustration of the last few days dissipate. "There's nothing to know, nosy. I met him last week and we went out. He needed someone to go to his niece's dance thing with."

Still standing there expectantly, Hailee said, "And?"

Slipping the little card out of the envelope, Skye turned to go into her office and set the package down. "And nothing.

This is the first I've heard from him again." She gestured at the flowers Hailee was trimming. "Arrange something. There really aren't any details. At least ones I'm going to divulge, so give it up. It's not like I have your juicy love life."

Hailee went back to what she was doing and Skye sat down at her desk and pulled the hand written card out.

Skye,

I'm so sorry I haven't gotten back with you. Please forgive me. I'm still stuck with the federal auditor. But my mind is stuck somewhere in the vicinity of your porch. Please know I'm thinking of you - just in case the auditor never leaves. I had a wonderful evening with you,

Gage

For several seconds she held the card and looked at the bold signature, thinking back to that sweet, warm moment on her porch. She felt herself flush and put a hand to the cheek he'd caressed with his own. That had been better than any kiss she'd ever had. It was wonderful to know he was thinking about it too. And that he admitted it. That was sweet of him.

She set the card aside and opened the package and smiled again as she pulled out a beautiful tin soldier nutcracker. It was the perfect gift to commemorate what she hoped was their first date. It was kind of him to find it and send it to her when he was as busy as he was. It was just what she'd needed to mellow her out and help her to focus better on what she was supposed to be doing instead of wondering why he hadn't called.

Hailee came to the door of her office and poked her head inside. "What did he give you?"

She held up the tin soldier and got up and took it out and set it near her work table where she'd be able to see it as she arranged. "What is it?" Hailee obviously didn't see the romance in the whole deal.

"Haven't you ever seen the Nutcracker ballet? That's where he took me the other night. It's a ballet about a tin soldier nutcracker like that one."

"Oh. That is so sweet. And he was sooo cute. Where did you find him?"

Skye laughed as she began to load arrangements from the cooler out to the delivery van and chose to answer obtusely. "That's what was in the package, silly."

"I was talking about the hottie in the car, Skye."

"Oh, I didn't see the hottie in the car. I was inside eating, remember? You're the one who found the hottie in the car. You say he was cute?"

Hailee rolled her eyes. "Skye."

"He was probably just a delivery man. Don't you think? After all, you do know delivery people."

"Men who look like that don't become delivery men. Movie stars maybe. And a delivery Jaguar? Sure, Skye. Hey, you're not dating a movie star are you?"

That made Skye really laugh. "I'm not dating anyone, Hai. I went out with him once. And he's a chiropractor, not a movie star. Stop pestering me and get going, you little romantic. I'm sure by the time you get back I'll have more to deliver and then we need to take the flowers over to Hurricane for the Delaney wedding." They loaded the vases into the compartments built into the back of the van to hold them and Hailee waved as she finally pulled away and left Skye to put the finishing touches on the wedding flowers she was working on, next to the brightly colored tin soldier.

That night, Skye took the tin soldier and a paper sack full of Chinese take out over to Mama Woo's and ate dinner with her. Several times over the past few days Mama Woo had tried to get Skye to admit whether Gage had kissed her that night and Skye had smiled, but she would never tell her anything. When Mama Woo saw the nutcracker, she tried again. Skye just laughed as she served up the dinner and got out Mama Woo's medications.

Skye had picked up some photos for Mama Woo earlier in the week and Mama Woo went over and pulled several out of one of the packets and showed them to Skye as she was getting ready to leave. Some of them weren't centered and not terribly well focused, but one had turned out perfectly and Skye asked her if she could have a copy.

"Take them with Missy. More lovely couple I never see. You look like magazine at grocery store." Skye didn't say anything in reply, just looked again at the picture. There was definitely something about him.

She tucked the photos into the pocket of her jacket, called to Kitty and locked up behind her, and then she squared her shoulders as she got ready to go back across to her house in the dark of the late December night. As she stepped out, she scanned the short alleyway as she quietly spoke to the dog in German and then watched her closely, trusting to the dog's senses much more than to her own to know if danger waited outside. When the dog looked back at her and stepped out, Skye glanced around one more time and then hurried across to her own door and let them in and then locked back up behind her. Once inside, she sighed as she tossed her keys on the shelf beside the door.

It was an uncommonly beautiful night out there. A waxing moon played hide and seek with mystical, ethereal clouds and the effect was mysterious and romantic and wistful. She looked out the window where the beautiful moon now showed through the bars that covered her windows like the bars of a jail and tried not to feel bitter that she now felt she had to live like a prisoner while Shane had all the freedom in the world to enjoy the spell of the moon.

She sighed again. It wasn't right. It wasn't fair. But it was what it was and she dressed for bed, reminding herself that one of her spiritual gifts was a happy, positive outlook regardless of what the world chose to do around her. Shane had already taken a good portion of her freedom. She'd be darned if she was going to let him take her sunny attitude as well.

She had much to be grateful for, even if there was a psychotic man threatening her in the name of love. She had so many wonderful blessings from her health, to the gospel, to the fact that she had been blessed to be born an American with all the marvelous opportunities that so many in this world only dreamed of. As she brushed her teeth and puttered around her bed room, she counted her blessings and by the time she had read her scriptures and prayed, she could look back out at that fascinating moon, even through her bars and enjoy its sweet spell as she and her tin soldier settled into bed.

At four o'clock in the afternoon on Christmas Eve, Skye pulled in the big flower pots and tugged the heavy metal gate across the front of her store and secured it. If any hostess in town hadn't picked up her Christmas dinner centerpiece, it was now officially too late. Miss Daisy's was closed in honor of the Savior of the world's birth. Skye ran across to Mama Woo's and let herself in. "Sulee, I'm going to make a last minute run to the grocery store. Is there anything you'd like me to pick up for you when I do? Anything you forgot for our Christmas dinner tomorrow?"

Mama Woo smiled, albeit tiredly from her living room chair. "No. I fine dear. Have everything. But thank for asking." Skye came further into the room and put a gentle hand to the old woman's head.

"Are you feeling okay, Mama Woo? You don't sound like yourself. Or are you just tired? You don't have a fever."

Mama Woo smiled again. "I fine, Missy. Sometime Christmas just make me little blue. That so silly, doesn't it? Just sometimes homesick of family more than usual. We not had much at Christmas, but had each other. I know they in wondaful place, but I miss." Tears escaped from her faded, wrinkled eyes and slipped down her cheeks as Skye knelt beside her chair and put her arms around her and cried with her.

Skye didn't say anything. What could you say to someone who had seen her own children killed in front of her eyes in the most brutal fashion? What does one say to comfort someone whose loved ones had been tortured and murdered? Skye didn't even know how to grasp what this dear, sweet old woman had witnessed, let alone how to cope with it. She knelt beside her and they wept together for all the things that could have been if only the world would learn to embrace what the Christ child had offered all those centuries ago. Skye prayed as she knelt there, both to know how to comfort Mama Woo, and how to help in some small way to promote the sweet peace of Jesus in this crazy world around her.

That was one of the reasons she loved the plants and flowers. It was a way to bring happiness, and peace, and a sense that all was right in the world and that God was in His heaven and had blessed His children with many miracles like living, growing things.

At length, Mama Woo wiped at her tears and gently pushed Skye away. "Go, do shopping now, Missy. No feel sorry for me. I miss, but it sweet pain to sit here in memories. At least have family small time. Some never blessed with family at all. Let me remember and think on them and enjoy all good heartache. You go. Give me few hours to open heart for those days and times before I lose so much."

Skye patted the soft, creased cheek. "All right then, you remember and savor the good times especially. I'll be back soon." With that, she let herself back out and gathered up her purse from her house, put Kitty in the car and headed out.

She was at the meat counter, thinking about splurging on lobster tails for the two of them and wondering if something that festive would mock Mama Woo's heartache or help it, when someone touched her on the arm and said, "Hey, Skye."

For just a moment she thought Shane had found her and she started to spin and was half way to hitting Gage Garrison under the nose in a Tae Kwan Do strike when she realized it was his voice she was hearing. She gulped to swallow that instant adrenaline hit from the fear, took a deep breath and smiled to try to recover her cool. "Oh, Gage, you scared me. I had no idea anyone was right there."

"Sorry about that. Merry Christmas. Did you get the tin soldier?"

"I did. Thank you very much. He's the perfect memento." She looked at him closely and wondered if he was sick or just completely bone tired as she asked, "How did your audit turn out?"

Gage grimaced. "It hasn't turned out, yet. I've been working sixteen hour days since the ballet. The only reason I'm not still a prisoner of my office is that I think the guy's wife finally put her foot down and ordered him to come home. At least since he's a federal employee he gets to take several days over Christmas, so I have a bit of a reprieve to try and catch up. How did you do? Did you make it through all your Christmas orders?"

She glanced at her watch. "As of about twenty minutes ago." She smiled. "There were a couple of orders that never got picked up, but I only stay really late for bowtie impaired chiropractors. And I had some imperative last minute shopping to do before all the grocery stores closed. I've been working so much that I would have had to eat cold cereal for Christmas dinner if I didn't get here."

He nodded with a grin. "I know exactly what you mean."

She was still studying him and said, "Are you okay, Gage? Is it just that you're not in a tux, or are you as hammered as you look?"

He laughed at her brutal audacity. "I guess I can trust you to always level with me, anyway. I'm fine, just incredibly tired. But thanks for asking. Are you going with the lobster or king crab?" He nodded at the case in front of them.

"Neither probably. I was thinking about the lobster, but Mama Woo is a little depressed this evening. She's been thinking about her family and sent me to shop so she could have some time for the sweet, painful memories. Lobster sounds great, but it might not be appropriate. She's not really in the mood for festive."

"How much time does she need for her sad memories? Do you have time to come eat lobster with me before she needs you? I could definitely use some festive and I'm ravenous. What do you say?"

"I'd say sure, you can never have too much festive when there's lobster involved, but Kitty is in the car, so maybe another day."

"Kitty can come too. We'll even share our shellfish."

Skye laughed and shook her head. "All right, we'll come, but the dog isn't getting any lobster. That's taking festive over the top. So, are we going to have cold cereal with the lobster or should we find something else to go with it?"

"Definitely something other than cold cereal."

Half an hour later, they checked out with ridiculously few groceries for how long it had taken them to shop as they talked. They had settled on a prepackaged wild rice pilaf, asparagus that was outrageously expensive in December and a package of Poppin' Fresh breadsticks that Gage planned to make some cheesy, garlic thing with while Skye broiled the lobster with scampi butter. In keeping with the festive idea, they bought sparkling cranberry and pomegranate juice and for desert they were going to make a chocolate mousse pie together. Skye wasn't exactly sure how it would turn out, but she was definitely willing to give making it with him a try.

She followed him to his house in her car and although it was in an exclusive neighborhood, it was understated and welcoming and not at all a place that made a point of being affluent. As they carried the groceries into the kitchen from the garage, Kitty's toenails clicked on the stone tile in the mud room and Skye was glad to notice that his kitchen floor was hand scraped wood and the dog wouldn't damage it.

Gage left them in the kitchen while he went to get out of his suit and Skye looked around at his beautiful home as she began to unload the bags onto his granite countertop. It was elegant, but there was something that almost seemed forlorn in the big, perfectly decorated rooms that appeared to be completely unlived in. It was like walking into a decorator model and not one thing seemed out of place except in the kitchen and great room. They were the only rooms that looked used and had a homey feel.

Putting the butter into the microwave to soften, she was just about to start to dig into his cupboards to find a cutting board and knife when he came back in wearing a pair of faded jeans that looked perfectly broken in, a Southern Utah University sweat shirt and a pair of brown fleece slippers. It was a new side of him she hadn't seen, but if anything he looked better than ever, even as weary as he obviously was.

He stopped at a keypad in the doorway and pushed a couple of buttons. The sound system of the house began to emit soft Christmas music as he crossed to the fireplace and began to load it with crumpled newspaper and logs. The beautiful Christmas tree in front of the window must have been on a timer because it had already been lit up as they walked in from the garage. Even though it was simply a drab brown fall landscape outside, the tree, the fire and the carols indeed made the house feel as if it was the night of the Christ child's birth.

Conversation came incredibly easy as they cooked together there in his kitchen beside the fire with the dog looking on. Skye made the scampi butter and got the lobsters ready to go under the broiler and then began to make a creamy sauce to top them as Gage crafted his breadsticks. Then together they made the crust for the mousse and then the filling and put it into the freezer to chill while they finished cooking.

She knew he was exhausted and couldn't help yawning over and over again and she wasn't surprised when she looked over at him and found him asleep in an easy chair where he'd taken the washed asparagus to trim and snap. She finished making the rice pilaf and then went and gently took the asparagus and finished getting it ready to go into the microwave while the lobster and breadsticks cooked.

When everything was ready to go into the ovens, she looked over at him again sleeping so deeply and decided to wait while he napped for awhile as he so obviously needed to. Going to his chair, she eased back the lever to recline it without waking him and then gently covered him with the fleece throw that had been tossed across the back of the couch. She covered the food with plastic wrap and then wandered around the great room looking at photographs and nick nacks that gave her a little more insight into the man who was sleeping so soundly there across the room.

There was a family portrait of what were obviously his parents and siblings and their families because the family resemblance was remarkable. There was Gage and his parents and two sisters and their husbands with two children each and then a younger version of Gage who could have been a twin except for something that made Skye think there was a huge dose of mischief behind those eyes. His dad looked to be a handsome, robust, middle aged man with a touch of gray at his temples, and his mother a shorter, sweet faced, motherly type, although she sported a trendy hairstyle and a veritable rock for a wedding ring. There were also several other photos of Gage with friends and in one she recognized the ballerina Sophie and what had to be her parents.

After puttering around the room for several minutes, Skye stopped by the book shelves and found herself studying the volumes there. It was amazing what you could discern about a person by perusing their literature. Gage was obviously LDS and had a section of religious books with all the titles she had come to recognize in her short six months of having been a member. He also had shelves and shelves of others she didn't recognize but knew they had to be inspirational because of either general authority authors, or the titles and content. In addition, he had a respectable collection of self-improvement and attitude books by the likes of Stephen Covey and John Maxwell and Og Mandino.

He'd kept several textbooks from college, and had a section of classics ranging from Shakespeare's cadre to Huckleberry Finn and For Whom the Bell Tolls. Finally, he had a shelf that was widely disparate from fly fishing technique, to political works, to westerns, and mysteries, and the Lord Of The Rings series. That he was well read was apparent by the scope and sheer volume of the wall of bookshelves. After seeing his library, she glanced back over at this man who had just become even more intriguing. Why was this man still single? From what she'd seen, he seemed to have it all.

Her stomach growled and she glanced at her watch and wondered if Mama Woo was okay at home alone on Christmas Eve. Still hesitant to wake him, Skye built up the fire and took his Bible and settled down in front of it to read the Christmas story with the crackle of logs and the quiet carols adding to the spirit.

Glancing up at his luxurious home, she had to wonder how Mary and Joseph would have appreciated the peace and warmth and ease that surrounded her. How uncomfortable had the young mother been in such humble circumstances as they were in that night? But that lack of pretention had all been a part of the plan from the start and maybe the very simplicity of it all had indeed been comfortable. At any rate, Skye knew God had sent His Son in the exact manner He intended and the world had been changed forever that night. She finished the story and sat there in the peace and relative quiet to contemplate that wondrous night and how grateful she was for all it meant.

Finally, deciding she'd better get moving on, she went to wake Gage, but then decided to have everything right ready to eat before she woke him. She put the lobster and breadsticks in and then microwaved the asparagus and reheated the pilaf. When everything came out and Gage's house smelled marvelous, she went to wake him.

She touched him on the arm and softly spoke his name, but he didn't stir at all and she gently shook him. He still didn't even break the deep, heavy breathing he had settled into and she hesitated and wondered if maybe she shouldn't wake him after all. He'd be embarrassed, but there were worse things. She touched him gently on the face and still he only sighed and went back to sleeping soundly.

With that, she turned back to the neatly set table and began to put everything away but stopped herself momentarily. When he woke up he would be more hungry than ever and if she put it all away, he'd be likely to eat cold cereal and save all of this and invite her back. She didn't want him to settle for cold cereal. She wanted him to be able to wake up and slip a plate into the microwave and eat well, right then.

Resolutely, she seated herself and bowed her head and prayed and then quietly ate her festive dinner with the dog looking on and the music and crackling fire and Gage's deep breathing as a background. Surprisingly, the meal was good and even with Gage only sleeping beside her; she didn't feel nearly as alone as she did eating at home with only Kitty for company. Leaving the chocolate mousse because it would keep, and in hopes of being invited back sometime, she rinsed her dishes and cleaned up and then made Gage a plate, covered it and put everything in the fridge.

With his house returned to order, she added wood to the fire and closed the glass doors. She left a short note, turned down the music, turned out the lights and quietly let herself out, locking the door behind her.

She found herself humming along to the carols on the radio as she drove through the streets strung with bright decorations and even the traffic signals seemed to be in the spirit of the thing as she looked down the rows of red and green stop lights.

In the alley behind her shop, she sat in her car for several minutes thinking about Gage and the Christ child and even Santa Clause and what life had been like before she'd begun this insane existence of trying to stay one step ahead of a love struck maniac. Deciding not to dwell on the negative when it had been a really nice evening, she looked up at Mama Woo's window and then around the alley to double check that she was alone as she got out. "Come on, Kitty. It's Christmas Eve. The night the Savior was born. Let's go take care of Mama Woo, shall we?"

Chapter 3

It took a few minutes of very soft Christmas music and the lingering smell of broiled lobster as Gage was beginning to wake up to finally get him cognizant enough to realize where he was. Looking around in the dimness of his home, he glanced up at the clock on the microwave and groaned out loud. It was one-thirty-six in the morning. Skye and Kitty were long gone. He pushed aside the throw she must have placed over him and mumbled as he pulled his chair upright, "Oh, you've really done it this time, Garrison. This will certainly go down as her most memorable Christmas Eve ever."

Clicking on the lights under the counter, he sniffed the lingering aromas that made his stomach demand attention. The kitchen was completely cleared and he opened the fridge, wondering what had happened to their Christmas Eve feast. Next to the foil wrapped bottle of sparkling juice he found the plate she'd made with a bright Post It stuck to the top of the plastic that covered the perfectly broiled lobster. "Gage, I tried to wake you, but you were pretty gone. Dinner was wonderful. Thanks for having me. Merry Christmas, Skye". He groaned again and ran a hand through his hair, wishing it wasn't too late to call and apologize.

He put the plate into the microwave, poured himself a tall glass of milk and leaned back against the counter to drink it as he waited for his belated dinner. At least the note hadn't sounded too angry. It didn't mention being contacted again either, but at least she hadn't been completely ticked off at him.

At the first bite of lobster, he closed his eyes and savored the perfectly seasoned and cooked delicacy. Never in his life had he had lobster like this! It was a pity she wasn't here to compliment on it. Who'd have thought that a beautiful and entertaining florist could cook, too? He made his way through the rest of the heavenly dinner, thinking about the intriguing woman he had rudely fallen asleep on and hoping she'd be as resilient about this as she'd been that first night when he'd shown up after she'd closed up shop. At least as a business owner herself she'd probably understand having those days when you worked yourself under the table.

Finishing, he rinsed his plate and loaded it into the dishwasher, then sighed and stretched his back and rolled his neck as he reached for the kitchen lights. Before he turned them off, he noticed his Bible sitting open on the hearth near the fireplace and he wondered how long she had waited before finally giving up on him and eating and going home.

He crossed to the hearth and reached for the book and noticed that she had been reading the Christmas story. It had been a Christmas Eve tradition in his family his whole life and, in fact, if he hadn't been so completely and utterly tired, he'd have gone up to his parents' house with the rest of his family earlier this evening to read it together with them. He thought about Skye again. She'd made a couple of smart alecky comments about her life, but other than Mrs. Woo, he had no idea what her history or her family was like. Apparently, she was at least a Christian.

Picking up the book, he took it back to his easy chair and after adjusting his floor lamp nearby so he could see; he turned back to the start of the story and began to read it himself. Who cared if it was after two in the morning? It was Christmas. And when he thought about it, he'd bet both of his sisters and brothers-in-law were probably still up, putting together bicycles and doll houses the way his parents had into the wee hours when he was a kid. Moments like this were about the only time he didn't envy them being happily married and settled with children.

He slept in until nearly noon and wouldn't have even gotten up then except that his parents and younger brother Gabriel showed up, pounding on his door and singing, with a fruitcake and a plate of his mother's famous Christmas breakfast frittata. He opened the door to their merriment and had to laugh to himself to see that Gabriel sported a ridiculous looking beanie that had a piece of Mistletoe attached to the top of it instead of the usual propeller. Gage smiled tiredly as he glanced down at his rumpled jams and shook his dad's hand and said, "That is positively the worst singing I've ever heard this early in the morning. What are you three doing out at the crack of dawn?"

His mom looked him up and down and patted his cheek. "It's the crack of eleven-forty-five, honey." She handed him a fruitcake. "You look terrible. Are you sick?"

"No, Mother. Just really tired. But thanks for being honest. You know I hate these things. But you still give me one every single year."

Just as he was going to hug his mother, Gabriel laughingly said, "C'mere big guy. How about a little peck on the cheek for Christmas morning? C'mon."

Gage knew instinctively to dive behind his mom and then his dad and then made a beeline back into the house as he said, "Oh, no you don't, Gabe! Don't you even dare! Where in the world did you find that thing, anyway? You'll scare every woman completely out of the state!"

Gabriel went to tackle him the way he had since they were little boys and laughed. "The girls love it! You're the only one who's run from me."

Gage sidestepped him and said, "Please tell me that's because I'm the only male you've said that to. Stop messing around. The last time you tackled me in here you broke my leather couch and it's never been the same. You're going to knock my tree over and Marcy and Lauren will kill us. They spent one whole afternoon decorating that thing. What did you get for Christmas?"

Their parents seemed completely unconcerned that these two adult men were acting like ten year olds. They came in, shut the door and began to slip off their jackets, open drapes and turn back on some Christmas music. Gabriel kept after Gage until finally he took him down onto the thick carpeting, making the tree sway dangerously as he did so. Gage was still so tired that he didn't even try to wrestle back and finally Gabriel got back up in disgust. "You're too old to even give me any competition anymore, Gage. Look at you. One tackle and you're toast."

"I was toast long before you got here, tough guy, but don't kid yourself. I can still take you any day of the week when I want to. This morning I'm just too tired to care. I thought you were getting something pretty awesome for Christmas. Did it not show up?"

Gabriel got up and sprawled onto the couch with a sigh. "Are we talking about my new electric leathers for the bullet bike? They are sweet! And no you can't borrow them. What'd you get?"

Gage yawned. "I have no idea. I haven't opened anything."

At that, Gabriel hopped back up and went over to the tree. "Well, get with the program, dude!" He started to rummage around in the packages underneath it. "Geez, Gage. There are presents from like seventeen different women! You need to introduce me to these girls. I could try out my new, ultimate fantastic, super charged, turbo powered Mistletoe beanie." He was digging through gifts; shaking

44

them and putting them back down. "Jill, Jennifer, Candice, Shannon." He went on mumbling to himself. "Isn't this just a little bit ridiculous, Romeo? Did you have to get something for all of them back? Do they all know about each other?"

With a sigh, Gage got up and headed for the kitchen. "I haven't had two seconds to reciprocate. Sorry, I only bought something for one woman other than family and she's not under there anyway. Honestly there's one under there I can't even remember meeting. Do you know any Natalies?"

"Natalie. Natalie. The only Natalie I know was that saucy little thing we met up at Elk Meadows last winter. But she turned out to be a not necessarily nice girl. You haven't kept in touch with her, have you?"

Gage's dad settled onto the couch and began to channel surf as his mother put the plate she was carrying into the microwave and turned and asked, "So, who did you buy for? Anyone I know?"

Gabriel was still under the tree and Gage heard paper tear and his mom said, "Gabriel John Garrison, get out of his stuff. What are you doing?"

He laughed and Gage turned to see what was funny and Gabriel lifted up a pair of red satin boxer shorts. "You might not know her, but she seems to know you! Look at these babies! So how does Natalie know what size underveh you wear, bro?"

Their mother gasped and their dad chuckled as Gage said, "Oh, brother. Red satin? Holy criminently, who would even make something like that, let alone put them on?"

Gabriel looked inside the candy apple red shorts. "Made by Victoria's Secret. They probably cost sixty bucks. You must mean a great deal to this Natalie."

Their mother made a disgusted sound. "Well, I personally hope this woman doesn't mean a great deal to you, Gage. I think that's a very inappropriate gift!"

"Don't worry, Mother. I don't know any Natalies and I'll bet you twenty Marcy and Lauren sent them as a joke."

Their mother looked skeptical. "I don't know. Even they wouldn't spend sixty dollars on a practical joke. You never answered my question. Who did you buy for?"

Gage grinned, but all he said was, "Is there really such a thing as a sixty dollar pair of boxers?"

Gabriel piped in from under the tree. "Heck yes! The last time I was in Victoria's Secret shopping, I found lots of those sexy little lingerie things that were more than that."

"Gabriel!" Their mother stood in the kitchen in open mouthed horror.

He just laughed and pointed at her. "Gotcha!"

She closed her mouth and then stomped her foot in outrage as the three men laughed and the microwave dinged. Gage took the plate and sat at the table as his mom put a glass down in front of him and went to the fridge. She looked inside for a moment or two and then glanced back at Gage with a decidedly speculative look and he wondered what was in his fridge that would make his mom look at him like that.

Getting a carton of orange juice, she brought it over to him and asked almost off-handedly, "So, who did you have the fancy dinner with?"

Gage smiled lazily even though just thinking about falling asleep last night made him want to groan again. "Oh, a friend. The one I bought the gift for." He took the juice and poured a glass and almost spilled it from smiling as he drank while his mom watched him like a hawk.

"A friend like who?"

"Just a friend. Did you like your books? I even went to one of those book signing things at Deseret Book to get you that signed Traci Hunter-Abramson. I think I was the only man in the store."

"They were very nice, thank you. I can't wait to start them. Have I met this friend? Is she in your stake?"

Gabriel joined in from under the tree again where there was more paper tearing, "Hey, maybe that's where you found Natalie. Or Annalise, or Heidi, or . . . "

Gage interrupted him, "We get the picture, Gabe. But typically, women who shop at Victoria's Secret don't shop at Deseret Book."

Gabriel gave him a wicked grin. "How do you know, Gage? You been hanging out at Victoria's Secret a lot?" Their mother made the sound again and their dad laughed from in front of the TV as Gabriel went back to opening presents. "Hey, Gage. There are actually some pretty cool things here. Check this out." He held up a fly rod. "It's from someone named Annalise. It's a Saint Croix. Apparently you mean even more to her than to Natalie. The gift is great. The card is pathetic. *Dear Gage, maybe we could "hook" up more often*, with little quotation marks around the hook. That's even tackier than red satin boxers."

"You're even reading his cards? Gabriel, get out of his stuff. There might be something private in there."

He held up the boxers again. "Boy, I'll say. Ya can't get much privater than ling er eeee."

Gage laughed as she automatically corrected him. "More private. Not privater. And it's pronounced lawn jer ay, hon. They don't typically call men's unmentionables lingerie."

"Yeah, well, they don't typically call men's unmentionables red satin either, Mom. If that's not ling er ee, then I don't know my Victoria's Secrets."

From the couch their dad grinned and weighed in, "That's enough, Gabriel. Quit hassling your mother. She'll go straight home and put your name in the temple and make me fast with her for your eternal salvation. Let me see that fly rod." Gabriel handed it over and he whistled softly. "I'll be darned. That's a $150 rod. If you honestly aren't interested in this girl, Gage, you'd better give this back. It wouldn't be honorable to let someone spend that kind of money on you in this economy. Or do you not know this Annalise either?"

Gage rolled his eyes. "No. I know this one. She's actually very married to a business man over in Mesquite. She used to be one of my patients."

His mother made another sound of disgust. "I'm so glad you said used to be. That's awful."

Gabriel laughed. "Yeah, and talk about your less than honorable. What's really awful is earning the money so your wife can spend it on another man. What do you suppose this is?" He held up a completely unrecognizable blue ceramic blob.

Sighing, Gage said, "That must be from Heidi. It's supposed to be art. She's an art student at Dixie. She's in my ward, in fact, I'm one of her home teachers. She's like eighteen and straight off the farm in some little place like Norway."

They all three looked at him blankly and finally Gabriel asked, "Like Norvay Norway? What are you saying here, Gage?"

Gage shook his head. "I'm saying there's no one worth using your beanie on under that tree, Gabe. I mean, they're nice girls. Well, most of them are nice girls, but none of them are keepers. At least not that I can see. Keep opening. I'll watch and attempt to eat this festive hunk of twelve pound cake Mom brought me and you can take inventory. I want to open the gifts from the family, though." He stood and went to the kitchen and returned with a cleaver and heavy cutting board and his mother gave a squeal of outrage and then smacked him teasingly on the forehead. When the other two turned to see what was going on they burst into laughter.

As Gage took an exaggerated swing with the cleaver and the cake fairly flew apart, Gabriel raised a hand. "Hey, lob me a hunk of that Chinese fighting cake, Gage."

Gage tossed him a piece and his mother cuffed him on the forehead again as he tossed another chunk toward his dad, who said, "Easy, Gage. You could hurt someone doing that."

This time his mother marched toward her husband in mock disgust whereupon he neatly hauled her onto his lap and kissed her as he said, "Oh, settle down, Maren. You know we all love your fruit cake. Plus it has all those health benefits. Twelve servings of fruit and whole grains in one piece and weight training thrown in to boot. It's why the whole family is so darn fit. Gage never answered your question about whether the mystery girl is in his stake."

"He didn't, did he?" She turned in her husband's arms. "Gage, now be honest with me. Is this girl LDS and is she someone you could be serious with?"

Gage lobbed another hunk of cake to Gabriel. "I don't know and I don't know. I haven't had a chance to find out. That audit has stolen my whole life. All I know is she's adorable, and beautiful, and incredibly intriguing."

At that, all three of them stared at him and finally Gabriel whistled. "I never thought I'd see the day. That actually sounds like he's interested in this girl. It's been since Katie Barnhardt in the second grade, hasn't it?"

Gage grinned sheepishly. "It hasn't been that long. It's not a big deal. And you're right. She might not even be LDS. I've only seen her twice, but she is fun."

Gabriel ripped open another package before looking up with a grin. "So... Can I meet her?"

"Not on your life! But nice try. Who is that from?"

"Lauren."

"Gabe! I said I wanted to open the ones from the family! You turkey! What did Marcy and the boys give me?"

"More red satin boxers. You're gonna love 'em! Okay, I'm kidding. They're blue satin. But you're still gonna love 'em."

"Oh, stop. Can you be serious for once? Scoot over and let me under there. Hey, who gave me the tickets to Tuacan?"

"That would be someone named Tessa." Gage sighed again and Gabriel asked, "What? Do you not know Tessa either?"

"No. I know her. I just don't want to take her to Tuacan."

Gabriel scrunched his lips sideways, rubbed his chin and said, "So, we now have a social dilemma of ethics. Is one obligated to take the givee on the date? One of the great questions that have stumped superior minds like mine through the ages."

Gage rolled his eyes at his brother and reached back under the tree as his mother said, "Of course you don't have to take anyone anywhere if you don't want to, Gage. Grow up and ignore Gabriel. Tessa shouldn't be able to force a date you don't want, even by buying the tickets. Just give them to your dad and me and if Tessa asks you can tell her that. Then when you really do want to take someone to Tuacan I'll spring for the tickets. By the time you're twenty seven years old you can quit feeling guilty about dating games and just worry about finding the real her."

Gabriel elbowed Gage and laughed. "Yeah. What she said. Grow up and ignore me. Hey, you could give those tickets to me too, ya know? I'm the starving college student in the family. And I'm desperately trying to find the real her too. In fact, much more desperately than you. You're already married to your clinic."

Their dad gave a snort of derision. "Desperate doesn't sound like what we witnessed under our Christmas tree this morning, Gabriel. I believe you had an even bigger pile of unreciprocated gifts from girls than Gage here. Of course, there were no unmentionables, but at least none of them were bank rolled by the woman's husband either, were they?"

"Unreciprocated? What are you talking about? Why do you think I'm a starving student? I spent my life savings trying to reciprocate so no one will feel slighted. I'm not nearly so cold blooded as Gage here."

"I am not cold blooded. I'm just tired. And have matured to the point that I now realize buying a woman a gift just because she gave me one may not be the kindest thing in the long run."

"Oh, man! You mean I didn't need to spend all that money and do all that running around? Geez, Gage, couldn't you have given me this mature advice a few days ago?"

From the couch Maren Garrison laughed. "Gabriel, I do not believe fifteen identical four dollar boxes of chocolates equates to a lot of money and running around. And I believe you gave them to them when they came to your apartment to bring you something, didn't you?"

Gage laughed and elbowed his brother. "Busted. So, did you give anyone a real gift? Is there anyone special?"

"Would I be offering to meet your adorable, beautiful, incredibly intriguing and fun mystery girl if there were?" He opened the tin of homemade cookies Marcy had given Gage and helped himself as he talked, "I am going to be a tubbo from all these Christmas goodies."

Taking the tin and putting the lid back on Gage said, "So then stay out of my Christmas goodies. And away from my mystery girl, or I'll have to put the hurt on you."

At that, their mom said, "Careful, Gage. Don't challenge him. You know how he is, and the last thing I need is sons who don't speak to each other for the rest of their lives because of some mystery girl."

Gabriel began unloading the pile of gifts in his lap. "Ah, he can have the girl, but putting the hurt on me? This I gotta see." With his lap cleared, he leaned in and grabbed Gage and began to wrestle him and both of their parents launched off of the couch to grab the swaying Christmas tree in the nick of time.

With the tree stabilized, Maren leaned in and bopped both of them on the forehead again. "All right, knock it off you two. You're not ten anymore. You're gonna break the couch again or something. I swear, Con. I've been after these boys since Gabriel was big enough to roll over to stop this! Gabriel!"

She wacked him again. "Stop it this minute! Gage has a beautiful home here and you keep wrecking it. Now behave yourself. He may be older and sit behind a desk, but he's as fit as he ever was and this competition is ridiculous. What would be wrong with proving your manhood with a civilized game of chess?" Both sons looked up at her in disbelief for a second. "Okay, so maybe not. But could you at least not break so much furniture?"

Gabriel rolled out from under the tree and grabbed the tin of cookies again as Gage straightened his t-shirt and reclined on the floor. "Thanks, Mom. I'm honestly too tired to want to win this morning."

"It's not morning anymore, sweetie. Is the audit looking like it's winding down any?"

He groaned. "Not that I can tell. This guy is going to single handedly make me want to be a surfer dude and forget being a business man."

"Oh, I wouldn't go that far, hon. The surfing is probably great, but the pay stinks."

Gabriel laughed. "Yeah, but think of the girls on the beach, man!"

Conrad Garrison shook his head. "I'd guess that the girls wouldn't look so great when your belly was empty and the rent came due. Stick with the clinic, son. The auditor will eventually grow old and die."

Gage chuckled. "That's not really all that funny, Dad. I'm beginning to worry about that. The problem is there are a couple more where he came from when he finally kills over."

"Could be worse. You could be struggling to make ends meet like a huge portion of the world is right now."

"That's exactly what Skye said. In a round about way."

All three of them looked at him and his mom asked, "Do I know Skye?"

When the door shut behind his family an hour later, Gage picked up his cell phone, fully intending to call Skye and beg her forgiveness and then remembered he didn't have her number programmed into it. He dug out a phone book and looked her up, but she wasn't listed personally, so he looked up a number for Miss Daisy's.

There was no answer and he hung up the phone, wondering if it would be intrusive to show up at her house at one-thirty on Christmas Day and frustrated that he had to wait to try to apologize. After puttering for more than two hours he decided he needed to beg her forgiveness sooner than later and finally climbed into his car and headed toward her shop and apartment. The shop was locked up tight and no one answered when he knocked on her door in the alley so he decided to try Mrs. Woo's before giving up and going back home.

It was actually Skye who answered the door and for a moment they just stood looking at each other and then finally Skye smiled and opened the door wide. "Merry Christmas, Gage. You look much less hammered than you did yesterday. How are you feeling?"

"Foolish, and guilty, and several other things along that line. I'm so sorry I fell asleep and ruined dinner. Please forgive me."

"You don't need to apologize just for being dead tired, Gage. I've worked Valentine's Day and Mother's Day. I know what it's like to be dead on your feet. Come in, you're just in time. We're starting to make Christmas dinner. Mama Woo, look who dropped in."

The tiny Asian woman came around the corner of the kitchen counter to put an arm around Gage. "Welcome tired Docto'. Missy tell me you fall sleeping. You better now?"

Gage glanced at Skye. "Much better thank you. How are you? Are you having a Merry Christmas?"

"Oh, heaven yes. Beat Skye at cards many time this afnoon. Get many nice thing. Very merry." She escorted Gage in and offered him a seat before asking, "Missy no tell me you kiss. Did kiss? Or no?"

Skye rolled her eyes and looked away as she mumbled, "Mama Woo. Stop that this minute. You're embarrassing me." She turned back to Gage and tried to act like nothing was wrong. "Can you stay for dinner? Or do you have other pressing engagements? We're not even sure yet what we're having, but it will be good. Mama Woo is a marvelous cook."

"There's nowhere I need to be. Would I be intruding?"

Mama Woo hugged him again. "No intruding. Welcome." She gestured back and forth between her and Skye. "Need more handsome men here. Come to table and sit. I bring hiding treats."

When she would have walked away after seating him, Skye waved her into a chair. "You sit too, Mama Woo. I'll bring your secret stash of treats and you two can visit and watch me as I get dinner ready." She walked over and reached into a kitchen drawer and brought back a grocery bag and set it on the table. "Here Gage. You can try to keep her from overdosing on goodies. It makes her blood sugar go into fits so you'll have to ration her." She put a hand on Mama Woo's shoulder. "And you have to watch her or she'll sneak stuff and hide it under her apron. Don't ruin your appetites." She winked at Gage. "And don't you tell her if you kissed me or not."

"My lips are sealed. Unless she bribes me with hiding treats. Apron huh?" He smiled at Mama Woo and patted her hand. "I never thought of concealing goodies under an apron. I may have to try that sometime. What have you got in that bag, Mama Woo?"

Mama Woo gave a conspiratorial laugh and dumped her stash on the table and she and Gage spent several minutes trying to decide what they should indulge in that wouldn't ruin their appetites as Skye worked around Mama Woo's kitchen. He finally got up and went into the kitchen and began rolling up his sleeves as he asked, "What can I help you with, Skye? Give me a job and I promise I won't fall asleep on you this time. I wield a mean chef knife."

She set him up cutting celery and onions for the stuffing and then she took potatoes and a peeler to the table for Mama Woo to work on while she was sitting down. "Can you handle pealing these, Mama Woo? Or will it bother your arthritis?"

The tiny woman waved the peeler airily. "Heaven no. I fine. May take time, but I do."

The three of them spent a pleasant hour stuffing a roasting hen and making mashed potatoes and gravy and a beautiful green salad topped with cranberries and sunflower seeds and shredded mozzarella cheese. Then Mama Woo supervised the other two in making a rich pastry filled with nuts and butter and brown sugar for desert. While they waited for the chicken to cook, they played cards again and Mama Woo beat them both before she started to look decidedly tired. Helping her to her easy chair, Skye covered her with a soft throw and then came back and played cards again while the little woman slept.

When the chicken came out, she was still sleeping soundly so they waited almost another hour playing cards while she rested and then the three of them got out some fine China and ate a wonderful and companionable meal together. Gage didn't stay long after the dessert was served. He felt like he'd invited himself for long enough, but when he finally drove away and headed up to his parents' house he would liked to have stayed longer. It had been a wonderful, peaceful and satisfying Christmas afternoon.

Jaclyn M. Hawkes

Chapter 4

The day after Christmas Skye was back in the shop early doing wedding flowers. She had at least one wedding everyday except Sunday because of all the college kids who wanted to get married over the break in classes. It was a grueling schedule, even with Hailee's help and each night Skye checked on Mama Woo and then dropped into bed bone tired to start it all over again the next day.

One thing really helped to keep her upbeat and energized. Gage dropped into the shop at lunch time three days that week to buy flowers. If he hadn't invited her to lunch on all three of those days she would have wondered if there were a special someone he was buying all the flowers for. One of the days she didn't have time to eat, but she went with him the other two and it was ridiculously nice to sit across a table from him for that short hour or so and enjoy him and some down time before heading back into the rat race of that week.

By the time New Years Eve rolled around, she was too tired to do anything more than just check on Mama Woo again before crashing without even considering waiting up for the new year. She laid down wondering what Gage was doing to celebrate that night. They hadn't known each other long, but still, if she were honest, she was a little disappointed that he hadn't offered to do something with her to celebrate.

She hadn't intended to wake up to celebrate at midnight, but when she heard a gunshot and then Kitty barked, Skye sat straight up in bed, her heart pounding nearly out of her chest. She automatically reached behind her bed near her pillow to grip her own gun before a whole series of the bangs made her realize she was hearing firecrackers, not gunfire. Kitty barked again and Skye remembered she'd acted just like this on the fourth of July.

She spoke quietly to the dog as she plumped her pillows and laid back down. "It's just a new year, Kitty Kitty. We're okay. We're still safe. For the time being at least." Skye looked out the window again at the stars through the bars and sleepily wondered aloud, "What do you suppose this year will bring, Kitty? We're past due for Shane to find us. Where do you think we should go next? I've loved it here in St. George. This has been the nicest town to live in by far, don't you think?"

The dog got up and came over to the bed and put her nose up on it as if listening intently to what Skye was saying as she went on, "I've found so many people here to love and this community has been so good to me. It'll kill me when we have to leave."

Worry about Mama Woo had begun to weigh on her. The people in the ward were good to look in on her, but Mama Woo was getting older and more and more frail and there was no one in the world who would be around to truly take care of her. Skye always worried that when she had to run, Mama Woo would just be put into a care center somewhere and forgotten. The thought made her heartsick and she tried to push it from her mind.

It would have been nice to push Shane altogether from her mind as well, but that would be incredibly foolish. He was out there and she knew he was still looking for her and she needed to have plans in mind for that day when he would show up out of the blue. Not being prepared could mean her life.

She turned over on her stomach and put her hand on the dog's head. "I don't know what we'll do, Kitty, but God has watched over us so far. We'll get through this. But I so wish I could honestly settle down and get on with my life." She was only twenty five, but when she was growing up she never dreamed she'd be at this point in her life where having a serious relationship and eventually marriage and a family were completely out of the question. Who'd have thought she wouldn't even be able to do something as simple as phone her family when she wanted to?

When she finally dragged herself out of bed the next day after the luxury of sleeping in, she ate and then decided to go work in the shop even though she would be closed today so she could get a jump on the last wedding scheduled for January third. It was the last one, but by far the biggest of them all and was going to take everything she had to be ready for it even with what help Hailee could give once she was back in school the next day.

After making lunch, Skye put it in a basket and carried it across and ate with Mama Woo and then she and Kitty locked themselves in the closed shop and went to work. She was hoping Gage would drop by the way he had on Christmas Day, even though she was too busy to stop and make a big dinner with him, but then he hadn't really mentioned anything like that when he'd been here this week.

When she realized she was hoping to see him again she had to stop and think about just what she wanted from him. She turned off her radio and then paused as she really thought about it. He was so attractive and they had had such a good time together, but if she were honest, she had absolutely no business even thinking about getting involved with someone when there was every possibility Shane would show up soon. Not only would any relationship end abruptly, probably without much of an explanation, but she could definitely be putting anyone who Shane construed as competition at risk of becoming his target as well. Maybe even more so. After all if Shane could harm someone he professed to love, what would he do to another man?

Still unsure of what to do with her budding feelings for Gage, she sighed and turned her radio back on. Oh, well. It wasn't like he was madly in love with her anyway. A few minutes later when the shop phone rang and she recognized his number she sighed again and let the machine pick up, absolutely torn between wanting to talk to him and wanting to protect him.

****

The auditor was back. He'd been back for three days now and Gage was incredibly glad it was Friday night and he could bid the man goodbye for at least the weekend. Not that Gage himself would get to take a day off. He was back to working long overtime to try and catch up on his real work again. And his chiropractic practice had slowly ground to almost a complete halt between the auditor and the paperwork. Sometimes he wondered if that wasn't a good thing.

When the auditor finally packed up and left, Sandy wasn't far behind him and Gage wearily loosened his tie and picked up his cell phone, wondering if Skye would already have her evening completely full with a date with another guy. Skye answered and he could hear the tiredness in her voice even behind her cheery Miss Daisy's greeting. "May I speak with Tulip Von Snowdrop please."

Skye laughed and said, "I'm sorry Gage, Tulip isn't available. Tonight it's just plain old Skye. What are you up to?"

"I'm wondering if you already have twelve dates for

tonight or if I could interest you in dinner. We could bring Mama Woo with. Do you already have plans?"

"I don't have plans, Gage, but I think I'm honestly too tired to go get dinner. But then I'm too tired to cook, too, so I don't know what. I did the biggest wedding of my floral career today."

"I'm not far behind you although my day was with an auditor not a bride. Maybe we could just order a pizza and eat while we watch a movie to relax."

"That sounds marvelous. Your place or mine?"

"Well, you're welcome at mine, but if we went to yours we could take Mama Woo home when she needs to and you could just walk me to the door instead of having to be taken home when you're so tired."

"Yes, but I'm warning you. I only have a nineteen inch TV and then you'd have to go home instead of just being able to rest when you're tired."

"The TV is fine and I'd rather let you rest. Especially after Christmas Eve. You get Mama Woo and order the pizza and I'll be there to pay for it before it arrives. See you in a sec."

"Thanks, Gage. It sounds marvelous. Bye."

Gage was glad to go to her house so the night would be less tiring for her, but after settling into the little loveseat beside her in her small living room, he decided it was the all-time most uncomfortable piece of furniture he'd ever sat in, in his life. He couldn't say anything and after they'd prayed, they all three tore into the pizza and then put in the movie Mama Woo had chosen.

When Gage had told her to pick, Skye had laughed but wouldn't say why. When Big Jake came on starring John Wayne he was completely surprised. He turned and looked at Skye in disbelief, and she whispered, "She has a thing for John Wayne westerns. She thinks he's cute."

Gage raised his eyebrows and whispered back, "Cute? John Wayne?" Skye nodded with a huge smile. "Oh, I think he'd be so embarrassed if he heard that word."

Skye giggled and whispered, "Don't worry. He's dead. He doesn't mind a bit."

Still whispering he admitted, "You have a point. Does she do this often?"

"Oh, I've only seen this particular one about four times. It's actually pretty good except for when they... Actually, have you seen it?" He shook his head. "Oh, then I won't give anything away. You'll probably like it. It's definitely not a chick flick."

The movie was fine. The loveseat was excruciating and Gage was eminently relieved when Skye got up and complained, "I swear that seat was not made for the human body. Let me go find some pillows and blankets and let's see if the floor is any more comfortable. It's not usually so bad when it's just her and me. She sits in the recliner and I sprawl somewhere, but to actually sit in it's horrible. Sorry. I'll be right back."

She came back with about four fluffy pillows and two thick comforters and tossed them on the floor and Gage sat down on them and leaned back against the loveseat. "Much better, thanks. Where in the world did you get this thing?" He indicated the loveseat.

"The last owner left it. Now I know why, but it's too much hassle to move it out, so I've just left it. I guess I should get rid of it, huh?"

Gage smiled. "I'll bet your home teachers don't stay too long. Maybe it comes in handy. Are you LDS?"

"I am. But that hasn't really been the case. They usually stay awhile. I'll have to seat them in it."

"Do you go to a singles ward or a family ward?"

"Family. That way I can take Mama Woo."

"Let me guess. You have a single guy who your ward thinks would be the perfect match." She rolled her eyes and he laughed. "My ward keeps doing the same thing, but I go to a singles ward so it compounds."

Skye smiled patiently. "I'm sure they have good intentions."

The movie had only been playing about an hour when Mama Woo started to drift off and Skye got up and roused her and asked Gage to turn on a light for a minute while she helped her across the small room and to the door. Gage paused the movie and went and offered his arm to the diminutive Asian woman, and he and Skye and Kitty walked her home together. He waited for a minute or two while Skye helped her to her bedroom, and then they locked up her house and went back next door to Skye's.

At the door, Skye began to unlock it and he said, "I didn't even realize we'd locked it when we went over."

"Uh, well, it locks automatically whenever it's closed."

He glanced up at the bars on the windows and down at the dog she had put on guard as they walked out the door and wondered again what was with all the security. As they made it inside, Skye pulled the door tightly closed and then spoke German to Kitty again and the dog relaxed and padded into what must have been the bedroom. Skye sighed as she picked up the remote to turn back on the TV. "I know the security is a little over the top. Sorry. Do you want the recliner now? It's not as bad as the loveseat, I promise."

Deciding he'd wait to ask about the security until she was ready to tell him, he shook his head. "No, the floor is actually great with the pillows, thanks. Are you okay?"

"I might lounge on the loveseat behind you if you don't mind and watch over your shoulder. Are you still okay with this movie or do you want to watch something else since my little John Wayne fan is gone?"

"The movie's great unless you want to change it."

She pointed the remote. "I'm learning to really like John Wayne except that he's so condescending in some of his movies. Sometimes I wonder if he isn't single handedly responsible for all the men our dads' age who think it isn't masculine to say you're sorry. But he's definitely a star of epic proportion." As the movie came back on, she sprawled lengthwise on the seat behind him not touching him, but close enough that he could smell her perfume. It was the same one she'd been wearing on the night of the ballet and that scent brought back memories of that first night on her porch when he'd so wanted to kiss her. For a second it short circuited his brain and he missed a portion of the movie.

He got his concentration back for a while until she reached over his shoulder and asked him to hand her one of the scattered pillows. He handed it to her and once she had it adjusted he reached over and took her hand where it dangled over the edge of the seat beside him. After that he never really did pick up the story line again. He was too focused on the small hand with the calloused finger tips that he held in his. The more he was around this girl, the more he wanted to be.

As the credits began to roll, he turned his head and looked into the clear blue eyes that were only inches from his and for a second neither of them looked away. He finally glanced from her eyes to notice she was obviously tired and he stood up and began to fold the comforters and stack the pillows. Skye clicked off the TV and stood to clear away the pizza and soda mess. With the house back in order, they walked toward the door in silence and then when they got there, Gage turned back to look at her.

He put up a hand to gently squeeze the muscle above her shoulder as he said, "Thanks for agreeing to see me even though we were tired. It was nice. Someday we'll get together again when neither one of us is dragging. If this auditor has his way that will be four years from now, but I keep holding out hope." He smiled and shrugged. "He hasn't found anything really questionable yet. Maybe his superiors will tell him to quit wasting time and come on home."

Nodding she said, "That is a great attitude. Keep thinking positively and it'll all work out."

She smiled wearily and he left her shoulder and gently touched her where her smile curved into her cheek. He looked down into her eyes again and then slowly leaned and softly kissed the corner of her smile. "Goodnight, Skye Alexander. Sleep tight and dream of cowboys."

Jaclyn M. Hawkes

Chapter 5

He dropped into Skye's shop on Monday and Tuesday and bought flowers again and dropped bouquets off at both of his sisters' houses and took one to his mom. When he did it again on Friday, his sisters were both at his parents' house and the three women cornered him in the kitchen as he set the arrangements down. Lauren asked, "So, Gage, we're hearing talk about some intriguing mystery woman named Skye. And we're suddenly getting more flowers than we've gotten from our own husbands in years. We're just going to guess that this mystery Skye works at a flower shop. Is that a possibility?"

He folded his arms and leaned against his mother's kitchen counter. "It's a possibility. Why do you ask?"

"Have you stopped to consider that this girl may just be assuming you have a girlfriend who really likes flowers? Or that you are giving flowers to lots of different women. That could be a problem if you have romantic intentions toward her. Maybe buying flowers isn't the best idea in this situation. You may be just shooting yourself in the foot and making her boss a lot of money."

"She owns the shop, but maybe you're right and I should quit buying you all flowers."

"No! Don't stop! You're making our husbands squirm. It's been very good from our end."

"Hmmm. Well maybe I'll just have to be very clear about what my feelings are toward my mysterious florist then. But you girls owe me for making your husbands squirm. I may call in a favor sometime."

The three women looked at each and then back at him. "Fine with us. Just let us know."

The three women looked at each other again once he was gone and it only took a moment to decide they needed to go buy flowers at a certain shop called Miss Daisy's.

****

Hailee was out making deliveries and Skye was busy at her work table mid afternoon Friday when the bell on the door rang and three relatively familiar, beautiful dark haired women walked into her shop and began looking around. Even if she hadn't recognized them from the photos in Gage's home, the family resemblance was striking enough that she would have known who they were anyway. Realizing this was a reconnaissance mission, she was grateful her apron was relatively clean and that her hair and make up had gone well this morning. This had to be a good sign if they were checking her out. She must mean something to Gage to bring out all three of them.

Smiling happily, she greeted them, "Good afternoon ladies. Do you want to look around for a few minutes, or is there something I can help you with?"

One of the sisters replied, "Your shop is so marvelous! Let us look around for a little while until we decide what we want." The three of them browsed for several minutes and since Skye wanted to check them out as well, she took her watering can and went out into the shop to begin watering the many containers.

They bought a large arrangement and a bottle garden that had a miniature family of deer living in it and then left and Skye had to grin as she continued watering her plants. She'd just been inspected by his mother and sisters. Gosh, they were all beautiful ladies.

****

Gage himself walked in a few minutes later, laughing as he came right out and asked, "Have you had any interesting dark haired female visitors this afternoon?"

Skye grinned at him. "They just left. You almost busted them in the act. What's going on?"

"How many of them came?"

"Your mom and two sisters. Why?"

He laughed. "All three of them! Wow! We rated all three of them. Hmm."

"How did you know they'd be coming in this afternoon?"

"They were all at my mom's house when I dropped more flowers off. They were wondering why they had begun to get flowers more often than usual. They love it. They just wondered why all of the sudden." He smiled. "They were also worried that you'd misunderstand and think I have a girlfriend who loves flowers, or worse, lots of girlfriends who love flowers. I assured them I'd make it perfectly clear to you that the flowers are going to my mother and sisters."

Smiling back, Skye said, "That's good to know, Dr. Garrison, but don't stop now. Profits are way up since I met you."

"Really?"

She laughed and nodded. "A little."

"Well, profits aside, do you think I could just ask you out on a real date that we plan in advance for? I'll even promise not to be too tired or fall asleep on you."

Innocently, she asked, "You think I should say yes, even though I have plants to water and I told you I never date doctors or men as good looking as you?"

Unleashing a heart stopping smile, he replied, "Yes, I do. And if I need to I can go get Mama Woo to try to influence you as well. I'll make a deal with her that if she'll get you to say yes, I'll tell her whether I've kissed you or not."

Pausing in her watering, Skye's eyes sparkled as she asked, "Isn't that some form of blackmail? What's up with that?"

"Well, you could bypass any potential blackmail by just agreeing to go. Without making me grovel would be nice. You know I've never had a woman give me as hard a time as you do."

She bent into another plant. "It's good for you. Keeps you humble. How did you get away from the auditor?"

"You're not going to believe this, but I think he's done. It's given me a whole new lease on life."

At that, she stood upright and turned to him happily. "Oh, Gage, that's wonderful! In that case, I'll absolutely go. We should celebrate! Wait! Did they fine you? Are we celebrating or commiserating?"

"I don't know yet. I'll get the official report in a few weeks. But the prognosis is looking positive. He never found anything terrible that I'm aware of. Just to be safe, let's celebrate."

"Deal!" She put a hand on his arm. "I'm happy for you, Gage. This has been a miserable several weeks for you, hasn't it?"

He ran a hand through his hair. "The worst. Every time they audit me I think about just selling and letting someone else handle those kinds of headaches."

"Would you just go back to practicing chiropractics?"

He paused almost reflectively. "I don't know. The biggest money is in building and managing the building and the businesses, and I've learned there are some women who honestly think I'm their personal spa flunky instead of a medical professional. I'm like their weekly nail appointment or something. And to a couple of others I'm a bit of a fling that their husbands don't get uptight about because they think it's a doctor's appointment. Those ladies I won't accept appointments with anymore, but it's been a pain. It's like chiropractor groupies. I have a woman who actually flies home from wherever she's traveling at the moment for her adjustment. And I think her spine is fine. Sometimes in the mix of it all I forget that I have the ability to truly help people who are miserably in pain. All in all, I think if I had my preference, I'd build the buildings and get them up and running, and then sell for a big profit and avoid things like audits and malpractice insurance and chiropractor groupies."

She squeezed his arm and went back to watering. "I think I'm just the opposite of you. I know the money is in ownership and management, but I love the people and the actual flowers best. I love growing things and creating things and making people smile and feel peace. Plus, someday I want to quit working at all and just focus on having a family." She smiled at him. "I know. I know. It's old fashioned and politically incorrect, but it's what I want. It may never actually happen, but it's what I want."

He walked to the nearby sink and filled a jug with water to refill her watering can and said as he poured, "Well, Skye Alexander, going for what you really want is what life is all about. Not to mention that probably every single prophet has recommended that women stay home with their children if they possibly can. You can't go wrong by following the prophet's counsel. Why do you question that it might ever happen?"

Skye thought about Shane and the smile died out of her face. She tried to recall it as she quipped cheerfully, "Ah, that's a long and downer story and we're not going there right now. Right now we're celebrating your freedom. Do you want to go out tonight or plan something for the future?"

Gage got a mischievous grin. "If I promise not to tell Mama Woo if I've kissed you, can I have both?"

Skye chuckled as she watered more plants. "Sure, Gage. Just tell me what times and what should I wear, and I'll pencil you in."

After setting a date for Saturday of the next week to go on a sleigh ride and then have dinner up on the ski hill in a yurt at Elk Meadows, they ended up at Francesca's over another quiet bowl of clam chowder. This time Gage got his decadent dessert and Skye ended up sharing a few bites of it.

The restaurant was busy on a Friday night, so they left rather than sit talking, but instead of taking her home, Gage drove her to the golf course near his home. Shutting off the car, he turned to her. "Are you up for a walk with me?"

"Absolutely." It was a cool evening, but they had jackets and Skye even had a pretty scarf she wrapped around her neck as he helped her out of the passenger side of the Jag.

As they set off down the path, Gage reached for her hand, and folding her smaller one into his larger one felt like the most natural and right thing in the world. They walked without talking much, pausing occasionally to look up at the stars in the clear January night sky and marvel out loud at the incredible universe spread out above them.

When she started to shiver he took her back to the car and after settling her into the leather passenger seat, he went around and got in, turning on the heater as well as the heated seats to help her warm up faster. It was still only eight forty and when he offered her a cup of hot cocoa at the IHOP she accepted gratefully and he held her hand again as they walked inside. The dinner crowds had thinned and he asked for an out-of-the-way booth and was hoping she would open up to him a little more about the long and downer story she hadn't wanted to get into earlier.

Steaming cups of cocoa with mounds of whipped cream on top were placed in front of them momentarily and Skye picked hers up to wrap her still chilled hands around it. Gage didn't say anything, just looked at her from across the table and she looked back at him for a few moments and finally said, "What?"

He was patiently quiet and then said, "What, what?"

"Why are you looking at me like that?"

He shrugged. "I'm not looking at you like anything. I'm just listening, Skye."

"What do you mean?"

Taking a sip of his drink while he still looked at her, he shrugged again. "I keep thinking there's something you want to tell me, but are hesitant about. I just want you to know I'm listening."

She tried to laugh that off, but it wasn't the incredibly cheerful, musical laugh she usually gave him and he small talked for a few minutes and then waited again. Finally, he asked, "Why do you question that settling down to be a mom may ever happen for you?"

For a moment she looked almost spooked and then gave him a hesitant smile. It wasn't full blown, but he could tell she trusted him. She looked over at him and then softly said, "Do you remember in the Wedding Planner when Jennifer Lopez said something about how those who can't do, teach, and those who can't wed, plan?" He nodded. "That's kind of my situation only for different reasons. And with me it's those who can't receive, arrange."

Gage could feel himself narrow his eyes as he tried to figure out what in the world she was saying. Surely she wasn't intimating that she didn't think anyone would marry her. As gorgeous and fun and dynamic as she was, that was ridiculous.

Just when he was finally going to question what she meant, she asked, "Gage, can I tell you I've had so much fun with you these last few weeks? I think you're handsome, and smart, and interesting, and absolutely sweet."

He sat up, wondering where this was going all of the sudden. He thought they'd had a good night. "But what, Skye? Why does that sound like the preface to 'but I just want to be friends?'"

She hesitated for several seconds and then asked a weird question out of the blue. "Gage, do you remember that first night with you in the tux and me teasing you about not going out with doctors anymore?"

"Yeah, something smart alecky about how the last one had turned out to be a stalker or something. Why?"

This time when she looked quietly back at him he almost thought she was the one listening, waiting for him to open up. He was a little lost again and kept trying to go back over what they'd just been saying to figure out what he'd missed. Finally, she added simply, "I wasn't joking."

He narrowed his eyes again, still struggling to understand what she was trying to get through to him. At length he admitted, "Skye, I need you to help me understand what you're trying to tell me. I'm sorry, but I don't get what you're saying."

She sighed and looked away and then met his eyes again. "I'm from Portland, Gage. My family is still there, in fact. After high school I went to Portland State University. I have a degree in horticulture. There's a medical school there and I met this guy I started going out with. He was in his last year of med school. Was going to be an orthopedic surgeon." She looked down at her hands in her lap for several seconds and then looked back up at Gage. "For a while there, I honestly thought I was in love with him."

She hesitated for what felt like a long time and then continued, "This is a long and incredibly ugly and involved story that you don't really need to be bothered with, so I'll shorten it to the cliff notes. He'd gotten his MD and was taking some specializations and then one day he was hurt skiing. Long story short, he became a narcotics addict and he changed drastically. I don't know if it was the chemicals or if he'd always been crazy and I just hadn't seen it, but when he wouldn't even admit there was a problem, I finally said I was out of there."

She stopped and swallowed hard. "He went berserk. He nearly killed me. I was in the hospital for a couple of weeks and then it was months before I healed. Physically at least. He was in jail and I tried to move on, but something like that changes you. I went back and got a minor in criminal psychology. I'm not sure why. I guess I was just trying to understand what he was thinking and how to never let anything like that ever happen again. I also got a black belt in Tai Kwan Do and I'm a lifetime member of the NRA now.

"Before he got out, I had a restraining order put on him, but he hadn't been out for twenty four hours when he started to hound me. The cops could never catch him. It got so bad that finally, I told my family goodbye, took the last of the cash out of my savings and disappeared. That was three years ago. This is the fourth place I've been, the fourth business I've started so he couldn't trace my ID, the fourth time of trying to meet new friends and make an apartment secure and finding escape routes for when he shows up. And he will. He's brilliant except for damage the drugs have done to his brain, which sadly is a lot. That brain damage and the money issues the drugs have brought on are probably the only reason he hasn't found me here already."

She looked up into Gage's eyes. "I've been here thirteen months. That's two months longer than the longest it's ever taken him." She stopped speaking and put her hands on the table but then she put them back in her lap, still without saying anything.

It was an almost incredible story and Gage sat there, heartsick and trying to take it in. It explained all the security and those little glimpses of fear he'd seen a couple of times like when he'd startled her at the grocery store. She was watching him closely and he looked up and met her eyes. "So help me understand how you compute this to never being a mother. This has to end sometime, doesn't it? Can't they find him and lock him up?"

"Oh, they will. Or actually he'll find himself when he shows up here one day. He'll try to get me to go with him and when I refuse, he'll go crazy again. They'll put him in rehab for a while or lock him back up and I'll have another couple of weeks to figure out how to completely uproot my life again." She shrugged her shoulders but her face was desperately sad as she said, "It's the ultimate form of footloose and free."

Giving him a lopsided heartbroken smile, she went on, "A family isn't even a remote possibility. A boyfriend hardly is if I'm honest. What guy would want to get involved in a mess like that, knowing I'll either die or disappear one day? And a boyfriend would probably be in even more danger than me. Shane would completely freak and kill us both."

Gage was quiet for several minutes as he tried to process what he had just heard and then asked, "Is Skye Alexander your real name?" She nodded. "And you're sure he's still after you, even though you haven't been in touch with him for thirteen months?"

Nodding without facing him, she answered, "The police here keep in touch with the police in Portland. They've been keeping an eye on him and it isn't hard to tell that he's still looking."

"Does Hailee know?"

"Enough to know that if I tell her to leave and stay away, she's to do it immediately, without question."

After that, there was a long pause. He had no idea what to say. What could you say to something like this? How do you wrap your brain around such a hellacious thing when the woman across the table seemed like the most happy girl with the best attitude he'd ever seen? She was talking matter-of-factly about someone trying to kill her!

As he struggled to know how to react, she was watching him intently and even though he didn't know what to say, he knew he needed to say something. She drained her hot chocolate and began wrapping her scarf around her neck and he reached across the table and took her hand to stop her. When she looked up into his eyes, he said the only thing he knew to, "Skye, I'm so sorry."

She shook her head and pulled her hand away. "Don't pity me, Gage. I have a wonderful life here and I'm happy. And I have a great deal to be thankful for, including the fact I survived. A lot of women aren't that lucky. And it brought me to Christ. In a way I'm grateful. I had a friend who tried to share the gospel with me in Portland, but I wouldn't listen. Maybe I had to go through what I've had to, and end up here, to be teachable enough to listen, but I am eternally grateful for the chance to have the restored gospel."

"I don't pity you, Skye. I admire you. But don't expect me to say fine, it was nice knowing you, see ya later, because it's not going to happen. I think you probably already understand that."

She met his eyes. "That would be the wisest course of action, and you know it. That way neither one of us will get hurt emotionally and at least you could stay safely out of harm's way physically."

He gave a minimal shake of his head. "This is all too new to me to know what is wisest. But I know what I want and it's not to walk away. Not only that, but even if I wasn't interested in you romantically, I could never turn my back and not feel like the biggest low life on the planet."

"Being chivalrous is the last thing we should be focused on in this, Gage. There are far more pressing concerns. What kind of low life do you think I'd feel like if something happened to you because of me?"

After considering this for a few minutes, he said, "I'm glad you told me why you're so careful, but you need to know that I try very hard to be proactive and make the best decisions I can with the best judgment possible after weighing the options. I don't intend to be reactive in this situation either. And while I intend to be much more careful about keeping you safe, I'm not going to let this guy control my decision making. There's potentially too much at stake."

"What do you mean?"

He met her gaze openly. "I think you know exactly what I mean, Skye. So don't try to push me away, which was where you were headed with that little speech about how much fun we've had together but... Wasn't it?"

She paused and then admitted, "Yeah, it was, Gage. And while I do respect your right to use your best judgment, you have to respect mine as well."

"So, what does that mean?"

The waitress came by with fresh cups of cocoa topped with cream and Skye took hers absently and dipped a finger into the frilly whipping cream before she said, "I don't know, honestly. Sometimes I have no idea what I should be doing. But I do try to listen for personal inspiration and I have to have faith that Heavenly Father will get through to me even when I am not hearing as clearly as I would like to. I've come to enjoy you which only makes me even more torn. I guess for now, let's just see how things go, huh?"

"Yes and no. Let's see how things go, but let's also have a contingency plan in place for when you'll need it. I'm sure you already do, but is there any way I could be in on what you intend to do if he shows up?"

Shaking her head, she said, "How do you plan for something like that, Gage, when you have no idea what he'll do or when or where? The best I know how to do is keep my apartment secure and Kitty and a gun handy and have the police's number programmed into speed dial. Oh, and carry cash, always. Other than that, I just have to be ready to think on my feet so I can get away."

"Why haven't they kept him locked up if he's done this over and over?"

"Because the system has to operate within the law and sadly, sometimes humans don't even have as much protection as animals. It's always a first time in a new jurisdiction. The bottom line is, this man is sick. He's an addict with a horribly sad problem. With most addicts, they don't need incarceration, they need treatment. Only Shane isn't one who can be turned loose. The police just don't always understand that."

"Even with the restraining order and records of past behavior in other places?"

Skye shrugged. "I guess not. Sometimes it makes me want to scream and swear and rail at the unfairness and trouble of it all, but really, I have two options. Let it destroy my happiness. Or not. I'm choosing the not."

He reached across the table and took her hand again and met her eyes once more. "I think that's my favorite thing about you, Skye. You choose the not." He rubbed the pad of his thumb across her neat short fingernails. "It's a gift. I hope you never change. It makes the world around you a better place." After a moment, he almost whispered, "They say life isn't about waiting for the storm to end, it's about learning to dance in the rain. You have dancing in the rain down to an art."

She gave him a small smile and said softly, "Thanks."

Pulling up in the alley behind her shop, Gage watched her thoroughly scan the alleyway and for the first time, he understood some of what she was up against. It made him want to put his arms around her and guard her from the entire world. Her great attitude was in the forefront again as she glanced at Mama Woo's darkened windows and turned to him on her porch and thanked him for taking her. "I had a nice night, Gage. I'm sorry I kind of ruined it with my tale." She was looking up at him and even in the dark he could see the stars reflected in the depths of those sky blue eyes.

Stepping closer, he pulled her into the protective circle of his arms. "You didn't kind of ruin it, Skye. I'm glad you told me. It's something I need to know to help keep you safe."

She stilled in his embrace and then said softly, "Yeah, but you'll probably never think of me the same again."

He leaned slightly back and looked down at her. "No, you're right. My thoughts toward you change every time I see you. This time, I have an even greater respect for you. You're a survivor both physically and emotionally and it's incredibly refreshing. A lot of women in your position would be bitter and angry."

"I have my moments, occasionally."

"What? You're human?" He tried to keep it light at the same time he was trying not to want to kiss that wistful sound out of her voice. "We all have our moments. But I'm willing to bet your grumpy moments are rare and short lived."

She moved into his chest and rested her cheek against him as she nodded. "I have been blessed with a cheerful heart, thank goodness. I inherited it from my mom. And I'm so grateful. Sometimes I watch other women have these moody, dark attitudes and I feel so sorry for them. Being grouchy can't be all that fun."

Gage chuckled at her deep philosophical insight. "No being grouchy isn't all that fun. You've got that right. Someone should copyright that and make signs and pass them out at medical clinics."

That made her laugh. "I'm sure that will help the people who already feel lousy. They'll probably straighten right up!"

"Or maybe not."

"Surely not everyone at your medical clinic is that grouchy. Maybe you're just tired."

"Is that a nice way of saying I'm the one who's grouchy?" He pulled back from her and smiled at how sheepish she looked.

"No. But sometimes when you talk about your work, you don't sound as if you enjoy it all that much." Gage stopped and thought about that, and finally Skye said, "Count your blessings Gage. It will make you grateful, and gratitude in turn makes you feel happy. A happy heart isn't really something that you're either blessed with or not. It's a decision. Choose happy. There are millions of men in this world who dream of being as successful and smart and handsome and competent and talented and..."

He reached up and put a finger gently on her lips. "All right, all right. I get the picture. I have a great life here and you don't pity me either. You're right and I should have your upbeat attitude. I should remember that some of the guys I went to school with are just barely hitting their strides in their practices and they rent clinic space."

She smiled against his finger and he had to join her as she said, "See? You made a decision and your gratitude has already made you happier."

He gently ran his finger across her lips, watching her eyes and instantly forgot all about his practice. He was happy, but it definitely had more to do with the beautiful, sweet girl in his arms and her tempting mouth than making a choice to count his blessings. Or maybe she was one of his blessings. She definitely made him smile. Actually, she made him want to kiss her smile. As he caressed her lip, her smile mellowed and her blue eyes seemed even clearer still as she watched him back. It had probably only been a second or two, but it felt like long enough to drown in those deep blues.

At length, he slowly dropped his head until his own lips gently captured hers and her eyes closed as he finally kissed her the way he'd never wanted to kiss another girl in his life.

The way he'd dreamed of kissing her since that first night on this same porch.

Later, as her door shut behind her and he heard her shoot the dead bolt, he hurriedly glanced around and mentally berated himself for standing right out here in plain sight and kissing her until his brain had stalled. Even after what she'd told him tonight, kissing her even for just those few minutes had made him forget literally everything else, including the fact that potentially she wasn't safe.

Vowing to never let that happen again, he drove the several minutes across town to his house knowing exactly how the Brownie and Mad Martigan in Willow had felt after being powdered with the Dust of Broken Heart. He could suddenly understand just how a mighty warrior could stop in the middle of a battle and start spouting poetry. He felt like the very air around him had been permeated by that same sweet, cheerful heart that she made a decision to be blessed with.

Meeting her had made him blessed with it as well by association and it was amazing how much energy that released into his life. She'd commented about his attitude about his work, but until Skye, he hadn't even realized his attitude had been lacking. It was like the vibrance of her spirit reflected on everything around her and made the very air sparkle with her enthusiasm. Suddenly he could recognize that he'd lost some of his passion for life, especially where his practice was concerned, and as he pulled into his garage and let himself into his house, he committed to working on that. He thoroughly enjoyed being around Skye and he certainly wasn't going to be the one to dampen the attitude around her.

****

Skye locked her door, dropped a gentle hand to Kitty's head and stood quietly in the dark for a moment, testing the feel of her house to ensure all was as secure as it seemed. Reassured by Kitty's peaceful demeanor, she wandered back toward her bedroom, wondering how long her lips and her finger tips would tingle like they were from being kissed and caressed by Gage.

As she got ready for bed, there was a very lopsided battle going on between her heart and her head about how she should be dealing with a certain handsome chiropractor. There was this quiet, logical part at the back of her brain that kept trying to override the much more overt romantic part of her brain. The part of her brain that made her want to waltz to the soft radio as she brushed her teeth.

There was something about Gage that had a remarkable effect on her every time she was around him. Some combination of his confidence and his intelligence coupled with how attractive he was made her whole universe move just a little faster, while at the same time there was this understated sense of power and control that mellowed her and made her feel incredibly secure. Almost dangerously so.

As she picked up her Book of Mormon to read she gave herself a mini lecture about being unsafely carefree around Gage. What she'd said about Shane's reaction to a perceived competitor had been realistic. Gage could be in even more trouble than she was in this mess. And he'd never met Shane. He had no idea what he could really be in for.

Her mind registered all of this on some level, but a few minutes later after saying her prayers, she was still struggling to squelch the thoughts of how nice it was to be kissed by him tonight. She honestly hadn't known she could feel like this. That few moments on the back porch had been too enjoyable to even comprehend. Gosh, how had she gotten to be her age and not felt like this before? And what was this feeling anyway?

She stretched and yawned and smiled with her eyes closed and snuggled deeper into her down duvet. Dead tired, she felt herself relaxing into the softness of the bed after a full day and let out an almost inaudible sigh. This was such a sweet, comfortable feeling. The pillow case felt cool and smooth against the cheek that had been leaning against his strong chest tonight. She drifted closer to sleep. Gage Garrison was an incredible kisser.

****

The security guard at the Portland City offices noticed the snowstorm that interrupted the picture from the security camera that was covering the elevator to the west wing, but it only flashed for a second and then went back to the clear picture of the empty hall as it should be at three-forty in the morning. He watched it closely for another couple of minutes and then passed it off as the inevitable computer glitch that occurred in these tricky electronics. Just in case, he'd take a stroll up there and check things out in a few minutes. It would help keep him awake. But it could wait. He was just now texting some coed from the U of O he'd met online earlier. He'd only be texting for another few minutes anyway.

Chapter 6

Skye carefully herded her six year old primary class into the classroom after sharing time and tried to get them to settle down and focus on what she was trying to teach them about families. She was having a time of it and not only because their attention span was in the four minute range. For some reason this lesson made her more conscious than ever of the fact that her family here consisted of herself, a tiny, elderly Asian woman and a dog, and her own mind was wandering.

As far as that went, Mama Woo just wasn't herself lately. Skye had only known her about a year, but she'd never known her to struggle to get up out of a chair like she did this last little while and every move she made seemed to take her breath away. Skye made a mental note to get her in to her doctor and then tried to focus back on the six year olds which worked for a while.

She'd finally gotten Mama Woo off of her mind and then couldn't help thinking of her parents and brothers and their families back in Portland. Sometimes she missed them desperately. Her mother taught English at an inner city school that was as tough as they come and she was in that long stretch of January and early February between holidays when the days seemed to drag on forever for the students. Skye knew her mother was probably trying every trick in the book to keep the kids on task and see if she could get a light to come on inside a few of them.

Her dad was the city manager and they were plenty well enough off that her mother didn't have to work, but still, she worked tirelessly to try and make a difference to the at-risk kids she taught.

Skye wiped at a rogue tear that insisted on escaping from her eye and smiled at the children in front of her who were looking at her like something was definitely wrong with her. And something was. Why couldn't she focus any better than this, this morning? What would Gage have thought of her after their talk about choosing happy? She hurriedly finished the lesson and got out crayons and paper and had the class begin pictures of their forever families and she sighed and began to pack away her manual and get out the animal crackers she had brought for a snack. That was one thing about a six year old. A snack could fix anything.

Once she had turned the snackers back over to their parents, she collected Mama Woo from the gospel doctrine class and helped her into the chapel. When they were seated, Mama Woo studied her face for a few seconds and then patted her hand gently before looking up to the pulpit where the second counselor in the bishopric was opening the meeting. Now what had that look been about? Surely Mama Woo hadn't been able to tell that Skye was missing her family this morning, had she?

Back at Skye's house an hour and a half later, she settled Mama Woo at the kitchen counter with a premade pie crust to fit into the pan while Skye worked on the ingredients for a quiche to put in it. It was a beautiful, peaceful Sabbath afternoon and usually Skye loved working together with Mama Woo like this, but part of her brain kept thinking that she wished Gage was here cooking with them.

She hadn't spoken to him since he'd dropped her off late Friday and she wondered if he'd decided after hearing about Shane that she was not worth the possible danger. After the way he'd kissed her, she didn't think so, except he hadn't called. But then it had only been a day and a half. Her train of thought was high jacked back to that night on her porch as she remembered how incredibly nice it was to be kissed that way and it took her a minute to realize Mama Woo was watching her with a quizzical look on her face.

Coming back to the present, Skye looked down and realized she'd chopped the crumbled bacon in front of her into micro particles and she looked up at Mama Woo with a sheepish grin as the little woman smiled and teased, "Where you head this afnoon, Missy? Why you pink when you chop that bacon to smush? You thinking 'bout handsome docto' Gage? Yes?" Skye grinned and began to gather up the minute bacon pieces as Mama Woo made a clucking sound in her throat. "I think he cernly kiss you, Missy! Why else you can't remember be nice that poor bacon?"

Skye's grin grew into a full blown smile. "I am not telling you, Sulee. You're supposed to keep things like that private. Don't kiss and tell, remember? Do you want onions and two kinds of cheese, or just Provolone in your pie there?"

The little woman waved a hand. "All cheese. More merrier. No need tell me. Sulee can see eyes. He good kiss you, no? Mus be. Kiss your mind gone, all way."

Skye laughed and went to dig in the fridge. He'd definitely kissed her mind gone, all way. That was for sure. She had gone to bed that night thinking that she needed to stop seeing Gage for both of their safety and yet she hadn't been able to think of anything but him since.

She was thinking of him again a few minutes later when the doorbell sounded. That old panic jumped in her just for a moment. She didn't get many unexpected visitors. She quickly glanced at Kitty who stood in front of the door to the alley but she wasn't growling and, in fact, her snub tail was wagging as she stood there.

Skye wiped her hands on the apron she'd put on over her dress and went to peek through the peephole. She glanced at Mama Woo who had on that knowing smile again as she opened the door to see Gage standing on the small porch with a long baguette in his hands. They just stood there looking at each other for a minute and then he asked, "Am I too late to help cook Sunday dinner? I brought French bread and I'm a good chopper."

Shaking her head with a smile, Skye said, "You don't need to bring bread or chop something. Come on in. Mama Woo was just asking about you."

"Is she still wondering if I've kissed you?"

Skye flushed and dropped her eyes with a guilty smile. "Actually, no. For some reason she's decided that we've definitely kissed, but I haven't said a word. I promise."

Gage chuckled and tipped her chin up so she had to look at him and then gently touched her lip as he drew his hand away. They looked at each other for another few seconds and then finally Gage handed her the bread. "I wasn't sure what to bring. Tell me. What do you bring to a woman who is a florist? It's not like you want more flowers."

Taking his hand to pull him inside, she smiled. "Oh, but you're wrong, Gage. Just bring wildflowers. Wildflowers you've actually picked. That is the purist form of gifting. Wildflowers and chocolate. Chocolate kisses." She grinned up at him. "And other kisses. That works too."

He stopped momentarily. "Are we talking other flavors of Hershey kisses? Or just other kisses?"

She looked at him for a second and then turned back to her little kitchen and said over her shoulder, "Uh, yeah. Do you like Quiche? Mama Woo and I kind of make our own version that has everything in it but the kitchen sink."

He followed her as he said, "I like all flavors. Of Quiche. And stuff." Skye glanced back at him, wondering if he was saying what she thought he was. He definitely was. She flushed again and went back to her chopping as Gage slipped off his suit jacket and began rolling up his sleeves as he visited with Mama Woo.

On Tuesday, Hailee had an early out day and so Skye took advantage of having her available and she took Mama Woo in for a check up. When the doctor asked what the problem was, Skye couldn't even pin point anything. "I'm not sure, Dr. Hallam. I sometimes just think she isn't acting like herself. Does that sound crazy?"

The middle aged doctor shook his head with a smile. "Actually, it doesn't sound crazy at all. Okay, Mrs. Woo. You haven't had a really good physical for a while. Let's give you a good look over and see if we can tell why you have your young friend worried."

An hour and a half and several different tests later, Skye loaded Mama Woo back into her car with a heavy heart. Although Mama Woo had been exceptionally healthy for a woman who had been through what she had in her life, Skye's concerns had been founded. It hadn't taken Dr. Hallam more than a few minutes to determine that for some reason Mama Woo's blood pressure had become dangerously high. In fact, it was high enough that she was at considerable risk of having a stroke. He immediately put her on new medication and asked Skye to bring her back in in just a couple of days to be tested and if she had any concerns at all, to get her in immediately.

As Skye helped her out of the car, Mama Woo looked up at her and said, "I sorry, Missy. I sorry to be problem for you much. Thanks for help."

Skye hugged her gently. "You're not a problem, Mama Woo. I'm just worried." She smiled at the little woman. "We're all the family each other's got here, Sulee. I should be taking better care of you."

Mama Woo patted her hand. "We have much family, Missy. Some in other places, but all sealed. No worries. Some day all back together. You with yours, me with family. You see."

"I know, Sulee. But let's do better with that blood pressure okay?"

****

Gage broke away late in the morning on Tuesday to run some errands and hopefully talk Skye into going to lunch with him. He tried her cell as he drove, but she didn't pick up and he headed for her shop. When he made it there, she was nowhere in sight, but the pretty red haired girl she had working for her was in and came to help a man who came in just ahead of him. Gage waited and was a little surprised when the somewhat scruffy man approached the counter and asked hesitantly, "Is this the shop that has the agreement with, uhm, AA?" He held out a business card with something written on the back. "I was told if I brought this here I could get some flowers for my wife."

The red head smiled at the slightly flustered man. "This is exactly the right place. Just one moment and I'll grab you a bouquet." She went into the cooler and came back out with a bunch of flowers wrapped in plastic. She tucked in a packet of preservative as she said, "Choose a card, sir." She indicated the small cards on the counter and when the man had chosen one, she handed him the flowers with another smile and said, "Good job. You must be doing well, if you got one of her cards. I hope your wife enjoys these. Have a good day, Sir."

The man took the flowers and headed out the door without money being exchanged and Gage glanced at him before turning back to speak to the young girl. He must have looked confused, because the girl volunteered, "Skye has an agreement with Alcoholics Anonymous here. If they can stay sober, she'll provide free flowers with a note from their counselor. It's nothing fancy, but it's a way to help them as they try to get back on track with their lives. Sometimes the wives get a little thrashed in the mix of things."

"I imagine they do." Gage was surprised and glanced back out the door again and then back to the young woman. "When do you expect her back? Skye I mean?"

"I'm not sure. She took Mama Woo in to the doctor. I could give her a message if you'd like."

"Is Mama Woo sick?"

"You know, I 'm not sure. I know Skye is really concerned about her."

Gage left hoping something hadn't happened to Mama Woo. She was the only family Skye had right now.

He finally caught Skye on her phone as he was leaving work that night and she told him what was going on with Mama Woo. He could hear the worry in her voice and asked what he could do to help. "Actually, I was just going to deliver flowers to some of the widows here in my ward, but I hate to leave her alone right now. Are you busy tonight? Doctor appointments always stress her out anyway."

Gage arranged to watch over the tiny Asian woman for her, hoping he could also watch over Skye when she was through delivering flowers to the widows. That sounded just like something Skye would do. Take flowers to ladies who weren't likely to get them often. The more he got to know her, the more intriguing she was to him.

That same thought crossed his mind late Friday afternoon as he rode with Skye to deliver bouquets to a nursing home not far from her shop. As they walked into the facility that reeked of disinfectant carrying the arrangements, several of the residents called out to Skye and he realized she must have come there quite often for them to be this familiar with each other. Skye stopped in to visit with several of them as she delivered the flowers and Gage could see how happy they were to see her.

While she finished visiting, he brought in the rest of the flowers from her van and then paused near a pile of huge rocks and sand and tubing that littered the central courtyard of the facility. It was an eyesore and he wondered why the otherwise tired and flat lawn was such a mess. He would have thought the pile would have been a liability issue.

As he wandered back into the building, a school bus pulled up outside and Gage was surprised to see a whole troop of older teenaged boys climb out and come inside. He was even more surprised as they spread out to visit with the old folks. From what he was hearing, they weren't familiar with each other, but the boys didn't seem to hesitate to converse anyway. Seeing these kids act like this gladdened his heart. He wished he'd have been like this in high school. Then he hadn't realized how lonely some of these old folks could be. For just a second he felt guilty because now as an adult, he did know, but didn't do something about it nearly enough.

He'd lost Skye somewhere among the residents and was just looking for her when she came out of a room toward the man who had unloaded with the high school boys. As Gage approached them, he noticed the logo on the man's shirt was Washington High School Athletics. Shaking the man's hand, Skye introduced him as the boy's football coach and Gage was completely non-plussed as Skye whistled and then gathered the boys around her and went out into the courtyard with them as he and the coach brought up the rear.

Outside, Gage didn't understand for a minute what was going on, but he had to smile to see how the ever effervescent Skye shepherded the whole bunch of them to what he'd considered a rubble pile and began to direct the boys as they teamed up to lift and move the huge rocks and boulders. Slowly, over the next half hour or so, and with the help of a couple of gargantuan pry bars and a lot of groaning, the brawny young men turned the rubble pile into what appeared to be the foundation for a water garden and fountain. If Gage hadn't seen it himself, he'd have never believed it.

When the last of the huge stones had been satisfactorily placed, Skye gave the whole bunch of the boys high fives and fist bumps as they filed back out to their bus. Gage was smiling again as the bus pulled away at what he'd just witnessed. Only Skye could come up with such a solution to moving boulders without the aid of some monstrous piece of machinery. For a few more minutes, she moved smaller rocks around and neatly stacked the tubing to the side and then took Gage's hand as she headed back out to the van.

As he held the driver's side door for her, he asked, "So what does the football team get out of being the brute force behind your fountain?"

Skye smiled up at him. "They get to know these great elderly people and all the corsages and boutonnieres they can sell for prom in a couple of weeks. I promised them if they'd visit for a few minutes and help me with the boulders, I'd do a team fundraiser. I'm by far getting the best end of the deal, but they don't seem to mind. It would have cost me a fortune to hire machinery."

He came around and climbed into the passenger side of the van and then asked, "So what do you get out of this deal? Did the center hire you to build them a water garden?"

Shaking her head, Skye answered, "This is definitely not one of the care centers that can afford to put in a water garden. They can hardly afford to keep that ratty lawn mowed. I was bringing the flowers one day and decided they needed something to help cheer the place up. A pond and waterfall will do wonders for these sweet people. There's something about the sound of falling water that is good for the soul."

Gage looked across the van and smiled. There was definitely something about Skye Alexander that was good for the soul. He liked this girl enough that it almost scared him, except that being with her was the most comfortable thing he'd ever known.

In the middle of the afternoon on Thursday, he got a pleasant surprise when Skye called his cell phone. She hadn't done that and it had almost begun to be troubling. Her voice was even more upbeat than normal and it made him smile as she told him she'd had to call to give him the good news. Someone who had attended the huge wedding she'd done just after the first of the year had come in and scheduled a wedding that easily doubled that one's flower order for late March. She admitted that it would be a marathon event, but it meant that they loved her floral designs and he got off of the phone feeling as happy and proud as she had sounded as she told him. This girl was a one in ten billion as far as attitude went and he was becoming seriously smitten.

The next weekend, after going on a sleigh ride and then having dinner with her on the mountain, he liked her even more. The sleigh ride had been fun, but the dinner had been awful. The food was bad and only half cooked anyway and the yurt was uncomfortably cold and Gage had been on the verge of asking for his money back, but Skye had taken it all in stride with her usual sunny attitude. By the time he had her back to the alleyway behind her house, he had decided she was the most fun he'd ever had in his life.

Honestly, he just wanted to kiss her as they went to tuck Mama Woo in and he felt guilty for not being more solicitous of the gentle older woman. She needed this care and it was so good of Skye to watch over her, but after watching Skye smile through a night that had frankly been somewhat unpleasant, Gage wanted to kiss that sweet smile that didn't dampen even when her teeth had been chattering. She was an adorable good sport.

He asked her to go to church with him, but she taught primary and was worried about leaving Mama Woo to get to her meetings alone, so they settled on Skye going to church in her own ward and then once she had Mama Woo safely back home, she came just for Sacrament Meeting with him.

On the spur of the moment, he decided to take her up to his mom's house for dinner. He'd never brought a girl home to Sunday dinner in his life, and hoped if they just dropped in unannounced it wouldn't be that big of a deal.

It wasn't a big deal, but he probably should have warned Skye about Gabriel, although she dealt with his antics with that easy smile and sweet happy attitude, just like she dealt with everything else. Gabriel was in rare form, too. There was a moment there, as Gage introduced them when his little brother took her hand and literally bowed as he kissed it at length that Gage considered whacking him and warned, "All right, Romeo. Enough with the hand kissing. Let her go. She's with me, and she's going to stay that way for the whole meal, so give it up."

Gabriel finally let go with an exaggerated sigh and whined to their mother, "Mom, Gage is always so selfish. He made me stop kissing her hand when I was only halfway through."

"I'm sure you'll survive, Gabriel." His mother rolled her eyes as she wiped her hands on the towel she had picked up. "Just try not to encourage him. You must be Skye. It's so nice to meet you. Dinner isn't quite ready, but it should just be a few minutes."

Gage was just starting to slip off his suit jacket as Skye asked, "What can we do to help?"

They ended up mashing the potatoes and then helping with the green salad and it had been incredibly nice to watch Skye and his mother laughing together like they were old friends instead of just having met. For some reason, he really wanted Skye to be comfortable with his family. Well, most of his family. He had no doubt that Gabriel would have loved to have gotten chummy with her, but at that, Gage drew the line.

After dinner, Skye didn't hesitate to get up and begin helping to load the dishwasher and the way his dad stood beside her and rinsed dishes and handed them to her was like an unspoken seal of approval that she wasn't even aware of, but Gage was and it was a marvelous feeling. He had a great deal of respect for his parents' judgment and was grateful they were comfortable with her.

Gabriel was still a little too comfortable and as they were leaving, and he went into the hand kissing thing again, Gage said, "I should probably warn you, Gabe. She has a black belt in Tai Kwan Do so watch yourself. You get fresh with her and we're both going to hurt you."

His little brother only smiled bigger at her and said, "Aw, I can take Gage and sparring with you might be worth the pain." Gage wasn't amused, but Skye only laughed as she deftly pulled on Gabriel's hand and stepped to the side and instantly had his arm up behind his back for just a split second before she let him go as he grinned and said, "Okay. So maybe not. Dang, Skye, that was slick. Remind me not to mess with your girl, Gage."

"Yeah, I'll do that. Every time you reach to kiss her whole arm." Gage grinned and took Skye's hand as he led her back out to his car. As he opened the door for her, he paused before he let go of it and said, "Remind me never to mess with you either, Skye. You did that so fast I didn't even see what happened. For just a second there, he was speechless. And that's a first in my lifetime."

Once he was in the car, Skye commented, "I'll bet growing up with him was quite an experience. How much younger is he than you?"

"Five years. The older he gets, the more alike we look. He's definitely the cut up of the family. You never know what he's going to do next. Like hit on your date. Sorry about that."

She laughed. "You were the one he was trying to get to, Gage. It didn't bother me a bit. I thought he was adorable."

"Oh, great. Adorable. You're not supposed to tell your date you think his brother is adorable, Skye."

"Oh, sorry. I didn't realize that was the rule. But you have to admit he is." Gage looked across the car at her and she laughed again. "He's a tease, but I'm sure he wouldn't seriously challenge your authority. Relax, Romeo." Gage knew Gabriel truly was adorable, but that didn't stop him from being just a touch jealous anyway.

That night he noticed Mama Woo wasn't acting right. When he and Skye stopped to tuck her in that teasing smile hardly made an appearance and she didn't even try to remind him to kiss Skye as they went back out the door. Not that he needed any reminding where Skye's lips were concerned. Kissing her had become his favorite national pass time and he sometimes felt stupid about how much of his day he actually spent just thinking about kissing her. There were times when even his secretary noticed he was preoccupied.

Back inside Skye's apartment, he could see the worry in her eyes and pulled her into a hug, wishing he could somehow take it away for her. The best he could do was to offer to help her watch over Mama Woo. At least Skye knew he would be here for her if she ever needed it.

She did need it just a few days later. Skye was headed to the battered women shelter with some left over flowers and Mama Woo wasn't feeling great so Gage came by and sat with her. He hadn't minded a bit. Mama Woo was actually thoroughly enjoyable, but Skye was so grateful when she got home that he felt doubly rewarded. That night as he held Skye before telling her goodnight, he could feel the tension in her and turned her around and began to massage out the strain in her neck and shoulders as he asked, "Skye, is this work, or Mama Woo, or Shane that has you this uptight?"

For a second he wondered if she was going to answer him and as she tensed he looked around at her and realized she was trying to hide her feelings before she replied. At that, he moved right in front of her and looked in the eyes that she was struggling to keep from tearing up and said, "Don't,

Skye. Don't try to shut me out. We're past that by now, aren't we? Aren't we good enough friends that we can be honest with each other, even about the unhappy stuff?"

She didn't answer and instead dropped her eyes and he pulled her back into a tight hug. "You know, Skye. True friends are there for the good weather and the bad. It's only honorable. I know you're the most happy and positive human on the planet, but everyone has their moments. You've listened to me when I've struggled. I'm more than happy to return the favor." He pulled back to look at her and when she looked up, he asked, "You know that, don't you?"

She nodded and the tears finally overflowed her eyes, but it still took a few more seconds before she admitted in a whisper, "I do know, Gage. What I don't know is how to do that. I've never been very good at anything but the happy part. Talking about unhappy things always seems so wrong and selfish to me."

"But, Skye honey, that's what people who are in a relationship do. They give and take. They stand by each other through the happy and the unhappy. As long as it's not all one sided, that's actually what helps friendships to be stronger. Didn't you see that in your parents' relationship growing up?"

Nodding again, she leaned into his chest. "I did see it in their marriage, Gage, but I always tell myself that if I'll just choose happy, I'll never need to admit to bad weather."

"I'm no psychologist, Skye, but that sounds like a recipe for eventual disaster. Can anybody ignore their own needs forever? If my mother or sisters tried that, they'd be fine for a while and then have a nuclear melt down." He went back to massaging her shoulders as he watched her quietly. Finally, he said, "Okay, Skye. Be strong if you feel like you need to. But please know I'm here if you ever want to talk, all right? Turn around. In the mean time, enjoy the benefits of dating a chiropractor. Let me work on the tension."

Several minutes later, he asked, "Better?"

"Incredibly better. Thank you. I didn't realize chiropractors knew massage too. That was heaven. Thanks."

"Honestly, Skye. As tight as you are, you should probably come have a few sessions with the massage therapist. Especially before you head into the next couple of weeks. Won't Valentine's Day be hyper busy?"

She turned back to him and snuggled into his chest. "Mega hyper busy. I'm hiring two temporary helpers and it will probably still be grueling."

"Well, call me if you need a massage and I'll arrange it. I have an excellent therapist on staff."

"Thanks. I just might. Although my hours will be insane."

"I can arrange insane appointments. I'm the boss, remember? Plus, Cara knows I'll make it up to her somehow. So don't hesitate. Stress does terrible things to the human body."

She nodded wordlessly and he hugged her tighter. As the silence drew out between them, he could feel her almost melting against him closer still and she felt incredibly good there against him. She fit perfectly here inside the circle of his arms.

When she finally looked up at him, leaning to brush her cheek with his was instinctive and then he gently took her chin in his hand and watched her eyes as he finally touched his mouth to hers.

He wanted her to know he was there for her, whatever she needed, and he only intended to kiss her gently and softly, but after a moment, it felt like he needed to kiss her more insistently to help her know that he would handle whatever she needed him to. She needed to know this emotion was as strong as it had to be.

At length, when they finally pulled away from each other, he cupped her cheek with his hand and said quietly, "Whether it's work, or Mama Woo, or Shane, or even all three at the same time, I'm here if you need me, Skye. I'm here."

She searched his eyes and after a moment nodded. "Thank you."

He leaned to kiss her one more time. "Goodnight, Skye. Sleep well. Dream about me."

Chapter 7

The next Saturday morning, when he called to ask her to come play racquetball with him, she told him she was working on the water garden at the care center and when he dropped by, he was amazed at what she was up to. The ground inside the stone perimeter had been dug out to form a small pond that was simply a rubber liner at the moment and Skye was putting together the workings of the fountain that would circulate the water from the pond to the top of the small water fall she had created. She was dusty and smelled of plumbing cement and was unspeakably beautiful as she crafted what would obviously be a striking water garden when she was done.

Even at this rough stage the balance and beautiful design was apparent and he asked. "Do you ever do these on contract anymore? Could you be hired to build one for my clinic?" He grinned at her. "I'll spring for the football team labor so you don't have to make a load of boutonnières."

A shadow seemed to cross her face, but she said, "Sure, I could do that."

He wondered what had caused the concern he'd seen and finally asked her over a late lunch, "Why did you hesitate over building me a water garden? You don't need to feel obligated."

For a few seconds she seemed to be thinking about her answer and then said, "No, I love to create them. They can be such a comfort to people at times. I've seen what an effect they can have and a health clinic would be perfect." She hesitated and then looked up at him and continued, "I'd love to do it sometime after Valentine's Day."

After watching her eyes, he knew what she wasn't saying was that she didn't know if she'd even be around here then because the old boyfriend might have shown up. He almost asked her right out if she was planning to keep up this friendship that had steadily grown since that first night of the ballet, but then he decided against it. He knew her well enough by now to know she honestly cared for him, but that probably meant that she planned to do everything she could to keep him from being harmed by this Shane person. In a way, it was sweet of her, but if she ever really did up and leave without a trace, it would devastate him far more than he cared to admit.

He had asked her what her plan was that first time she'd told him about Shane and she'd said then that she didn't know what she'd do. She probably felt the same way still. He went back to eating after deciding to do a little poking around of his own.

That night he started digging on the internet. He didn't know the old boyfriend's last name and had to start with her name and it took some searching, but he eventually found the original judgment for the first time Shane had gone ballistic on her and what Gage read made him literally sick. She had glossed over the details when she'd admitted the story to him over cocoa that night, but the facts were appalling. She was indeed lucky to be alive after that kind of an attack.

The man's name was Shane Cainan and after reading of the failed attempt to punish him the first time, Gage pulled up everything he could on the guy to see if he could get a handle on just what Skye was dealing with here, but it was ineffective to say the least. To read addresses, financial records, degrees and criminal records couldn't give him a feel for what to expect from this madman.

After stewing over it for several days, he finally showed up at her flower shop at closing time on Thursday evening with Chinese take out and asked if he could invite himself to dinner again. After eating and visiting with Mama Woo, he and Skye went back to her little apartment to watch a movie, but they didn't make it through the movie very happily.

She knew something was on his mind and once they were securely locked inside with Kitty. Skye turned to him and asked, "Is something wrong, Gage? Where has your smile gone?"

With a sigh, he took her hand and led her to the excruciating loveseat. "I'm sorry, Skye. There's nothing really wrong except that I know you're planning to leave here abruptly sometime when your Shane shows up and I have no idea how to deal with that. In the first place, I can't spare you."

He gave her a sad smile and rubbed a thumb across the back of the hand he held. "And it twists my chauvinistic need to protect you all to smithereens. I feel like I should be figuring out how to keep you safe from him, not how to learn to live without you once you drop off the face of the earth again." He gave her another humorless smile. "How's a decent guy supposed to come to terms with this?"

She leaned her head against his shoulder with an almost inaudible sigh. "How's a decent girl supposed to answer that, Gage? I already feel guilty for seeing you. If I truly was a decent girl, I'd have quit a long time ago to keep you from becoming a target. I'm just being selfish and I know it, but I'm enjoying you so much."

With the way this conversation was heading, Gage began to wonder if he shouldn't have just kept his mouth shut and continued to dig for information on this Shane on his own.

The last thing he'd wanted was for her to tell him she no longer wanted to see him. It wouldn't work as long as he could see in her eyes that she cared for him, but he didn't really want to fight her over this. He knew she was an incredibly strong woman, in spite of how exquisitely beautiful she was.

When her phone rang and she took a call that must have been someone in her ward he was glad for the interruption and dug through the movies on her entertainment center while she talked. Starting the movie would be wiser than hashing this all out tonight. That would probably be a no-win situation.

That night, he Googled private investigators in the greater Portland area and the next morning on the way into the clinic, he phoned a couple who looked promising and arranged for one of them to discreetly check into this guy and see if he could find out if he really was still looking and how close he was if at all possible. He thought about just checking with the police both there and here, but worried they'd just think he was helping Shane try to find her and wouldn't tell him anything.

In a way, he felt somewhat underhanded about doing this behind her back, but he was no longer willing to just accept her walking away from him. He'd come to care about her far too much in the last couple of months. For the first time in his life, he was thinking about time and all eternity. He would never have told her that. She would have just run from him, but he was thinking it.

Saturday she put the finishing touches except for the plants on the water garden she'd been designing and then they went cross country skiing and then back to his house and had a candle light dinner beside the fire. Between the brilliant sunshine and the magnificent mountains, and then the ambience over dinner, he was still thinking that he'd like to keep spending glorious days like this with her forever if there was anyway possible. The more he was around her, the more he realized she was the most sweet and happy girl he'd ever known.

The only thing that marred their date was the ridiculous call he got that evening at nearly nine p.m. from a woman requesting he come in to the clinic and give her an emergency chiropractic treatment. It was the married woman who had given him the expensive fly rod at Christmas and he'd learned from experience that she probably had absolutely nothing wrong with her spine, and was, in fact, looking for something much different than a chiropractic adjustment.

He recognized the number and, in fact, didn't even take the call until she persisted. The third time she tried to reach him, he finally picked up and told her it would be impossible for him to come in, that he was in the middle of a personal situation.

He hung up with an apologetic smile for Skye. "Sorry about that. Now you see why sometimes I'm a little cynical. I inadvertently called her back on my cell phone once when she called the answering service and now she has my personal number. The last emergency she had, she showed up in not nearly enough clothing and made sure I knew her husband was out of town for several days. For a minute there, I wished I had called the night security guard to come in to my office with us."

Skye laughed and said, "What you need is a good bulletproof answering service that would stop them in their tracks. How often do you have to go in for legitimate emergencies in the middle of the night?"

"I only have about six patients who I'd honestly go in for after hours any more. And they're all either really good friends or little old ladies and children. The answering service shunts all of the other calls to one of the other chiropractors in the office. It's not very fair, I know, but it's one of the perks of being the owner."

"It's fair when you're the one with the costs of ownership. Enjoy it. You've earned it. If any of the others don't like it, let them start their own clinic. You know they probably won't. Personal initiative is pretty rare in this world and when you've done the work, you shouldn't feel guilty about enjoying the benefits."

They had gone on to talk of other things, but as he drove to his house after taking her home, he had to appreciate how nice it was to always have her encouragement. She didn't just choose happy – she also spread it around.

It took the PI several days to get back with him and by the time he did, it was the week before Valentine's Day and Skye had already begun to work those insane hours she'd spoken of. All the investigator had found was that this Shane Cainan was indeed still obsessed with Skye, but he himself seemed to have fallen off the planet and the PI couldn't find out where he was at the moment. Neither of those facts was very comforting to Gage and he considered hiring security for her building. He ultimately decided against it for the time being because he worried it would only make Skye more uptight than ever, and that was the last thing she needed in her life this week.

At least the PI had sent him a photo so that now he could at least recognize the guy if he saw him. Blonde and big, the guy looked to be well over six feet and had to have weighed close to two twenty. It was no wonder Skye had gotten her black belt; he was certainly no ninety pound weakling. Gage studied the face for a minute, knowing this guy would have to be considered handsome and tried to figure out how he felt about Skye thinking for a time she'd been in love with him. Even though the relationship was far more than over as far as she was concerned, Gage still couldn't help the touch of jealousy.

On the night of February eleventh, he got a call from Skye at ten-forty-five at night and when he picked up, he could hear the fear in her voice. He first thought Shane had found her until he heard her say, "Gage, I'm sorry to call so late. I'm running Mama Woo into the emergency room. Something is wrong. I'm worried she's having a stroke." Her voice cracked and then a second later she asked, "Is there any way I could stop by your house and have you give her a blessing?"

"Sure, Skye. Better yet, I'll just meet you there. I'll see if my dad or Gabriel are still up and bring them with. Do you need help getting her into the car? I could be there in minutes. Or should you just call for an ambulance?"

"No, I'll be fine. I'll see you there in a minute. And Gage."

"Yeah."

"Will you pray for her? I'm so worried."

"I will, Skye. I'll pray for both of you. I always do."

It took her another few seconds to whisper, "Thanks."

Gabriel came with him and for once he wasn't clowning around. Mama Woo's ghostly pallor and the obvious pain and confusion in her eyes had all of them absolutely sober. Gage walked into the emergency room and automatically wrapped Skye into a close hug to try an offset the fear he could see her struggling with. He stroked her back and whispered, "It's going to be all right, Skye. The doctors will know what to do."

After giving Mama Woo the blessing, Gabriel left to return home, but Gage stayed with Skye and when the doctors had Mama Woo stabilized and admitted her, he went up to the room with them. Once she was in and settled, he thought about offering to watch over Mama Woo and encouraging Skye to go home and rest, but he knew without even asking that Skye couldn't do it. Instead, once the lights were low and Mama Woo seemed to be resting, he showed

Skye how to fold out the funny little single futon into a miniature twin bed and then he rounded up some hospital blankets and encouraged her to try to rest there beside her sweet little adopted grandmother. She was exhausted and they both knew it.

It took only a couple of minutes for her to drift off to sleep after he assured her he would wake her if anything changed and then he sat down in the chair next to the wall to watch over both of them as they rested. This was not a convenient time for Skye to have to pull an all-nighter, but then sometimes life wasn't convenient. At least he would be able to give her some moral support tonight and take the day off tomorrow. He wished he was able to give Skye the day off as well. Unfortunately, the floral demands of Valentine's Day would preclude that.

The next morning, he drove Skye home so she could work with a promise to bring her back to get her car later when she wasn't too tired to drive and then he went back to the hospital to be with Mama Woo. She was much better and they were talking about letting her go home in a few hours if she stayed as stable as she'd been these last few hours. She had been having something the doctors were calling TIAs or mini strokes and the doctors had assured Skye she'd done the right thing to bring her in when she did.

Gage actually asked Gabriel to come back to the hospital and drive Skye's car home for her so it would be one less thing she had to worry about. He brought Mama Woo in his car and then he called in a favor from Cara, his massage therapist. He had her bring a portable massage table and come right to Skye's apartment and give her a massage over her lunch break. It wouldn't necessarily make up for the lack of sleep, but at least it would help with the muscle tension that had built up and was making her miserable.

When he brought her a hot lunch to wolf down afterwards, her sweet, tired smile of gratitude was more than worth the last fourteen hours.

At nine-thirty that night, when Skye finally finished with the orders she had to get ready for the next day, Gage met her at Mama Woo's door with a tender hug and another hot meal. As she ate, he carefully broached the subject of the night shift.

Skye needed sleep, but he knew she also needed to know Mama Woo was still okay. If she stayed here at Mama Woo's, she'd know her tiny elderly friend was okay, but Mama Woo's apartment didn't have near the security measures Skye's did. After a tired discussion, Skye finally gave in to the idea that Gage was going to sleep on Mama Woo's couch just in case. What he would do in the event of a murderous intruder wasn't really the issue. He knew Skye would simply rest better and she apparently did too.

Far too weary to argue, she had simply given him a long, gentle kiss goodnight and then she and Kitty had disappeared into Mama Woo's spare room.

Tired as he was, he woke up several times in the night to check on Mama Woo and then went back to sleep, but he was still in guardian mode and woke with a start when Skye gently woke him up by kissing him goodbye in the morning. It was only six thirty, but she was wide awake and beautiful as she bid him a cheerful good morning and then she and the dog headed across the alley.

After watching her let herself in safely, he went back and crashed on the couch again and then when Mama Woo got up at a little after eight and was looking markedly better, Gage went home and showered and headed in to work.

At noon, he showed back up at Skye's shop just a few minutes after the pizza he'd had delivered. He sat with Skye and her helpers and then took his lap top and went back to Mama Woo's for a few hours. Her blood pressure had been stable every time they'd checked it and when she smilingly shooed both Skye and him out that evening after dinner they accepted without too much fuss.

Inside Skye's living room, Gage just held her for the longest hug and then kissed her softly and said, "Goodnight, Skye Alexander. Sleep tight and try not to dream of flowers."

Without even realizing it, Gage fell into the role of chief personal assistant. Over the next two insanely busy days, he made sure Skye had real food in front of her at meal times and that she knew Mama Woo was well cared for, and then he had Cara come in again after work on the thirteenth. It was the insane hour of eleven thirty by the time Skye got off and he simply kissed her goodbye before Cara got started so she could just relax and go to sleep afterward.

With Mama Woo seeming to do better, and Skye over the top busy, Gage put in a huge, long afternoon at the office on Valentine's Day. He had no idea how to even try to celebrate the occasion with Skye and they had, in fact, simply decided to figure that out in about three days from now when things had slowed back down to normal.

Skye was keeping the shop open until ten o'clock, so he took dinner in to the shop and to Mama Woo at about six and then went back to the clinic to keep trying to catch up on what he'd left unfinished during this crunch time.

At nine-thirty, he came back and started watering the huge flower pots that Skye and Hailee hadn't had time to tend to for a few days. He was completely bow impaired, but he could handle watering for her. At ten, he pulled the huge sentinel pots inside and almost ceremonially shut the metal gate, turned out the lights, and led a thoroughly exhausted Skye back into her apartment. Even Kitty appeared to be beat.

As Skye kicked off her shoes and sat down to eat the Clam chowder he'd brought her from Francesca's, she rolled her neck and said tiredly, "I don't think I want to be a florist forever. Being a florist makes Valentine's Day very unromantic. I think I'd like to just go back to having a quiet date instead of working like this." She bowed her head to ask a blessing on the chowder and Gage automatically said it.

He made it a fast one, but he lost her anyway. By the time he said amen, she had fallen fast asleep on her folded arms and some of her hair was dipped into the soup. He smiled and pulled the bowl away and carefully mopped the chowder out of her hair with a napkin and then picked her up and gently carried her to her bed and covered her up, jeans and all. Back in her tiny kitchen, he covered the chowder with some plastic wrap and then put it and the Hershey's kisses he'd brought for dessert into the fridge. Turning out the lights, he had to smile again. He knew just how she'd feel in the morning. He had experience with this kind of thing from Christmas Eve.

Leaning to pet Kitty at the door, he said, "Watch over her, Kitty, Kitty." He said the German words he'd heard Skye say so many times to put the dog on guard and she took on that alertness, then he let himself out and made sure the door locked behind him. So it hadn't been the most relaxing Valentine's Day on record. It was still the only one in his whole life when he'd truly had a Valentine and it was unbelievably nice to be in love. Even dipped in clam chowder Skye was incredibly intriguing.

Jaclyn M. Hawkes

Chapter 8

The football team did a banner job on their fundraiser and Skye ended up with an order for seventy eight corsages and boutonnières. She'd had no idea they'd be able to sell that many and she was glad she'd had a couple of weeks to recuperate from Valentine's Day before prom night rolled around. Mama Woo had been put on some medicine to thin her blood and she was finally feeling and acting like the old Mama Woo.

Gage called to see if he could spirit Skye away for the evening and she laughed and told him about the huge pending order for the next day. "Sorry, the football players are making me earn their brute strength. It's going to be another late night with the flowers."

His deep chuckle came over the line and then he said, "I'd offer to help, but you know I'm hopelessly bow impaired. I could come and wipe the clam chowder out of your hair afterward though, if you'd like."

Skye groaned and said, "Oh, don't remind me. I'm so sorry. Please forgive me."

"It was actually very comforting after Christmas Eve."

She was sitting in front of her little TV elbow deep in roses and carnations when he called her cell phone to tell her he was on her porch with a pint of ice cream from Cold Stone.

He walked in wearing a pair of well broken in jeans that fit him to perfection and actually did try to make a couple of bows and then gave it up as hopeless and settled onto what he'd affectionately named "The Excruciating Loveseat" as Skye laughed and said, "You're better at making bows than I would be at fixing kinked backs."

He sat in the loveseat restlessly for nearly a half hour before giving that up as hopeless as well and pulling over a kitchen chair and saying, "There's a long standing tradition here in St.George. After every football fundraiser, the devoted admirer of the local florist celebrates by buying her a new sofa."

Laughing, Skye unburied her lap from the mound of flowers and wire and tape and went in search of the pile of pillows again. She tossed them on the floor and asked, "How long has this long standing tradition been long standing?"

He sprawled onto the pillows with a mellow sigh. "Oh, forever. I think the pioneers came up with it. Oh, no, it was that loveseat the pioneers came up with. I think it was made by the mean father of a courting-aged daughter and he designed it to make her suitors leave within minutes. She probably never did get married, poor girl. Then it's just been handed down from mean father to mean father. I think you inheriting it was a mistake. At any rate, I feel the need to replace it for you. Can I have you for a couch shopping excursion soon?"

Skye's gut reaction was to say it didn't really matter. She probably wouldn't be living here for a whole lot longer. She'd already been here almost sixteen months and she expected Shane to show up any day now. But she couldn't face walking away from Gage or even face saying that to him and instead simply said, "Sure, anytime, but you aren't buying it. I'm buying it or no deal."

He was watching her closely and she was almost a little surprised when he softly said, "We'll figure that out later. It would be stupid to agree for the traditional couch purchaser to abdicate his responsibility but I'm too stiff from sitting in the excruciating loveseat to argue just now." Something in his eyes said he knew exactly what she'd been thinking.

When she finally finished with the flowers and the tips of two of her fingers were literally bloody, he hauled himself off of her pillows and helped her carry the flowers all back into the shop and put them into the plastic cartons and into the cooler. The hug as he told her goodnight lasted and lasted and she knew without a doubt that he had known what she was thinking.

The next afternoon, she was in the walk-in cooler putting the prom flowers into boxes to deliver to the high school when she felt the air move as someone opened the door behind her. Fear exploded into her veins and as a hand touched her shoulder, she spun and struck and then kicked all in the same motion. She turned to follow up and then run and was appalled to realize she'd just knocked Gage across the cooler and solidly into the iron door behind him. He was leaning against it in surprise and trying to suck back in some of the air she'd just literally kicked out of him.

"Gage! Oh, I am so sorry! Please forgive me. You scared me! I had no idea you were even here."

After another minute of bending to try and breathe, he wheezed, "I did get that impression."

She came to him and put an arm around him. "Are you okay?"

Nodding because he still didn't appear to be able to breathe all that well, he admitted, "I'm not entirely sure. I've only had broken ribs once, but this is painfully reminiscent." He finally straightened almost up. "I'm sorry I scared you, Skye. I was just going to help you lift the boxes. I thought you heard me talking to you."

"The cooler fan is too loud. I didn't hear a thing. I'm so sorry." She put a hand against his side and he groaned and she added, "You probably do have broken ribs, Gage. I'm so, so sorry. Can I take you to a doctor?"

He tentatively straightened with a grimace. "They can't do anything for ribs anyway. I'll be fine. Are these the boxes?"

Watching him closely, she handed him a box and then wanted to swear. She had really hurt him. Not only had she totally kicked him with everything she had when he had been trying to help her, but her heart was still racing so fast that it literally hurt. She put a hand to her chest and reached for another box.

He was watching her as closely as she was watching him and she hoped he couldn't see how afraid she still was. That reaction had been sheer naked panic and she hated to have him see her like that. Even for only a second.

Once they were out of the cooler, they took the boxes to the minivan and loaded them into the back and then both looked at each other again for a second. Quietly, she said, "I'm so sorry, Gage."

He pulled her into a hug. "Me too, honey. I had no idea walking in like that would scare you. I guess that should have been a no brainer. I'm sorry, I wasn't thinking." He leaned back to look at her and asked softly, "Are *you* okay?"

She dropped her eyes and nodded and then shook her head and leaned into his chest and whispered, "I thought you were Shane."

Rubbing over her back, he murmured, "I know."

Hailee arrived and came in all bubbly and chattering and then she stopped and looked at the two of them for a minute and asked, "What's going on? Is something wrong?"

They both shook their heads at once and Skye pulled away from Gage and said almost too cheerily, "No, everything's fine. The van is loaded for the high school. Can you deliver the flowers for their prom? There's a Post It taped to the console with Coach Littleford's phone number on it. Call him when you get there and he'll send a couple of strapping young star athletes out to help you." She smiled at the pretty red head and hoped she couldn't see how upset Skye had just been.

Once Hailee was gone, Skye turned back to Gage and again, the hug lasted. They may not be going anywhere near discussing the subject of Shane, but they were both worrying about it anyway.

Back inside the shop, he went over to look at the photo of Ireland taped to the door she had just slammed him into as she'd kicked him. She came to stand beside him and mused, "Someday I'm going to visit that beach."

"Yes, it's beautiful. You've never been before? To Ireland?"

Walking away toward her work table, she answered, "No. I've never been to Europe at all. Actually, I haven't done much traveling in the last few years. I've been trying to fly under any radar that could be traced."

"So how have you been able to work? You said Skye is your real name."

She shrugged and shuffled through some papers. "I've never worked for anyone else I'd have to produce documentation for. By working for myself, I've been able to have everything under Nevada corporations and Nevada really is as persnickety about letting out information as is rumored. The only places that have record of Skye Alexander are the state of Nevada, my credit union account and the IRS. I have fraud alerts at the state and the IRS so theoretically, no one can get information from them and I was upfront with the ladies at the credit union and I honestly think my information has stayed in house with them. When I came, I deposited quite a bit of money so they didn't pull credit or anything like that."

She gave him a sad smile. "The corporation owns everything and I use a lot of cash. So far, so good."

He looked at her quietly for several seconds and then changed the subject back to traveling. "I went to Ireland right after I got out of college. It's marvelous. The friend I was going with backed out at the last minute, but I went anyway. It was a little lonely sometimes, but Ireland was incredible. I'm going back there someday too." He gave a small smile and admitted, "If I could swing it, I'd stay at the little cottage right on the ocean from the movie The Secret of Roan Inish. It probably isn't even there anymore, but wouldn't that be so cool? Have you ever seen it?"

She smiled. "The movie or the cottage? The movie was great. It would be incredible to stay there, wouldn't it? That would be about as far as you could get from the hassles of day-to-day business."

He reached out and gently touched the photo. "That is the allure of it, isn't it?"

After another second or two of gazing at it, he gingerly turned with just a hint of a grimace of pain and she felt guilty again for hurting him as he asked, "I was wondering if I could steal you away tonight since I couldn't last night. It's not to the prom unfortunately, but the symphony is performing. It would be great to see you in that marvelous little black dress again."

She tried to lighten the almost sad mood he seemed to be in suddenly. "If you want a prom, we could always hang a disco ball over the excruciating loveseat and slow dance in my living room. Does that mean you'll be in a tux again? I thought I was going to have to get security to hold the other women back that night."

At that, he did laugh and shook his head. "Would a suit do? I think I'll pass on the tux. But I'll take you up on that disco ball. Do you happen to have one? A disco ball, I mean. And are you saying you can go?"

"What? You mean everyone doesn't just happen to have a disco ball? Of course I'll go to the symphony. I love it."

"Do we have time to shop for your new couch and go to dinner first?"

Coming back to him, she stopped and looked up into his eyes. "Couch shopping would be great. But are you up to it with those ribs? I'm so sorry."

He leaned down to kiss her and then smiled. "I'm probably more up to that than dancing under the disco ball."

Once he left the shop, Skye wished she could bring back Gage's smile. It had been seriously missing after she hurt him in the cooler. And she didn't think it was the pain from the cracked ribs that had stolen the smile. It must have just been the whole stalker issue.

The disco ball might be just the thing to cheer him up and when Hailee got back, Skye grinned and asked her, "So, where do you think I could find a disco ball this afternoon, Hai? I was teasing Gage about having one and it would be a hoot if he showed up and I really did."

The vivacious red head laughed and said, "The drama teacher has one I'll bet he'd let you use. We're not using it tonight. Do you want me to call him and see?"

"That would be awesome if you would. Tell him I'm willing to rent it from him and I'll be careful with it."

"It's a disco ball, Skye. It's not like you need to worry about cracking the glass. It's already in a thousand pieces."

Nodding, Skye laughed at her. "You've got a point there."

When Gage showed up, he literally busted up over the spinning glittery ball hanging there above the painful loveseat and then groaned with the smile still on his face. That one belly laugh had been worth all of the struggle she and Hailee had gone to to hang the dang thing. It may have already been in a thousand fragments, but she had had to work not to drop it as they hooked it to the ceiling.

His mood had improved markedly over the last few hours and as Skye gently put an arm around him while they laughed together, she resolved to keep choosing happy for the duration of the night.

It was this issue of Shane hanging over her that tended to strain things. It made them both worry and there was the unspoken question of their relationship. They'd become more than very good friends over these past months. She wasn't exactly sure just how much more, but she knew she was in love with this handsome, laughing man and she knew the look in his eye sometimes spoke of far more than a platonic friendship. Sometimes that look was actually a little frightening. If she let herself go there, she could see forever.

Neither one of them had said the L word, and they weren't going to—but that was only because it would make the foolishness of it blatant. They felt how they felt and it was undeniable at this point, but they both knew that sometime soon she'd be gone and it would be over. It would kill her, but she would do it to keep Gage safe. Whenever she really dwelt on it, she felt incredibly guilty for possibly putting him in a lot of danger just because she was selfish and was enjoying him so much. Then she'd feel incredibly heartbroken over the thought of walking away from him. It was depressing her to the point that she struggled to choose happy. It was troubling enough that lately she had simply decided not to let her mind go there. Her mind or her heart.

She put the thought that she shouldn't be spending time with him aside as she slid into the luxurious leather seat of his car. In her head she knew she shouldn't be, but in her heart she also couldn't face the thought of life without him. At least not tonight. Tonight she was going to enjoy dressing up and going to the symphony with an incredibly gorgeous and good man. Then when he brought her home, she was going to make him laugh again with an impromptu prom, listening to the classics station on the radio in her tiny, tiny living room. She would try to face ending their relationship later.

Furniture shopping together probably wasn't the best idea if she was serious about putting the brakes on their emotions. Strolling hand in hand through the beautiful showroom only made her think about having a home with him. He was unbelievably comfortable to be with, and tonight, with both of them dressed up, she was more aware than ever of how attractive he was. Not only that, but the latent look deep in his eyes was frankly a little volatile. Somehow, it was a ridiculously heady feeling to know he desired her. That they were able to actually choose a couch at all was amazing with the amount of electricity charging the air between them.

Slow dancing under that silly disco ball didn't have exactly the effect she'd expected either. She'd been planning to make him laugh when she turned it on and the lights off, but laughter hadn't really been his reaction as she stepped into his arms to a romantic old Journey song. They'd joked about the prom, but the slow, warm ache she felt was definitely not an adolescent, high school feeling. Neither was the deep, almost molten need she glimpsed at the back of his blue eyes. This man was definitely not a mere kid.

Another old ballad came on by Chicago and maybe it was a good thing Gage's ribs were painfully sore, because she about wanted to slide right inside his suit coat with him and she didn't doubt he knew it. They danced even closer and when the song finally ended and a commercial came on, Gage quit dancing at all and leaned down to kiss her, completely oblivious to the obnoxious lights spinning around them. No, laughter was definitely not the feeling that frissioned between them.

Skye moaned in pleasure and forgot everything but just the feel of his kiss. He had an incredible kiss.

The fact that the next song was a classic disco tune by The BeeGeez was probably a good thing. It definitely brought them back to earth. Gage finally raised his head with a reluctant sigh and glanced up at the ridiculous mirrored ball, grinned down at her, groaned and said, "I'm sorry, Skye, but I am not up to any Saturday Night Fever moves just now. Which is good, because dancing is positively *not* what my mind is on. You and that dress and those exquisite earrings against your skin..."

He leaned down and kissed her softly on the side of her neck. "You're making me crazy just now. You look good tonight, Skye. You look really good. And you feel better than good. And you smell like..." He paused to breathe in and then kiss her again. "And I can't even begin to describe how you taste. It would bury us."

He looked into her eyes for what felt like eternity and as her heart began to beat even more furiously, he started to say something and then hesitated and kissed her again almost hungrily and then pulled away and said huskily, "As much as I would like to stay here and be buried with you, I should go. You are far too tempting."

He pulled her close again and she laid her cheek against his chest as she struggled to slow her breathing. He was right. He should go.

And she knew exactly what he had been going to say to her and as much as it thrilled her to know he felt the same way about her that she felt about him, telling each other would be a mistake. It would only make walking away that much more painful when the time came. Much as she didn't want to, she really should send him home now. Laughter was so not the effect he was having.

After a few more minutes of holding her, he pulled away, took her hand and led her to her front door, and then turned and looked down at her. The need in his eyes had ratcheted up a notch from volatile to explosive and he leaned and slowly kissed her one more time and said, "Goodnight, Skye Alexander. Sleep tight, and dream of kissing me."

Jaclyn M. Hawkes

Chapter 9

Gage stepped out the door and paused to listen for her dead bolt again and then ran a hand through his hair and wanted to swear in frustration. He wanted to turn back around and tell her he loved her and needed her and couldn't live without her, but her safety had to come first and they had to deal with this fool Shane Cainan –both to assure her safety and to free her up to be able to accept his proposal when he finally felt like he could make it. Man, he never again wanted to see that gut deep fear he'd seen in her eyes this afternoon when he'd frightened her.

And tonight… Holy Moses she had been something else tonight. He'd thought she looked smoking hot that first night. Getting to know her all these weeks and months had only made that initial attraction blossom until tonight it had threatened to detonate on them. Who would have thought he could feel that kind of physical attraction under a silly disco ball? He laughed in spite of himself and shook his head as he stepped down off of her porch. She never failed to entertain him. Walking back to his car he shook his head again and let out a huge breath. Just how good she had felt in his arms had been almost too entertaining, and he was sure the way he was feeling right now was not what she'd had in mind as she'd hung the thing.

Glancing up at Mama Woo's still darkened window, he started up his car and pulled toward the end of the alley. He would definitely never listen to those songs again without remembering her tonight. He really wanted to get on with his life now that he was sure he'd found her.

As he put on his blinker to pull into the road, he suddenly had the most uncomfortable feeling and looked all around but there was nothing that seemed out of the ordinary. His PI in Portland still hadn't been able to ascertain anything more than that Shane Cainan was still not around. His credit card records showed he had traveled extensively for months, and that a couple of those trips had indeed been to both Utah and to Las Vegas. Whether that meant he knew Skye had come here remained to be seen.

Gage hesitated before pulling out, wondering if he should go back and check on her and then shook his head. No, he shouldn't go back there. The privacy of both of them living alone was nice, but with the way he was feeling just now it could be dangerous as well. He picked up his phone instead.

When she answered, he wasn't sure what to say to her and finally decided he just needed to be honest. Safety for her could mean her life and he said, "I'm just pulling out of your street, but I had this strange feeling. I'm not sure how to explain it."

Skye laughed softly and said, "I'm not sure strange is the way I'd describe how I'm feeling, Gage, but I'll be fine once my heart rate gets over slow dancing with you."

That wasn't exactly what he was trying to convey to her, but at least he had confirmed that she wasn't feeling anxious and he chuckled softly and said, "I absolutely know what you mean. Who would have ever thought a disco ball should come with a disclaimer to use at your own risk? Have a good night, Skye."

"You too."

Still smiling at himself, he pulled out without worrying any more.

When he picked her up to go to church with him the next afternoon, he laughed again as she asked him to help her get the thing off of her ceiling. She admitted sheepishly that it was too dangerous to keep up there and Gage thought to himself, *yeah, but it's the beautiful dancer who's dangerous, not the thing falling on someone.* On the way out the door, she picked up a flower arrangement to take to his mother after the meeting.

They'd just pulled up to the front of his parents' house for dinner when his phone rang. He glanced at it and made a sound of disgust, put it back down and undid his seatbelt. Skye glanced over and asked, "Chiropractor groupie?"

Nodding, he was surprised as she picked up the phone and accepted the call. In a professional voice that had just a touch of nasal boredom, she said, "Physician's answering service." Gage couldn't help the smile that broke out as she went on, "I'm sorry, Dr. Garrison isn't available. Dr. Potawatame is on call this afternoon. Should I have him call you back at this number?" There was a pause and then she continued with even more of the nasal, "Dr. Potawatame is quite new. He's the shorter heavyset man with the comb over. He has a bit of an issue with halitosis, but I assure you, he's a wonderfully competent chiropractor."

There was another pause as Gage struggled to control the roar of laughter he could feel erupting. Finally, Skye said, "Very well. Have a good evening then, ma'am."

She closed his phone and matter-of-factly put it back in the console and grinned at him. "She wasn't sure about Dr. Potawatame. She said she'd call back if she was dying." He finally laughed out loud and came around the car to let her out and they were both still laughing as they walked through the front door of his parents' house with Gage carrying the flowers.

Gabriel was there again. He came over to greet them and Gage stepped in front of Skye and said, "One, Gabe. One little kiss, and then leave her alone or your dead, dude."

Gabriel's eyes lit up and he asked happily, "Really? I can have one?"

In the sternest of voices, Gage repeated, "One!"

Laughing good naturedly, Gabriel said, "Cool!"

Gage stepped out from in front of Skye as his parents turned to greet them. They were all caught by surprise as Gabriel moved to Skye, put his hands on her shoulders and proceeded to plant an enthusiastic kiss on her shocked lips. Skye gasped, Gage swore, and his mother let out a small shriek of disbelief and outrage.

The kiss only lasted an instant and then Gabriel walked away chuckling as his mother bopped him soundly on the forehead and Gage added, "I thought we were talking kissing her hand, Gabe!"

Cheerfully, Gabriel replied, "Oh, well. You should have stipulated that, bro. I thought you wanted me to kiss her right on that beautiful mouth." He glanced at Skye with a grin. "Although, she doesn't really pucker up too well. I think I musta caught her by surprise. Sorry about that, Skye. Next time I'll give you enough time for anticipation!"

Gage's mother let out another sound and wacked Gabriel again as his dad laughed softly.

At that, Skye looked back to Gage with raised eyebrows and smiled as Gage returned, "Oh, no! Not a chance, Romeo! You aren't getting within ten feet of her ever again! Geez, she'll never dare come to Mom and Dad's at this rate!"

His mother was still completely flustered and said, "And I wouldn't blame her!" She turned to Skye and added, "I'm so sorry, Skye. Please, just ignore him." Still giving her younger son the look, she added, "Gabriel John Garrison! Straighten up this minute!"

He sounded legitimately straightened for a moment as he answered, "Oh, all right. You guys take all the fun out of kissing. Give me a job, Mother and I'll help with dinner to redeem myself.

Skye smiled as his mother said, "That's a start, young man. Hadn't you better wear an apron so you don't ruin your suit?"

A moment later when Gabriel put the apron on as a cape and tried to leap toward their mother, saying, "I'll save you! Give me a vegetable peeler!"

Even Gage couldn't help laughing at his antics and then at their mother as she dramatically rolled her eyes and sighed and said, "I swear, Gabriel! You act more like a seven year old sometimes than a twenty two year old. What exactly are you peeling? The soup is already made."

"Fine. Then I'll save you with a spoon instead of a vegetable peeler. What else do you need done?"

"Set the table please, honey."

Gabriel made another ungainly leap toward the china closet and his mother let out a squawk of panic, "No! No leaping with the stemware! You do the silverware and maybe Gage could bring the breakables."

Gabriel smiled and put his arm around his mother and in a wheedling voice asked, "Could Skye help me set the table, Mother? She wouldn't break anything."

At this, just as Gage was going to threaten his younger sibling, Skye replied sweetly, "Oh, I don't know. I've been known to make a few dents from time to time. On guys who got too chummy."

She smiled, but met Gage's eyes apologetically and he grinned and wrapped an arm around her shoulders and gave her a squeeze as he added, "She isn't setting the table with you, Gabriel. I'd hate to have to trounce you at Sunday dinner. Mom would be mad at both of us for weeks."

Their mother nodded in agreement. "Yes, I would! And I imagine Skye wouldn't be far behind, so don't challenge him, Gage. Gabriel, put the apron on over your front and come whip this cream instead of setting the table. That should be safe enough."

Gage chuckled. "Are you sure, Mom? A spinning electronic device with the potential of flipping an oily substance to the far corners of the universe? That sounds like trouble to me. I'm thinking the napkins or something. What do you think, Skye?"

Ever upbeat, Skye replied, "I think Gabriel could handle all of it with complete competence. Anyone who can leap like that? Hey, I'd guess he could do anything well. No?"

Gage rolled his eyes this time and grinned. "That's what I get for asking the queen of positive speaking. You're making me wonder if you didn't plan that whole kissing thing with him."

Skye laughed. "I believe Mama Woo may have been in on that one as well. It's a vast right wing conspiracy."

"I suspected as much." Gage laughed with her and without even thinking about it, bent to kiss her himself, then laughed again when he saw the look that passed between his mother and brother as he added, "We should have brought Mama Woo to dinner with us. She'd know how to handle Gabriel."

Skye agreed, "She definitely would."

Chapter 10

Actually, when Gage took Skye home a while later, Mama Woo wouldn't have been up to dealing with Gabriel at all. She didn't look good and when Skye took her blood pressure, Gage gave her a hurried blessing and then they immediately took her straight into the hospital again. Even on the blood pressure medicine, this time she was through the roof.

The doctors were able to bring it back down relatively quickly but decided to keep her for observation anyway and as they settled her into a room for the night again, Skye turned to Gage and said, "I'm not nearly so tired tonight as I was the last time. And she's better too. I think we'll be fine. Go home and sleep in a real bed so you won't be wiped out in the morning. I'll call if there's any change."

Gage studied her eyes for a moment, wondering if he should mention his concern that there wasn't security here at the hospital to speak of and then decided against it. Skye knew better than he did what she was up against and he wasn't going to be the one to bring that fear back into her eyes. He hugged her for several long minutes, wishing he could tell her how he was feeling about her and then went back to his car with a promise to come in the morning and pick them up.

He prayed for both of them as he drove back home and then called the hospital and asked for the security department. After explaining who he was, hoping his medical background would give him some legitimacy, he explained that Skye was staying there and had a stalker and asked that a little extra caution be taken around her just in case. The man in charge assured him they'd be diligent and Gage was able to go in and go to bed with some semblance of peace of mind. In the morning, he took a box of Krispy Kreme donuts into the security people to add to his verbal appreciation and then gratefully took Skye and Mama Woo safely home.

Her new couch was delivered late that afternoon and Gage wanted to practically celebrate as the delivery men loaded up the excruciating loveseat and hauled it unceremoniously away to the dump. He would definitely not miss that miserable thing. The new couch, on the other hand, was going to be marvelous and it was probably a good thing they had Mama Woo with them that night as they ate dinner at Skye's and then watched another John Wayne movie. This one was McClintock and Mama Woo was incredibly funny as she cheered during the mud fight and then at the end when John Wayne was chasing Maureen O'Hara. Even though Gage had never seen the movie, he thought Mama Woo was every bit as entertaining as it was.

Pulling out of her neighborhood as he left, he had that same uncomfortable feeling he'd had the other day and he called Skye back again. This time, he simply said he was anxious and asked her to have whoever she was in contact with at the police department have the local patrols beefed up around there for the night. Skye had agreed with a hesitant voice and he felt terrible. He hated to scare her, but he'd never forgive himself if he ignored this feeling and something happened.

On an impulse, he pulled to the curb where he could see down her alley and just parked there watching for over an hour. He never saw anything suspicious and when he noticed the police were indeed cruising by there occasionally, he went on home to bed.

When he stopped by with lunch the next afternoon, he kissed her tenderly and apologized for being uptight, but Skye shook her head and admitted, "No, I was actually feeling uncomfortable too, Gage. It's much better to be too careful than not enough. I appreciate it."

He still wished he could wipe away that fear he saw at the back of her eyes.

As Skye and Hailee prepared for the huge wedding coming up in just over a week, Gage was dealing with more work issues of his own. One of his hired physicians was being sued for malpractice and another one had been indicted on drug possession charges, and then one of the public restrooms on the lower level had a toilet supply hose blow and cause a flood. Someone noticed it right away, and insurance covered it, but the resulting mess and clean up was still a major project. He was working longer hours than ever when what he really wanted to be doing was guarding Skye.

Even after the several talks he had had with her about being grateful, or maybe because of them, he was still thinking more and more about making some major changes in his career. The bottom line was he worked to make money and as long as he wasn't forgoing any big personal dreams, it really made the most sense to do what produced the greatest amount of money with the least amount of headaches.

He knew it was important to feel like he was making a valuable contribution to society, but he also had to take into account that someday he wanted to marry this girl and have a family and he wanted to be able to focus on them eventually and not on the hassles of business. At least not this many hassles.

It didn't even surprise him anymore when Skye's face popped into his head now when he thought about moving on with his life. Even knowing that she needed his assistance from time to time in her life didn't change that. In fact, it seemed to enhance his need to watch over her and rescue her occasionally.

He felt that need to be her knight in shining armor again when the compressor on her walk-in cooler went out the day before the huge wedding she was doing the flowers for. She had thousands and thousands of dollars worth of flowers sitting in it and he was surprised that she was literally in tears as he walked in to bring her lunch. She'd just gotten off the phone with the repairman who had been her last hope and there was no way they could get it working before it was too late to save the wedding flowers.

It was the first time he'd ever seen her succumb to discouragement, even a little bit. That almost worried him, as up-beat as she usually was, but the situation truly would discourage most people.

Thinking quickly, the first thing he did was call and order a load of ice blocks and then the second thing he did was wrap her in a tender hug. As he kissed her tears away, he assured her, "If they can't fix the cooler, we can certainly bring in a reefer truck and simply load the flowers into it. Everything will work out fine."

Then, as she hurriedly ate the Mexican food he'd brought, he rubbed her neck and shoulders and let her get back to work while he made the arrangements for the refrigerated big rig. He even arranged for the temporaries to come again and help move everything over and help out for those two days. More than anything, he wanted the temps to be the one's to dismantle everything after the wedding was over so Skye would be able to finally rest when the creative genius had taken it all out of her.

****

Even with Gage's support and the temps, the big wedding was still the marathon undertaking she'd known it would be. It was a wedding that would have made the society pages if St. George had had such a thing and Skye had turned the ranch it was being held at into a bride's fairytale dream. The effort had indeed been huge, but the satisfaction Gage saw in her eyes as they finished setting everything up seemed to be worth the gargantuan effort she'd put into it.

The gratitude he saw that night as she lounged on her new couch and toasted marshmallows over a candle on her coffee table was worth even more. They both knew that if he hadn't made the arrangements he had, things could have turned out vastly different and she would probably still be long at the reception site instead of here beside her miniature fire eating cheese and crackers and s'mores.

Even with the extra help, she was tired to the bone and he tried not to laugh as he watched Kitty lick all the cheese off of one of her crackers without Skye realizing it. He tossed the cracker to the dog, set the rest up on the counter and then made Kitty go lay down somewhere else as he took the pretty stemmed goblet full of cranberry juice that was just about to tip from Skye's exhausted hand. He hauled her to her feet, blew out her candles and kissed her gently. "Come on, Cinderella. You've done too much and are going to turn into a pumpkin. Kick me out so you end up in your bed in something comfortable instead of here on your couch in your clothes."

She was tired enough that for once she was a little whiny and said, "I don't want you to leave yet, Gage. Stay just fifteen more minutes. Please."

Her wanting him to stay warmed his heart, but she really was all in. "Honey, if you weren't talking, you wouldn't be awake in fifteen more seconds. You're beat. I'll come see you tomorrow. I promise."

Sleepily, she asked, "Promise?"

He nodded. "Promise. Hailee will be here and we'll take the afternoon off and go pick wildflowers and have a picnic and then go to a musical at Tuacan. It's Kiss Me Kate and you'll love it."

"What if it rains?"

"Then we'll dance."

As he led her to the door, she sighed and softly said, "I would really like that."

She buried her head in his chest and he just let her rest there as he kissed her hair and said, "Goodnight, Skye Alexander. Sleep tight and dream about weddings."

Standing on her porch, this time he had to admit to himself that he didn't want her to dream about weddings she was doing the flowers for. He wanted her to dream about her own wedding, to him, across the altar at the temple where they'd both be dressed in the whites of eternity. He had no problem anymore facing the fact that he wanted to marry her and be with her forever. He'd only known her for a little over five months, but he grew more sure every single day. Skye Alexander was definitely a keeper. She probably looked marvelous all in white.

The only thing he had trouble with was seeing his way past this idea that she was going to up and disappear and leave him behind without any idea of where she was going. He could even deal with her leaving for a while if he knew she was safe and that he'd get to be with her eventually, but right now, he knew taking Gage with her wasn't part of the game plan.

Even if it was, he couldn't just go with her anyway. He had a chiropractic practice and a medical clinic to run. Facing the fact that he wanted to marry her and that right now he couldn't even plan to be with her and make sure she was safe, made him realize that the changes he'd been thinking of needed to be made immediately. He needed to cut back now, before she needed him at a moment's notice. If he ever felt differently, he could start doing chiropractics again, but for the time being, he needed to sell both the practice and the building and he should do it while the economy of St. George was wide open because of its record growth. He'd known it for a while. Now he just needed to get it done.

He was in his car and was just about to start it, with his thoughts still full of marrying Skye and some personal freedom, when a car pulling slowly past the head of the alley caught his attention. It was crawling along and the hair on the back of his neck began to stand on end and the anxiousness was immediate. Without hesitating, he called the police and explained what his suspicions were and he was transferred to an officer who was familiar with the situation.

After Gage had explained what he thought was going on and was assured that both Skye's home and shop front would be closely watched by patrolling cruisers, he then arranged for an off-duty police officer to literally stake out her alley for a couple of days. That was the only way he could think to try to ensure her safety tonight when she was literally too tired to even try to protect herself.

Still wondering if he should call her and tell her what he suspected, he prayed and decided against it again. She was probably already asleep. She'd done everything she knew to protect herself and tonight she desperately needed to rest. Knowing that Shane may be around would only scare her from that. As long as she was closely guarded, he decided to let her sleep.

He stayed put until both the staked officer arrived and the cruisers had come past a couple of times and then he finally pulled away and went home. Leaving her right now felt almost traitorous, but then he needed to sleep as well if he was going to be any good for protecting her in the light of day tomorrow.

Sleeping had been a good theory, but it didn't exactly happen as he'd hoped. Even as tired as he was from working long hours at his clinic and then trying to fill in the gaps for Skye, once he prayed and finally got into bed, he laid there and worried about Skye's safety and then worried that the day they had been dreading where she up and disappeared was here.

The thought of her being gone made him literally sick and that kept him from sleeping as well, on top of the worries.

Who knew how many hours, he laid there struggling to find enough peace to rest and it wasn't forthcoming. There weren't a whole lot of solutions to be found there in the darkness of his lonely room. Her safety was paramount and had to be the top priority, but that still left him knowing he'd waited too long to let her know how he was truly feeling about her and to what depth. He'd never even told her he loved her, let alone asked her to stay with him forever.

She knew it. She knew he loved her. He knew she knew it, but he should have told her. He should have said the words out loud. Before this crazy Shane showed up and forced them to rip their whole lives apart to escape him. Gage had just worried that if he said it she'd decide she had to end their friendship to attempt to keep him safe. Which wasn't a frivolous concern. That was exactly what she would have done had he pushed her. The only ace in the hole was Mama Woo. Gage hoped having Mama Woo would influence Skye to not just leave him in the worst case scenario where Shane did find her and they couldn't keep him locked up.

Along with everything else, Gage should have made a decision earlier about selling out so he could have the freedom to be able to be with her to protect her or even run with her if they couldn't find a way to keep her safe and she did have to go. He'd wasted so much time feeling guilty for being ungrateful for his success that he may have completely missed the window and now it was too late.

No. It wasn't too late. It couldn't be too late. No matter what, it couldn't be too late. There was too much at stake here to ever give up. He'd walk away from his responsibilities here before he'd walk away from her, if it came down to that. She was worth ten thousand practices and buildings.

He turned over in frustration and punched his pillow into shape for the ninetieth time and then felt foolish and humbled himself to get back out of bed to kneel beside it and ask his Father in Heaven just what in the world he should be doing with this whole situation. God knew. He knew everything and right now, He was the only one who had any answers as far as Gage could see.

Prayer helped and the measure of peace it brought was truly heaven sent. Gage still wasn't sure how everything would work out, and that anxious feeling hadn't gone, but at least he'd been reminded that God was still in control and He still was all-powerful and still all-knowing. Maybe Gage didn't have all the answers, but he knew one thing. He was going to begin at first light doing all the things he'd foolishly put off. Moreover, he was going to move forward in his life with faith and trust that God would help both him and Skye attain their righteous desires as long as they were willing to be obedient and work for them. God promises blessings for those who live the way He wants them to and of all the people Gage knew who were striving to follow the Savior, Skye was the best of the best.

Gage never did really fall asleep, but at least he'd gotten some rest in by the time his internal alarm went off telling him it was time to get up and get started with the rest of his life. The first thing he did was to call the officer watching Skye's apartment and double check that all was clear there and when he was assured that they'd seen no sign of Shane, Gage breathed a huge sigh of relief. Now to work on the rest of his plans.

Knowing his neighbor would be leaving for work at a few minutes to seven, Gage caught him in the driveway and after the usual pleasantries asked, "Hey, Wade, did you ever sell your cottage up in Snow Canyon?"

"No, we decided to wait and remodel it first. We've never gotten around to doing anything with it."

"What would it take to talk you into renting it for a couple of months?"

His good neighbor shook his head. "I won't rent it to you, but you can use it for as long as you want. You've done a million things for us and we never even get up there." He looked down and took a key off the ring in his hand and handed it to Gage. "The code to the gates is 1084. You've been there before and know which one it is. Enjoy it. Gotta go."

As his neighbor pulled away, Gage mentally checked the first life changing item off of his list and went back and got into his own car to keep working on the rest. He stopped at his credit union and got a thousand dollars in large bills and then went to his office.

After assuring her that he wasn't sick, just tired, he gave a list to a thunderstruck Sandy that entailed how he wanted her to go about setting up listing his clinic and arranging to sell his practice. At her look, he said, "I'll explain later." While she was still in shock, he asked for a new employee cell phone that had never been issued to anyone before and with that in hand, thanked her and went back to his car. Now to find a way to get Skye to listen to him without dumping him or thinking he'd lost his mind.

Her shop didn't open until nine but she was already there inside working around and when he knocked, she smiled and began to unlock the big gate just as she had that very first night of the ballet. He must have had a pretty serious face, because by the time she got the gate free, she was looking at him in concern, put a hand up to his forehead and asked, "What's wrong, Gage? Are you sick? You don't look so good. Has something happened? What are you doing here?"

Taking her hand and pulling her back into the shop, he only stopped when he got clear in to her work table where she'd been arranging roses in vases for the display case. Finally, he turned and looked into her worried eyes and then asked quietly, "How did things go here last night? After I left."

She shook her head in confusion. "Fine, why? I went to bed and slept like the dead until just a little while ago. What's going on?"

Still wondering how he was going to say all the things he wanted to, he finally just pulled her into a hug and breathed against her hair, "I saw someone driving slowly past the top of the alley last night as I was leaving and it kind of freaked me out. I've worried about you all night." He pulled back and looked down at her and continued, "I called the police and they've been watching your house, but I should have just watched too. I didn't sleep anyway."

She didn't say anything, just looked up at him as if she was trying to get inside his mind and finally, he said, "I arranged to sell my clinic and my practice this morning, Skye. I need to make some changes in my life. Please don't think I'm ungrateful, but I can't keep up this pace and do the things I need to."

The concern, mixed with confusion on her face changed to include full out worry as she tentatively asked, "Things like? What's going on with you, Gage? Why are you so intense? Is all of this just because of a car cruising by slowly last night? What else is going on?"

He looked up and then rubbed the back of his neck with a hand as he sighed. Finally, he looked back at her and took her by the shoulders and leaned to kiss her with all the frustration and worry and concern he'd been feeling. For a moment, she kissed him back and then pulled back again and asked gently, "Just tell me, Gage. Why are you here this morning? What's going on? Is something going on?"

He gave a humorless laugh and shook his head. "Yeah. Something is going on." Looking into her eyes, he took both of her hands and after studying her for a moment, he asked, "Will you marry me, Skye?"

Her eyes widened, but for several seconds, all she did was continue to look at him and then finally, she put a hand up to his cheek and sadly shook her head and quietly said, "You know I can't marry you, Gage. You know I can't. Why are you doing this?"

"Why can't you, Skye? You love me. Why can't you marry me?"

She sighed and looked down and admitted, "I do love you, Gage." A second later, she looked back up with tears in her eyes. "That's why it would be such a mistake. Because I do care so much for you that I would never do that to you. Drag you into this mess on a permanent basis." She sadly shook her head and went on, "I knew that very first night that I had no business dating, but you were pretty persuasive and it was just going to be that night." She gave him a sad smile. "And I've loved every minute with you. Which is my only excuse for letting us get to this point. I'm sorry. I just..."

After struggling to get control of her emotions, she whispered, "He would kill you, Gage. And I don't know how to end this. I don't know how to ever find a way to be safe enough to move on with my life. He's obsessed and he's crazy, but the police either don't believe it or just can't spare the manpower or time. I'm sorry, Gage. This is my life. I'm sorry."

Dropping her hands, he wrapped his arms around her and leaned his head against her hair and said, "You don't need to be sorry, Skye. None of this is your doing. And I hate to burst your control bubble, but we're way past the it's been fun, have a nice life stage. I'm already into this mess on a permanent basis. A way permanent basis. A forever basis. And I don't want to wait until all the storms pass. I want to dance with you in the rain." She looked up and he shook his head and went on, "Don't fight me, Skye. I'm not a child and you know it. Let's don't waste energy on arguing, let's just try to figure out what to do. I don't know why I was so anxious last night, but it was the most awful feeling. I swear it was a prompting, Skye."

She nodded in his arms and said, "God has a way of watching over us, doesn't He?"

Pulling back, he nodded. "Yes, Skye, but we still need to be wise about this. I know you're planning to just up and leave and do what you can, but I can't live with that. I've listed my businesses, but I can't just pick up and leave yet and there's still your shop and Mama Woo and Kitty and…"

He dug into his pocket and handed her the phone and keys and money and said, "I want you to take these and keep them with you. Like on your body with you. The phone has never been used, so it hasn't been tampered with and no one has the number except me. I can call from a pay phone somewhere so no one can get the number. The keys are to a cottage just twenty minutes or so from here in Snow Canyon Estates, but it's gated and secluded and there are several ways to get into and out of it in case you need to bolt. It's number 11 and the code to the gate is 1084 and after I leave here, I'll make sure it has groceries and dog food and everything you'll need."

He paused and in a pleading voice asked, "So if you need to run, could you at least consider holing up there for a little while until we see if we can catch him and deal with a few things like Mama Woo?"

He searched her eyes for a minute, but when she didn't agree, he went on, "And if you do need to leave, I want you to have some money to live on until we can make arrangements. If the clinic sells, I'll go with you."

She still just looked from the handful he'd given her to his face and back for a moment and then without saying anything, bent and pulled up the cuff of her jeans and zipped the key and money and phone into a little pouch she had strapped around her leg just above her ankle.

Standing back up, they continued to look into each others eyes and then Gage wrapped her back in his arms and whispered, "I love you, Skye. I love you and I'm going to do whatever it takes to try to help you get safe enough to move on with your life." He kissed her hair and went on, "But I want to be the one you move on in your life with. You don't have to answer me now, but know that that's what I want and maybe someday soon, we can get this all figured out." Pulling back and looking down at her, he softly said, "Let's figure it out and get married and I'll take you to the Roan Inish cottage for a honeymoon and then someday you can quit working Valentine's Day and focus on having a family."

The silence would have been unnerving if he hadn't seen the light that seemed to glow from her eyes in spite of the tug of war she was obviously fighting with herself over what to answer. Finally, she didn't answer at all except to reach up and softly kiss his cheek and say, "Thank you for helping me, Gage. I'm sorry, but I can't promise you anything right now, but I would love all of that with you. I so would love that."

She dropped her eyes for a minute and then looked back up. "In the mean time, we have to be a lot more careful about being discreet about you and me. If he's tracked me to here, he'll realize we're... That you..." She put a hand back up to his cheek and admitted, "That I love you and it will make him furious. That would be really, really bad. So we need to back off some."

"Meaning?"

"Meaning we should be doing what we should have been doing all along. Nothing that would make an observer think you're important to me."

Gage looked at her for a minute and then pulled away in frustration and swore under his breath. How could he agree to this? But how could he not? He ran a hand through his hair again and turned back to her and pulled her into his arms and kissed her briefly but passionately. Then he gently set her away from him, knowing that what he was feeling showed in his eyes. Turning, he almost ground out huskily, "I can do this for you, Skye. I can do whatever we need to for you. For a little while. But not for long. It'll kill me. You've become the light of my whole world. The universe will be dark without you close."

He sighed and walked over to the door of the cooler with its photo of Ireland and stood looking at it with his back to her. After studying it, he carefully removed it from the cooler and brought it back to her work table and taped it to the wall beside it and said, "I was so looking forward to picking wildflowers with you this afternoon." Glancing up, he gave her the brightest smile he could muster and added, "I'll make it up to you when this is over, I promise. I guess I'll see you later sometime. Think about me today, huh?" He began to walk to the door and said over his shoulder, "Be safe, Skye. I do love you."

Before he made it to the door, a car pulled into the parking lot at the same moment the shop phone rang. Even as he heard her sunny greeting when she picked it up, he recognized that the man in the car was Shane Cainan in the flesh. Turning back around, he caught Skye's eye and she must have understood instantly because she abruptly ended the call.

Pretending to study a group of large silk arrangements, Gage heard Skye's almost inaudible gasp and looked up as the big blonde man said almost quietly, "Hello, Skye. It's been a long time."

As Kitty began to growl softly next to Skye, Gage said brightly, "Now you charged me for all four of them, right?"

Without skipping a beat, Skye replied, "Yes, sir. They're all paid for. Was there anything else you wanted?"

Gage gave her a meaningful look and then asked, "Would you mind helping me get them to my car? I always worry that I'll destroy things this delicate."

"No problem, sir." Turning to Shane, Skye said calmly, "Let me just help this gentleman load his car and then I'll be right with you, Shane."

He almost sounded soft spoken as he answered, "I'll be right here."

Carrying two of the arrangements, Gage hated to even turn his back as he walked toward the door, literally willing Skye and Kitty to follow him safely to the curb. Opening the driver's side door, he put the keys into the ignition of the car and tossed his phone on the console. He pulled the seat forward to put the arrangements he carried into the back seat and then pushed the seat back and pointed across the driver's seat toward the passenger seat as he whispered, "Take Kitty and go. Call the police and go to the cottage. I'll act like you stole my car and see if I can stall him. Go!"

Skye leaned in like she was going to set the arrangements down and then quickly jumped in and Kitty leaped over her lap as she started the car and almost caught Gage's suit coat in the door as she pulled it shut, backed out and squealed away.

Looking after her, Gage began to yell and ran back into the shop to pick up the shop phone, ranting as he did so, "She stole my car! That woman just stole my car!" Shane went to charge out the door and Gage got right into his path and began to accuse him, "You were in on this, weren't you? You two had it all planned. You helped her steal my car!"

Shane tried to go around him and Gage shoved him away from the door. "Oh no. You're not going anywhere. You're staying right here until you call her and make her bring it right back. She'll go to jail and you'll be an accomplice. Make her bring it right back and I won't even press charges."

Still, Shane was all but ignoring him and tried to go around him. Gage finally grabbed his arm and almost threw him back inside the shop and roared, "I said, you're not going anywhere! Not until you arrange to have my car brought back. Now!"

When Shane shoved him back, Gage no longer had to feign the anger that shot into his veins at how strong this man was who had so hurt Skye. At least Shane didn't seem angry, just anxious as he retorted, "I had nothing to do with her taking your car! I haven't seen her in a year. Get out of my way! I need to go after her!"

The off-duty policeman Gage had seen as he'd pulled in earlier should have been here almost instantly and Gage wondered where in the heck he was as he tried to over power this hulking brute who was intent on reaching his car just a few feet away. Geez, how had Skye survived being assaulted by this Neanderthal? He was a mountain. Gage shoved him again and Shane slugged him and knocked him into a rack of gift boxes. It sent the whole rack flying across the floor and silently Gage swore as he tried to get to Shane in time to stop him from getting out the door.

He didn't make it. Shane got into the car and was backed out and leaving before Gage was even able to get a license number, let alone stop him. As the Ford Focus with Nevada plates that must have been a rental car sped out of the lot, Gage finally heard the siren he'd been expecting and began to pray as the officer realized he needed to follow the small Ford and flipped a u-turn and sped off as well. At least there was no way Shane's car could keep up with the Jag if Skye was able to get away safely.

Gage prayed they'd catch him as he began to clean up the mess. He was bitterly disappointed when another officer pulled into the parking lot just a minute or two later and admitted they'd lost him in rush hour traffic. Shane had been driving crazily and police department policy was to let him go rather than risk a wreck in a chase within the city with an unknown driver.

At the word 'unknown' Gage got angry. "Unknown?" He glanced down at the officer's badge and went on heatedly, "Unknown? Lieutenant Pederson, your department has known about this guy for over a year! He was the one I called you about just last night! She has a restraining order against him and he's attempted to kidnap her and assaulted her a number of times. How can you say he's unknown?"

Pederson tried to mollify him, "Look, calm down, buddy. Think about it. If you heard a news story about some cop killing an innocent bystander by having a high speed chase in the middle of St. George, you'd be disgusted and you know it. They couldn't chase him. We've got his plate number and a description and a general direction and we'll get him. We just won't do it at high speed. You got me?"

Gage sighed in disgust, gingerly touched the eye he suspected would soon be black and nodded, still praying. He desperately hoped he'd given her enough time to get away safely. He'd done his level best, he was just about forty pounds lighter than Shane had been and none of Shane's weight had been fat.

Chapter 11

Two hours and a ridiculous number of police reports later, Gage watered all of her flowers heavily and then dragged the heavy gate across the front of her shop and picked up the bag he'd packed for her. He'd called his own phone more than an hour and a half ago and found that Skye had indeed made it safely to the cottage and was securely locked in with the Jag hidden in the garage. It had been an unbelievable relief to hear her voice.

He'd been secretly pleased that she had especially requested he bring the nutcracker he had given her. He'd have to bring her another gift that was easier to snuggle with.

With a wry smile he put the closed sign in the window and locked up her door. For the time being, the shop was simply going to be closed until they could catch Shane and make certain he wouldn't be a threat to Hailee if she came in and opened it part-time.

Pulling the rental car he'd had delivered around to the alley in front of Mama Woo's, he knocked on her door. When she opened and invited him in, he could see the worry on her face and realized he should have come over earlier to explain. Once she understood that Skye was safe, he could see the worry dissipate but wished Skye were here to reassure her anyway. For that matter, he wished Skye were here to reassure him as well. Not being able to be with her and know she was safe was awful.

Gage took Mama Woo's blood pressure and seriously considered running her back in to the hospital. She must have seen it in his eyes, because she immediately began to assure him that now that she knew Skye was safe, it would come down. Hoping she was right, he was incredibly relieved when Mama Woo asked if she could go stay with Skye without Gage even having to suggest it. He'd been afraid she would insist on staying here but she needed to go be with Skye for both of their sakes. They needed to watch over each other right now.

After helping the little woman pack a bag, he double checked to make sure she had her medicine holder and then took her out and helped her into the car. They stopped for fast food for lunch and until then he hadn't realized he was ravenous from skipping breakfast this morning. He'd been just a bit uptight and looking back, he knew it was no wonder. He had indeed been feeling a prompting that he was eternally grateful he'd followed.

He checked Mama Woo's blood pressure again and was relieved to find it had dropped markedly and he stopped and they got the promised groceries for the cottage. After he drove around randomly for a while to make sure no one was following them, he finally, made the short drive up to Snow Canyon Estates and that gate locking behind him was almost as reassuring as Skye's beautiful face smiling from the door of the cottage as they got out of the car in the closed garage.

Hugging her and actually holding her and making sure she was okay was so sweet after this awful morning that he wondered if he'd ever be able to let go. He decided he was going to try not to think about having to leave her later. He didn't want to have to face that for awhile. The future was too tenuous at this point to waste worrying, when he could be enjoying the time he did get with her. It was too nice to be here close to her and enjoy her fussing over his tender eye that had gone several shades of blue and purple. He'd never gotten a black eye from being slugged before and if it hadn't been in such an awful situation, he'd have enjoyed her babying him.

Unfortunately, waiting didn't change that need to hold her and he was still incredibly loathe to let go of her at almost ten o'clock that night, but he needed to go. Even with a mid-afternoon nap, his sleepless night the night before had him feeling like he had sand in his eyes. And as much as he felt inclined to just stay here with them to watch over them, it was definitely a good thing that he needed to go in to the office. Staying here with her would only augment the attraction that had already been seriously added to on this fateful day. Both talking about getting married and then the intense emotional aftermath of Shane appearing had made them both almost clingy toward each other. As unbelievably sweet as that was, staying wouldn't have been prudent.

At the door out to the garage, Gage pulled Skye tightly into his arms and kissed her tenderly, but hungrily, and then said, "Goodnight, Skye Alexander. I love you. Sleep tight and think about marrying me."

He got into his rental car and headed back home, glad that other than getting big eyes, she hadn't seemed too upset to have him say that.

****

Skye shut the garage door behind him and after making sure the dead bolt was thrown on the house door, she leaned against it and sighed. *Wow. He loved her and wanted to marry her.* Looking back, she couldn't even believe where she was tonight compared to where her life was last night. Well, after her history with Shane, yes, she could, but this day had been quite a day, all in all.

She closed her eyes and remembered how Gage had looked as he'd asked her to marry him. She'd known he cared deeply for her, but she'd never dreamed she'd wake up this morning and he'd ask her to marry him. Even dead tired and with a bruised eye he was incredible. If this wasn't a life and death situation, she would definitely take him up on his offer to dance in the rain instead of waiting for the storm to pass.

Turning from the door, she walked back in to the main part of the cottage, grateful for Kitty's reassuring presence there beside her. Mama Woo had gone down to bed a couple of hours ago and honestly, Skye was more than a little nervous here in this beautiful, but strange cottage. The noises of the night were different and she missed the security measures of her apartment, prisonlike though they seemed to be. At least she knew that there an intruder would have their work cut out for them. Glancing around at the beautiful natural wood of the cottage, she hoped security here was adequate as well. As a last resort, she had her little Glock pistol.

Once settled into bed, sleep was elusive for her. It was easy to think laying there in the dark and quiet. Her mind went back over the events of the day and seemed to replay them time and again and in this strange place and after the stress and fear of it all, it felt surreal and twisted and incredibly frightening. Reaching out to the nightstand beside the bed, she touched the little gun Gage had brought her from her house just to make sure it was still there. Realizing her perspective was skewing with the darkness and fatigue, she wished she would have asked him for a blessing before he'd left here tonight. A blessing, coupled with his incredibly comforting presence would have helped. She was sure of it.

Gage. What to do about Gage? It would have been heavenly to be able to say yes to his proposal and simply move on as they'd talked about. He'd said they'd go to Ireland and then someday she could retire and have his babies. He hadn't worded it quite that way, but that was what he'd meant and it made her stomach do gymnastics just thinking about it.

She sighed and put her hand under her cheek. She'd never met anyone who gave her these sweet butterflies like Gage Garrison. He was handsome and sharp, but he was also considerate and thoughtful and it was a lethal combination where her heart was concerned.

At least today had gone relatively well, other than Gage's poor eye. She'd known this day was coming for months and months and had been dreading it, but it could have been worse. A lot worse. The effect Gage had on her world was incredible. His soft spoken strength and confident presence was amazingly comforting. He really was like her own personal soldier who was always rescuing her. Today had been big time rescuing. What would she have done this morning if he hadn't been there when he was?

She thought about that for a few minutes and then tried to make her mind think about something more positive, but then her head began to wonder what could have happened to Gage if Shane had shown up just two minutes earlier. If Shane had seen that passionate kiss, he'd have gone berserk and…

Skye's mind shied violently away from the thoughts of Shane harming Gage the way he'd hurt her those years ago when he'd gone crazy. She sat up in bed with a hand to her beating chest. If something like that ever happened to Gage… She shook her head and swallowed the horrible, huge lump in her throat and tried to make her heart stop beating so painfully fast. She had to be more careful not to ever let Shane know about Gage. She had to. She couldn't deal with something like that happening to Gage because of her. She couldn't.

Getting back out of bed, she knelt to pray again, both for Gage's safety and for the strength she needed to be able to resist him to keep him safe. It was going to be the hardest thing in the world to do, but she needed to stay away from him. She couldn't let Shane hurt him. Dancing in the rain before this storm was over could cost his life. Both of their lives.

****

As Gage drove home from the cottage in Snow Canyon, still in the rental car because they didn't want to take a chance on the Jag being seen by Shane, he called the police. When they told him they hadn't seen a sign of Shane Cainan, Gage was disgusted on top of being exhausted. St.George wasn't that big of a place. How could they lose a guy in broad daylight and then not find him again?

Just for the heck of it, he drove past the flower shop and then looked down their alley, but nothing appeared out of place, and he drove on home. He'd forgotten to get the garage door opener out of the Jag and he had to park in the driveway and get out and punch in the code to open the door. As he turned to go back to the car, he glanced up and down his own street. Even though he saw nothing here either, for some reason the hair on the back of his neck stood on end again and he wondered if he was just tired or if this was another prompting.

Looking around more thoroughly, he finally shook his head and got back into the rental car and pulled inside the garage. When the door closed securely behind him, he turned off the motor and leaned his head back against the head rest of the car. As much as he hated leaving Skye, it was really nice to be home.

Getting out of the car, he went inside and automatically pushed the button on his answering machine and then dug into the fridge as he listened. There was nothing of interest either on the machine or in the fridge and he settled for pulling out the milk and reaching for a box of cold cereal. That was going to be one of the benefits of stopping with the clinic rat race. He was going to eat a lot more real food. Eating cold cereal alone at the end of the night was not the way a healthy twenty-seven year old man was supposed to be living.

****

Shane Cainan watched the alley way behind the small flower shop for more than half an hour before finally approaching the back door and picking the shop's locks. The nearest other apartment was dark and silent and he wondered about that. In the last couple of days that he had been watching this building to make sure he had the right place, the other apartment had been lit up in the evening and he'd seen Skye cross back and forth twice.

He could have already grabbed her but he'd actually been hoping to have her come back home with him of her own free will this time. Lately, he'd begun to realize that just having her wasn't going to work. He needed her to need him as well.

He'd thought about it a lot over the last year and more since she'd disappeared this time and he really missed those old days when she'd been with him because she wanted to and they'd had such a good time together. She was the most upbeat person he'd ever met and her perpetually sunny personality had smoothed so many of the troubles out of his life that for a while there, he'd honestly thought he had a handle on his anger and the voices in his head for good.

It was going to be hard to win her back after hurting her so badly that time, but he really did love her. She had to know that by now after all the effort he'd gone to to find her each time she hit the road. She had to understand that he practically worshipped her and if she'd just give him one more chance, they could patch things up and live happily ever after.

If she'd just agree to come back, he could control his need for the pills, and ignore the voices. He was sure of it. He just

155

needed her positive input in his life again and he'd be fine. They'd both be fine. They could start back over where they left off and he'd finish his specialty work and go on to be the doctor he'd worked so hard to become and she could be the other half of his world again. They'd be a great team. They had to be. He didn't know how to even face the thought of life without her. That was why he'd been working so hard to find her in the first place.

Getting past the dead bolt had taken some doing, but he finally made it into the little apartment and he stopped for a moment and took a deep breath. Yeah, there was no doubt that this was Skye's home. He could smell that sweet perfume that had been haunting him these years without her.

He dug around and didn't find what he was looking for until he tried the little office out in the shop. What he needed was phone records and credit card bills and her calendar.

He never did find any credit card information and the calendar had only two doctor appointments on it, but with the phone bills he hit pay dirt. She only made calls to a few numbers and it would be the work of only a moment or two back out in his car on his laptop to find out who she called. Then hopefully, he would have her. He'd be able to find out where she went, because this time, he didn't think she'd completely blown out of the area again.

For some reason, the locked up shop and the mysteriously missing neighbor and even the dog she'd had with her spoke of more roots this time. Her shop was impressive and he couldn't imagine she'd just pull up stakes on an operation this big this time. Hopefully, she'd simply gone to ground somewhere nearby, thinking she could make him believe she'd run, but then she'd come back here.

It didn't matter either way. He'd gotten good about this snooping around thing and he hoped he'd find her this very night, if these cell phone records told him what he thought they would. He'd find out who her friends were and then find out which one she was staying with and then he'd talk to her. Nice and gentle like and she'd come around. She'd remember how it used to be with them. She'd remember just like he did every hour of every day since she'd been gone and she'd agree to come back. She had to. He couldn't live without her.

****

He had no idea what time it was, but it was deep in the night and the sound of his garage door opening brought Gage wide awake in an instant. For just a second, he thought maybe Skye had come to talk to him, but then he dismissed that idea. She would never walk into his house in the middle of the night without calling him first, and she wouldn't want to be out and about in the wee hours anyway. Whoever it was, it wasn't someone who was welcome, that was for sure.

Who in the world would try to sneak into a person's house by opening their big, noisy garage door? Reaching for his cell phone on the nightstand, he dialed 911 and found himself wishing he was a lifetime member of the NRA like Skye was and had had the foresight to invest in a hand gun of his own. As it was, he had to settle for reaching for the fireplace poker as he told the police he had an intruder.

Now that he was awake and his heart was racing in anticipation of facing whoever this was, he had to admit, the garage door didn't really make that much noise after all and it truly was the easiest way to get into his house. He never worried about the door into the house from the garage because the garage was locked. At least that had been the theory. And honestly, security had never seemed that critical until recently. Really, really recently.

Tonight was the first time he could ever remember thinking about whether his home was secure as he'd retired to bed. He'd heard there was a way to break the codes for openers, but had never considered himself much of a target for that kind of thing. This Shane guy was beginning to get old in a hurry.

He could hear furtive footsteps in the hall and once a floorboard creaked as whoever was there quietly opened every door they came to. He must have figured out that Gage and Skye were together and he'd either come here looking for her, or to put his competition out of commission. Either idea wasn't all that appealing to Gage, and he could feel a slow burning anger push the last vestige of sleep out of his head. Who did this man think he was that he could treat people this way?

The footsteps drew closer down the darkened hallway, and Gage silently stepped behind the door with the poker raised, wondering how long it would be before the police could get here. Physical confrontation with a weapon had never been a consideration for him, but right now he was wishing he'd been more of a trouble maker in school. Frankly, knowing how to knock this guy's block off would have been altogether satisfying right now. There was something about defending his home and Skye that brought out a warrior in him he'd never suspected existed.

As it was, after seeing him today, and reading the other day about what he had done to Skye, facing him was sobering. What was it they said about it being impossible to reason with madness? Physically confronting madness didn't make a whole lot of sense either. Gage shouldn't be feeling this urge to smash this man. It was contrary to all he'd been raised with and the years of schooling he'd had to become a medical professional, but that didn't stop the almost primal urge he felt to crush him and throw him out of his house on his ear.

The bedroom door opened so slowly and silently that at first Gage wasn't even aware it was opening, even though he was standing in the shadows behind it. When he did realize, the jolt of adrenaline that hit him was overpowering and he could feel himself almost getting jittery.

A head leaned into the room through the only partly opened door and after looking around in the near darkness, softly called Skye's name into the room. The hope and devotion Gage could hear in his voice were not at all what Gage was expecting and it took him back for a minute. This was not the crazy, vicious mad man Gage was expecting. He may have been crazy, but this guy was still in love with Skye. You could hear it plainly and it calmed the latent warrior in Gage enough for him to step close to the door so Shane couldn't push it open easily and calmly answer, "Skye isn't here. She's long gone. She ran so you couldn't hurt her and she would never stay at a man's house overnight and you know it."

Shane's head spun to look at him and Gage could tell that even in the dark, Shane recognized him. He let out an expletive as he said in surprise, "You! I thought you were just a customer. Why would she be calling you? What are you doing around Skye?"

For some reason, Gage decided to be honest with this guy and he said quietly, "Who Skye associated with is no longer any of your business, Shane. She was trying to have a life in spite of trying to stay away from you so you can't hurt her again. If you would leave her alone, she could quit running and get on with her life, instead of having to live in fear and stay away from all the people she loves. Did it ever occur to you that you've made her life a lonely, frightened hell?"

Shane shook his head and said, "She's the one who's chosen that. I've only been trying to find her to get her to come home. I love her and she knows it and if she'd stop hiding long enough for me to explain to her, she'd understand that I don't want to harm her."

In disgust, Gage almost ground out, "Beating her almost to death is a horrible way to show her you love her."

Again, Gage could hear the pure regret in Shane's voice. "I didn't mean to do that to her. It was the voices. And the drugs. I didn't mean to do it. I'm better now. I'll explain that if she'll let me."

Gage tried not to sound as completely repulsed as he felt when he replied almost fatalistically, "She's gone, Cainan. Long gone, thanks to you. She's never going to give you a second chance to harm her. Do you think she's stupid? Her entire life is geared around security. You've seen her apartment."

"She just doesn't understand. I'm better now."

Finally, Gage could hear the police sirens in the distance and began to speak to try and cover the sound, so they could catch him, "She doesn't ever want to see you again, Shane. You nearly killed her. She's never going to get over that. She lives in constant fear now and she probably always will because of what you did. Just go back home and leave her alone so that wherever she goes this time, she can finally have some peace and put down some roots. She's lonely and discouraged. If you really love her, just forget her and let her have a life."

"I'll give her a good life. And what do you care?"

At that, Gage hesitated and finally said, "I love her too, Shane, but that doesn't matter either because she has to keep running scared because of you. Even though I think she really cares for me, she couldn't stay. She has the world on her shoulders and now she feels like she even has to protect everyone around her. If you truly cared for her, you wouldn't do that to her. As long as you dog her, she'll never be able to have a real home where she feels safe and can settle down. You're ruining her life."

"I am not!" Shane finally began to get upset and he tried to shove the door open, but Gage's foot still held it. "I didn't make her choose to leave! That was her own decision. She'll learn to trust me again. I'll take care of her."

Truly feeling pity for this lunatic, Gage replied, "I'm sorry, Shane, but she's gone. Both physically and emotionally. She's definitely not in love with you anymore and she knew you'd find her and she's been planning to take off when you did. If you honestly care for her, give her the gift of freedom. Give her the gift of feeling safe for a change. Let her sleep through the night without fear. Let her look out of windows that don't have bars on them, or simply go for a walk. With you after her, she can't do that. Ever. She's a prisoner because of you. A very lonely prisoner with no permanent home or friends or family. That's not really the way to show someone you love them, is it?"

Shane made a sound of anger and tried to bull his way through the door, but still Gage held it as Shane roared, "I haven't done any of that! I've only tried to find her to bring her home! That's where she belongs anyway. Where is she? Tell me where she is!"

"Look, Shane, I tried to talk her into staying, but she has this strange idea that she had to go to keep everyone here safe. You saw how she took off, when she saw you. You're too late. If you don't give her the freedom I'm asking for, you're simply back to square one with trying to figure out where she's gone. Either way, she's never going to agree to be with you. What you did killed any feelings she had for you. But if you keep dogging her, she'll never feel like she can be with anyone else either and she'll spend the rest of her life alone and running. What kind of a life is that? If you really love her, you wouldn't do that to her."

Shane finally heard the sirens and for a split second he froze and then he glared at Gage and threatened, "If you're hiding her, I'll come after you! Stay away from her! Do you hear me? If she talks to you, tell her I'm sorry and that she can come back. That I love her and will never hurt her again. But you stay away from her!"

Knowing he was going to try to make a run for it, Gage shoved into the door to try and pin him and for several seconds the two of them fought for all they were worth as the sirens got closer and eventually pulled into the driveway with squealing brakes. Finally, Shane forced a meaty fist into the room and began to try to hit Gage as he struggled to hold the door. Most of Shane's efforts amounted to wild flailing, but occasionally, he connected and when he hit the already tender eye, Gage groaned but continued to hold the door, wishing he could swing the poker to knock him senseless.

Ultimately, it came down to the fact that Shane was simply bigger and heavier and stronger and had a longer reach than Gage and just as they heard the police slam into the house from the garage, Shane slipped free of the doorway and disappeared down the hall.

He must have gone for the French doors at the back of the house, and apparently, he didn't try to pause and unlock them. Gage heard a crash and wood splintering and then the shatter of glass and ran in to see two officers running out through the broken doors after Shane as another patrol car pulled to the curb in the front. This one didn't have a siren, but the flashing red and blue lights of both patrol cars lit up the whole neighborhood. At first Gage regretted that, but on thinking about it, it would be good for the nearest neighbors to be awake and alert in case Shane tried to get into one of their houses to escape.

Once again, the police lost him and this time, Gage had a mangled set of French doors to add to his black eye, compliments of Shane Cainan. Seemingly hours later, when the police came back and began their endless reports, at least this time, Shane had left evidence and a whole lot of criminal activity they could go after him for, and it gave Gage hope that once they did catch him, they would keep him longer this time.

From some of Shane's comments, Gage assumed he'd broken into Skye's place and Gage rode with the police to check it out.

There was no sign of forced entry, but he hadn't closed the door all the way when he'd left and the little apartment was still open. Even inside he hadn't made much of a mess, except for in the office of her shop and one of the drawers in her bedroom. When Gage realized Shane had been into the drawer that held Skye's under things, the disgust he'd been feeling ratcheted up to a deep, slow burning anger. Maybe Shane didn't see himself as a predator, but that only added proof that he was as crazy as Skye had intimated.

On the drive back to his house, Gage and the officer tried to brainstorm about what kinds of information Shane had gotten from her place. Gage had hoped not to have to admit to her what had happened, but there wasn't really any option. They had to ask her what Shane might have gotten that would put her at more risk, and she needed to know what was going on.

In a way, Gage dreaded talking to her, especially when it might lead Shane right to her. The main reason she had insisted Gage stay away from her was to keep Shane unaware they were involved. At least Shane hadn't gone berserk as Skye had feared and tried to kill him right then. His calm, almost pleading demeanor had, in fact, been almost puzzling for someone who could be as violent as that police report had shown.

Either he was a split personality, or he'd made some massive changes since this whole thing had started. Tonight, he had truly sounded like he thought he could somehow convince Skye to actually go back to Portland with him. Gage shook his head in amazement. Talk about your delusions of grandeur. This guy didn't seem to think that what he had done to Skye would matter after all this time if he could just talk to her. What a twisted sense of reality.

Still, his showing up here tonight and then evading the police yet again was incredibly discouraging, in spite of the fact that he had been surprisingly amicable. Initially, Gage had hoped they'd catch Shane and lock him up and find a way to keep him this time and Gage could talk Skye into staying in St. George and if not marrying him right away, at least making plans to move toward that.

Now, with Shane still at large, knowing Skye, she would be thinking about making a clean run of it again instead of hanging out at the cottage. And honestly, he couldn't expect her to stay locked up there forever. It would bring a whole new meaning to the word cottage fever.

At least she had Mama Woo to help her be inclined to stay this time. If he honestly faced the truth, she and Kitty were probably the real reasons Skye hadn't already blown this town. It would be much harder to disappear with a dog in tow, but Gage didn't think Skye would just get rid of Kitty as much as she tended to rely on her for security.

He needed to call Skye, but he was going to have to wait until he could use a phone he was sure wouldn't be monitored. Who knew what this guy was capable of with some funky electronics? Skye had mentioned he was brilliant, and he'd certainly had no trouble with his garage door opener or the locks on her back door. If Gage hadn't seen it with his own eyes, he'd have never believed it. He'd thought her little fortress was completely impenetrable.

With a tired sigh, he saw the last of the officers out and went into his garage to see if he had anything to somehow secure the French doors. There was nothing that would make him feel safe enough to go back to bed, but he desperately needed sleep and decided to just leave and go up to his parents' house. Then, after thinking about that, he decided he wasn't going to possibly put them at risk as well and instead, packed an overnight bag and after driving around the darkened streets of St. George long enough to believe no one was following him, he checked into the nearby Fairfield Inn.

Hating to have to do it, especially at almost three-forty in the morning, he picked up the room phone and called the new cell phone he'd insisted Skye take. She needed to know what was going on in case Shane had somehow figured out how to locate her.

Even at that insane hour of the night, once she understood that it was Gage calling, she was her typical upbeat self and rather than being devastated and upset, she graciously thanked Gage tiredly for letting her know what had happened. How emotionally honest she was being, or how she found the self-control to never let things get her down was a complete mystery to him, but it was still wonderful to hear her sweet voice and know that, for now at least, she was okay. He told her he loved her and then hung up the phone and gratefully crashed for the couple of hours remaining of this night.

At seven o'clock, when the alarm on his phone finally woke him through his overpowering fatigue, he rolled over and tried to wake up enough to make a halfway cognizant phone call to Sandy and let her know it would be awhile before he came in. He still owned the place, but there was no way he was going in there first thing this morning.

Jaclyn M. Hawkes

Chapter 12

Skye rolled over and put a lazy hand over the edge of the bed to touch Kitty on the head. It was nice to have such an ever dependable companion. The sweet, constant dog might be more of a blessing right now than ever. Skye rolled back onto her back and sighed as she looked up at the heavy wooden timbers of the cottage ceiling above her.

It had been two and a half days and the police still hadn't been able to catch Shane. This time, because of his other criminal acts, like breaking into Gage's and running from the police, there was actually more of a chance he'd be kept incarcerated for a little longer—if they were able to at least find him.

But it wasn't looking like he was going to be found and that left Skye with two options. Come out into the open and try to act as bait to catch him, or disappear again, an option that was heartbreaking, but beginning to look like the wisest course of action anyway. She was taking too much of a risk with the others involved here. If they didn't find him and she waited too long, Shane would figure out where she was and possibly harm someone else this time as well, even though his behavior the other night toward Gage was amazingly innocuous.

Skye still couldn't believe Shane had stood there in the dark calmly talking to Gage instead of becoming insanely jealous and violent. Something strange was going on there. It almost sounded like Shane was in complete denial about both Gage and thinking that Skye would ever consent to return to Portland with him.

She thought about Mama Woo sleeping there in the next room and felt incredibly torn. Staying might be endangering the little Asian woman, but either walking away from her or trying to take her with was out of the question. Skye didn't feel like she could just leave her, but Mama Woo's health was far too unstable to be able to flee like Skye had had to. Moreover, that didn't even address what to do about Gage.

He'd come to visit twice now and it had ridiculously hard to tell him goodbye both times, and then she missed him miserably in between. She'd known her heart was thoroughly involved, but she'd had no idea it would be this lonely trying to stay away from him. The idea of running again and leaving him behind made her positively heartsick. She closed her eyes again and sighed. There were times that choosing happy was harder than it sounded. How long was it going to be before she would feel as if her life was her own again?

With a long, languid stretch, Skye rolled out to kneel beside the bed, knowing she needed far more insight about what she had to be doing here than she could drum up on her own this morning.

Whether it was God making her decision simpler or just coincidence, when she got to the kitchen and began to say good morning to Mama Woo, she pulled up short. Her tiny adopted grandmother smiled but the left side of her face didn't wrinkle and join in and Skye knew almost instantly that she'd had another stroke in the night. Mama Woo must have been aware that something wasn't right as well because when Skye told her they had to go to the hospital immediately, she didn't even hesitate, just nodded quietly and turned to pick up her purse from the countertop.

Skye wasn't sure if it was safe to call Gage's phone and felt like her own blood pressure was going up as she pushed the opener and backed his Jag out of the garage. This wasn't the wisest thing to do as far as Shane Cainan was concerned, but there was no other option. Mama Woo needed to be seen immediately. Skye just wished she had Gage's steady, reassurance there beside her this time.

In the emergency room, they took them straight back, without even making them fill out any paperwork and Skye was immensely relieved to find that the attending physician was the same one who had admitted Mama Woo the last time. As they gave her the dose of the enzyme to try to reverse the effects of the stroke, he asked, "When did you have the stroke, Mrs. Woo? Do you know how long it's been?"

Mama Woo just shook her head with a hesitant smile as tears filled her eyes, and the doctor looked at Skye. Although Skye had no idea how long it had been, she hugged Mama Woo and said reassuringly, "It was sometime in the night, but I'm sure it will be in time." She smiled and with a Herculean effort, kept the tears out of her eyes and voice. "You're going to be okay, Sulee. This medicine will stop this thing in its tracks. You'll be good as new soon, just like the last times."

Mama Woo returned her smile, but Skye knew she didn't really believe what Skye was saying. There was something in those dark, wise old eyes that belied the words Skye was speaking and it was stronger than Skye's attempt not to tear up. The moisture welled and over flowed her eyes as she moved closer to the sweet older woman and hugged her close. "Oh Mama Woo. Help me think positively, would you? Heavenly Father is watching over us. You're going to be fine. We're going to be fine."

Nodding against Skye, Mama Woo agreed and said, "You right Missy. Sulee fine. No worries. You see. Worry about Missy. Not Sulee."

That was just what Skye was afraid of; that she had been the cause of Mama Woo's stroke. "I have an idea. How about if neither one of us worries about anything." She encouraged Mama Woo to lie back against the pillows and relax. "Let's think about happy things, Sulee. You are the sweetest gift to me and I love you. You're right. No worries."

Half an hour later, when Gage called the new cell phone, Mama Woo had been moved onto the second floor and finally gone to sleep, but it was still all Skye could do to keep the tears out of her voice as she explained what had happened and where they were. The concern and then reassurance in Gage's voice was incredibly comforting and Skye finally began to relax for the first time since she'd wandered into the kitchen that morning.

As he walked into the hospital room a few minutes later, looking like something out of a magazine, stepping into his arms was like coming home and was even more comforting. Right now, when it felt like her world was spinning out of control, Gage could make everything right again. Man, what she wouldn't give to be able to just enjoy him.

Remembering that she was going to be careful not to do things that would make an observer realize how they felt about each other, Skye began to pull away from Gage's tight hug and he let her go enough that he could look down at her. She felt like he was looking right into her soul and she looked away, hesitant for him to see either how she was feeling about him or how upset she was about what was going on with Mama Woo.

As Gage settled into one of the two chairs against the wall, he gently pulled Skye down into the chair beside him and looked at her deeply once more before asking quietly, "Are you okay?"

She nodded, but she knew he didn't believe her as he caressed her face with a gentle hand. Finally, he pulled her head against his shoulder and questioned what the doctor was saying about Mama Woo and Skye's voice cracked as she admitted that Mama Woo's blood pressure wasn't dropping the way it had before. She paused and then whispered, "What if I've caused this, Gage? What if it's me and the strange house and the stress of it all?"

He wrapped a gentle arm around her shoulder and said, "Skye, honey, you can't control the world. All you can do is the best you can do and then you have to let the rest go and be okay with it. The rest you have to turn over to God and let Him take care of. Remember?"

She nodded, but she couldn't help the tears that rolled down her cheeks and made a wet spot on the lapel of his suit jacket. It was easy to talk about letting go of the things you couldn't control, but sometimes it was terribly hard to actually do.

When Gage finally broke the relative quiet of the room, she could hear the regret in his voice as he asked, "Have you talked to security here yet? Do they know what's going on with Shane?" She shook her head without looking up and Gage gently pushed her away and got up and walked out the door. A few minutes later, he came back in and said, "They're going to be careful not to let anyone in or put her name on the list for the dispatcher, and their going to have security patrol this floor. I've also got an off-duty officer who's going to hang out here." As he sat down and gathered her back into his arms, he asked, "Did you get any breakfast?"

Tempted to hedge, she shook her head but said, "No, but I'm fine. I'm not sure I could eat anything anyway, but thank you for asking."

"Everything looks better after breakfast, Skye. In a minute I'll go down and get you something. Would you rather have protein or something sweet?"

She reached up and patted his cheek. "I've already got something sweet. How about a bagel, or something bland?"

He rolled his eyes and said, "Oh, brother. Sweet? I'm pathetic. You're ruining my reputation. A bagel does sound really good. I think I'll join you."

"Hey, at least I didn't say you were bland. Your car is in the parking lot. You could probably take it back now. It was very nice to drive. Thank you for letting me steal it."

Gage patted her cheek this time and said with a grin, "Stealing my car was nothing after you'd already stolen my heart."

"Oh, brother. That was way worse than saying you were sweet."

"Oh, it was not. That was actually pretty good as far as one liners go." He got up and walked to the door and glanced out. "There's a security guard out here, so relax and I'll be right back with something bland to go with my sweet car."

Several minutes later he came back in and handed her a bagel and cream cheese, a chug of milk and a breakfast sandwich with an egg and bacon and when she looked up at him, he said, "I'd feel stupid eating in front of you without getting you one too."

They sat in comfortable silence as they ate and then he picked up the mess before sitting back down and wrapping an arm around her again. She loved it, but it made her worry about Shane again and she reminded Gage, "We were going to not let anyone see us being a couple, remember?"

He gave a sigh that was almost a groan and said, "How could I forget? It's miserable staying away from you. But all bets are off with Mama Woo like this. We're in official crisis destressing mode and it's regulation."

Skye nodded. "Oh, I see. But there was a reason for deciding that, you know."

"I know, but it's almost worth possibly being killed to be able to touch you. And Shane isn't here and isn't going to be, so it's okay. Shush and enjoy it. I am."

She looked at him for a few moments, wondering if she should argue about this and finally settled for saying, "This isn't a joke, Gage. And it's not really polite to shush people. How are things going at work? Are you going to end up working all night tonight if you stay here with me?"

Shaking his head, he answered, "No, but even if I had to, that would be worth it too." This time, she rolled her eyes and then he continued, "You know what's wild? I've had three buyers interested in the clinic already. I thought it would take months to sell it. It looks like it might happen pretty fast. St. George is listed as one of the best places in the country to retire and so it's also listed as one of the hottest economies. The broker thinks the clinic might bring even more than it appraised for."

Skye studied him soberly and then asked, "And your practice?"

"I haven't had any takers for that yet, unfortunately. It's advertised on the web, but where it will make the most splash is in the trade journals and they won't even come out for several more days. That one I can have some of the other practitioners handle though." She was still watching him, wondering if what he was saying was that if she left, he was still planning to come with her. Which was ridiculous. All of this was.

There was no way she could go if she needed to with a tiny old Asian woman, a dog, and a devoted chiropractor. It was beginning to sound like the exodus of the Israelites or something. And it was all a moot point anyway with Mama Woo lying there so ill anyway. Skye glanced at her blood pressure reading and sighed again. Still through the roof. She almost wanted to wake Mama Woo up and have her smile to see if the enzyme was working to reverse the stroke or if they had been too late. She dearly hoped they hadn't been too late.

Gage was still there with her at one o'clock the next morning. He'd left her side only long enough to go back to the cottage early that afternoon and take Kitty to his mom's house. It was a good thing he was still there, because he knew to take Skye's hand and pull her to the corner of the room and hold her tightly when a warning alarm sounded on one of the machines hooked up to Mama Woo and the room suddenly filled with medical personnel.

Skye wasn't sure what was happening and she looked up at Gage in fear, but he only shook his head sadly and whispered, "She's having another stroke, Skye. They're doing all that can be done, but it looks to be a massive one and her heart keeps stopping. Just pray. That's all we can do." He put his head close to hers and hugged her tighter and she knew he was indeed praying and she closed her eyes and joined him.

It may have been all they could do, but it was all that was needed, wasn't it? She fought her fear to remind herself that God was in control here, just as He always was and that His will would be done. That didn't necessarily mean Mama Woo would walk away from this, but at least Skye took some comfort in remembering He was indeed in charge.

Seemingly hours later, the alarms quit going off and slowly the room emptied down to just Mama Woo's nurse and one other technician who was entering information onto the computer in the room as the nurse read off numbers and readings. Through all of it, Mama Woo had never woken up, and Skye tried to read the screen above her bed to understand just how she was doing.

Her blood pressure had dropped finally, probably due to the number of medicines they had just administered in the organized chaos of that crazy short while, but all of their faces had been frighteningly sober as they'd worked over her and then left and Skye wasn't deluding herself that Mama Woo was fine this time. Her heart rate was slow and labored and the pallor of her skin was a sickly gray, and even in her sleep, the abnormal pull of the muscles on one side of her face made her nearly unrecognizable. Not only had the enzyme not reversed the signs of last night's stroke, but it hadn't helped to prevent this massive one either and Skye dreaded finding out how bad Mama Woo was when she finally woke up. Three of the other digital lines on the monitor above the bed had flat lined or were intermittent and Skye didn't even dare ask what that meant yet. All she knew right now was that she felt an incredible weight of responsibility for having brought all of this on. There was no doubt that the stress of the last few days had heightened Mama Woo's blood pressure.

When the technician finally left, Skye hesitated and then asked the silent nurse what had just happened and was gently told that Mama Woo had indeed suffered a massive stroke and had almost died. The nurse glanced up at the monitor above the sweet little woman's bed and shook her head and sadly admitted, "I'm sorry, Skye, but she probably won't ever come back out of this. There appears to be considerable damage and her brain isn't responding much. She may never even know you if she wakes up, which isn't terribly likely anyway. I mean, there's always the possibility, but..." She nodded at the monitor and continued, "That third line that only has occasional spikes is her brain activity. I'm sorry."

The nurse walked out the door and Skye studied the monitor for a moment or two and then turned back into Gage's hug like it was a sanctuary that she hoped would keep all of this from being real. Mama Woo couldn't be brain dead. She was getting older, but she was still vibrant and funny and sweet. Skye struggled to hold back the tears and fear and heartache, but it was impossible and she stayed buried in the strength of Gage's chest, letting him absorb the emotion that was drowning her just like his white shirt absorbed the torrent of tears. The sadness was choking, but the guilt was what was so overpowering. This was all her fault. Worry and stress over Skye and then leaving her home was what had brought this all on and Skye knew it.

She wasn't even sure what time of the morning it was when Gage folded out the miniature futon chair and went in search of linens and a pillow. She accepted his gentle kiss and encouragement to lie down almost woodenly and then collapsed into a restless dream filled place where the fear and sadness still filled the very air with an almost tangible anxiousness. She had no idea how many times she woke up and was upset, but every single time, Gage was there to speak to her quietly and softly touch her until she could go back to trying to rest again. Even his gentle reassurance was troubling in a way because it made Skye feel guilty for keeping him up all night, not to mention putting him in possible danger just by being with her. Even in the throes of this mess, Shane's existence was an ever present threat.

When Skye finally really woke up in the light of day late the next morning, for once Gage was gone, but her Relief Society president sat in his chair instead and she looked over at Skye with a sad smile and said quietly, "I'd say good morning, but..." She reached for Skye's hand and gave it a squeeze. "I'm so sorry, Skye. I know you love her so much."

Still half asleep, Skye glanced up at the monitor to be disappointed at seeing that Mama Woo's brain was responding even less than last night. She ran a hand through her tangled hair and sat up with a sigh. It hadn't just been a bad dream. Mama Woo really was laying there basically in a coma. It made Skye heart broken all over again and she had to fight to contain the tears that seemed to want to flood out of her eyes.

She wasn't a crier. At least not usually. Raining all over Gage last night had been the first time in her life she could ever remember doing that. She was the one who smiled into the face of adversity and found the rose colored lining on even the darkest of clouds. Staying happy in spite of any of life's storms was her specialty, but this morning her spirit felt incredibly tired.

Reaching for her purse, she dug for her little hair brush and attempted to tame her hair and then pulled it up into a haphazard knot with a clip and dug one more time for the toothbrush she carried. At least brushing her teeth and washing her face made her feel marginally better, and by the time Gage reappeared with another armload of breakfast, Skye had the waterworks firmly in hand.

Her Relief Society president stayed for another half hour visiting with Skye and Gage as the three of them ate and then sadly squeezed Skye's shoulder and asked her to call if there was anything she or the ward could do, before slipping out the hospital room door.

With her gone, Skye studied Gage's face as he quietly studied her own and then she gave a small smile and asked, "Do I look as tired as you do?"

Gage laughed and shook his head. "No, you actually look beautiful this morning in spite of it all. Am I that bad?"

She reached over and gently touched his eye that was starting to turn green and yellow around the edges and then leaned to put her cheek next to his the way he had that first night. "You look like a white knight who rescued the damsel, but at the cost of a night's sleep. I'm sorry I was so restless, but I'm so grateful to you for being here." She paused and then had to whisper, "I don't know how I'd have gotten through without you. Thank you."

He pulled her head back against his chest and wrapped an arm around her protectively again. "You'd have been just fine, Skye Alexander. You may have stumbled, but then you'd have just danced in the rain the way you always do. It's your gift. You're the strongest woman I've ever known and you pull it all off beautifully." He played with a tendril of hair that had escaped the clip. "You would have been fine, but a shoulder to cry on occasionally is a good thing on a bad night. Thanks for letting me be there. I've never gotten to be anyone's white knight. It's kind of nice. I just wish it was under different circumstances."

She nodded against him and said sadly, "Me too."

After a few more minutes, Gage looked over at Mama Woo sleeping so quietly and softly mused, "I wonder if she's already back with her family on the other side of the veil. Do you suppose that line softens when your spirit is somehow in limbo?"

Appreciating his kind way of dealing with the subject of Mama Woo's death, she was incredibly grateful to have that whole issue broached in such a sweet way. It was wonderful to be able to remember that for the one who leaves this estate, dying is a good thing in the big picture. Skye hoped Mama Woo was indeed with her beloved family in spirit. Skye had some small idea of how much losing her family had hurt Mama Woo. She'd be thrilled to be able to be with them again in a place that was immune from the terrible things of this earth.

Skye leaned up and kissed Gage's cheek and murmured, "Thank you for helping me to realize that for her this might be just what she would have wanted."

He looked down at her and said, "You're welcome. And you're right. This is sad, but she did miss her family terribly."

Nodding again and swallowing the lump in her throat, at length Skye could admit, "I know."

She finally talked him into leaving her to go home and get some real rest that evening at nearly eight o'clock. Before he left, he double checked with the security people and the officer who was lounging outside the door in a soft chair they'd pulled into the hall, and then Gage gently kissed her goodbye and was gone. Skye missed him, but in another way it was a huge relief. She knew she was where she needed to be right now, but she also knew Shane was still out there. Waiting. Probably watching. And she truly doubted the amiable demeanor he'd shown so far when he'd come into contact with any of them. She didn't doubt that he was trying to change to win her back. For a long time, he'd been very sweet, but she shuddered as she remembered his brutality of that awful attack. Somewhere inside him, there was still a maniac. Sadly, she knew all about that part of him.

Jaclyn M. Hawkes

Chapter 13

Taking a huge chance at being apprehended by police, Shane Cainan showered and shaved on the fourth morning after breaking in to Skye's shop and headed back up there. He was finally beginning to wonder if Skye truly had left the area. He'd been watching both her house and that pretty boy chiropractor and other than the guy going in to his clinic, there hadn't been any activity near either place when he'd been there. Shane hadn't been able to be both places at once, but from what he could discern, this Dr. Garrison hadn't gone anywhere near Skye if she was around and her shop was still locked up tight.

He wished he'd had put something on the guy's car the night he'd gone to his house so he could know exactly where he drove, but he didn't have one. He'd ordered a couple but they hadn't arrived yet and the car Garrison was driving was a rental. He expected it to be turned back in and have the Jag reappear. So far the Jag hadn't surfaced and Shane wasn't sure if that was a good thing or not. If it did, he intended to put a tracking device on it as well.

He'd also been monitoring the phone numbers he'd found on her phone records, but there hadn't been any activity at all between them. Even Skye's parents' phones hadn't been contacted.

Shane parked around the corner where the new car he'd rented to replace the one that had been identified wouldn't be obvious and then walked down to her alley and quietly knocked at the next door down from Skye's apartment and the one next to it. It was only eight o'clock in the morning and he hoped who ever answered wouldn't be mad that he showed up so early.

It was actually a young teenager and it appeared he was alone as he was just shrugging into a jacket and back pack when Shane asked him, "Hey, I'm an old friend of Skye's and am in town and wanted to see her, but I haven't been able to find her home and she isn't answering her phone. Do you have any idea where I could get hold of her?"

The youth shook his head and took a set of head phones out of his pocket and said, "She's been gone and we thought she went on vacation or something. Have you checked with Mrs. Woo at the apartment between us?"

"There hasn't been anyone there either. Is Skye friends with this Mrs. Woo?"

"Yeah, they're together all the time. I wonder if Mrs. Woo is in the hospital again. She had a stroke or something a few weeks ago and Skye had her in the hospital. Maybe that's why she doesn't answer her phone. When my grandpa was in the hospital, we had to keep our phones off when we were inside. I gotta get to class. Good luck trying to find her." The youth left and Shane tried the last apartment on the alley, but when no one answered, he walked back around the block to where he'd left his car on a side street and got out his laptop and checked into both Mrs. Woo and the where abouts of the local hospital.

After finding the information he wanted, he drove to the hospital and was just going to go inside and ask which room Sulee Woo was in, when he spotted the green Jag in the parking lot at the rear of the hospital. Knowing Skye and how hard she'd been to find, he was surprised she'd left it right out in the open. Maybe it wasn't the same car, but no, as he wandered closer, it still had the flower arrangements in the back seat that she and that pretty boy had loaded into it that day.

Thinking about him being with Skye made that slow, hot irritation that Shane was always struggling to control rise up in him again. He let it linger for a moment while he hated the thought of another man with Skye and then he actively squelched it as best he could.

He did hate the thought of another man with Skye, but she would have been disappointed in him for letting himself get angry and he tamped the irritation down. If he was ever going to be able to talk her into coming home, he had to keep a cool head. He had to remember that he had to be able to win Skye over from this man if he ever wanted her to stay with him and being angry would only drive her away.

Still wanting to key the beautiful car, he parked and walked into the lobby of the hospital. Not surprisingly, when he asked the receptionist what room Sulee Woo was in, the woman checked her list and looked up at him blankly and said, "I'm sorry, sir, but we don't have a Sulee Woo listed. Are you sure she's supposed to be here?"

He shook his head and apologized and quickly left the hospital. He'd expected they'd be trying to fly under the radar. Skye knew him. She knew how much he loved her and to what lengths he'd go to find her. He was just glad he'd gotten a little closer to being able to see her and talk to her. He went back to his car and started to hack into the hospital's computer system. The people may not tell him what he wanted to know, but the computer told him every time.

She was in room 216 and he literally rubbed his hands together to have that information. Skye was probably right inside this hospital right now. He thought about just walking right in and trying to talk to her, but a St. George city police car was parked in the lot nearest the entrance and he decided to wait and do a little more digging and preparation and try to go in later at night when there weren't quite so many people around.

There would be maintenance people here in the middle of the night. Maybe he could pose as one of them to get inside. At any rate, he decided he was going to watch that car. He had no idea how long they would keep this Woo woman, but he intended to be here if Skye walked out before he got inside to see her. The relative privacy of the parking lot would be perfect to try to explain to her.

Skye never came out, but a number of different police officers went in and out and sometimes even cruised the lot and after moving his car several times so he wouldn't look too suspicious, Shane finally decided he needed to leave for a few hours. If they were going to release this Mrs. Woo, they would have already done it, and if Skye was going to leave for the night it would probably still be awhile.

When he came back at nine-thirty that night, he was disgusted to realize the Jag was gone. He pulled into a parking spot and pulled up the hospital system again and breathed a sigh of relief. The Woo woman was still listed for room 216, so hopefully, Skye would come back again in the morning. Just to be sure, he drove around and checked the lot, but there was no sign of the beautiful green car.

Parking again, he hacked into the security system of the hospital and looked around until he found the cameras that serviced the second floor. He'd just been going to plan a way to get into the room, but he was glad he'd done it when he spotted the uniformed police officer lounging in the hallway. Maybe trying to go inside tonight wasn't the right plan. Unless there was a criminal in the hospital, which he doubted in this sleepy little town, the Woo woman's room must be nearby. Skye had never had a cop hanging out nearby full time before, but then he hadn't ever been free to find her and she hadn't waited to run before either.

Shane didn't know who this Mrs. Woo was, but he was glad she'd needed to be hospitalized right now. Shane could wait until Skye came or went. He could simply sit here and watch the security cameras to know when she would. This was turning out to be much easier than he'd thought it would be.

****

Mama Woo's condition hadn't changed except to become even more tenuous by the next day and when Gage came in late in the morning, Skye was surprised to see the bishop of her ward walk in with him. Gage came and kissed her although he had a frighteningly serious face and the bishop shook her hand before taking the other seat while Gage stood next to hers. They small talked for a few minutes and then Skye began to tell them how Mama Woo was doing, but then Gage told her he'd already spoken to the doctor on the way in. He glanced up at her bishop who admitted that the doctor had actually called him at his home that morning.

Confused, Skye looked from one to the other of them and then Gage explained, "Your bishop here holds the power of attorney for Mama Woo, Skye, and he's also the one who has to make any big hairy decisions about Mama Woo's health."

He left it at that and she looked back and forth between the two of them again and then breathed a huge sigh of relief and almost whispered, "Please tell me you're saying I don't have to be the one to decide when she's taken off the machines."

Gage just kept looking at her sadly, but the bishop nodded his head and said gently, "You don't have to decide, Skye. Thankfully, she spared you of that when she got all of her legal things together before you ever moved here. She didn't know who to ask and since I was her bishop and also a physician, she listed me as the power of attorney over everything." He paused, but then continued hesitantly, "But she also has a Do Not Resuscitate clause that comes into play here legally. That's why the doctor called me this morning. They didn't have her living will until last night and he felt he needed to tell me honestly how she is doing. She has stipulated she doesn't want to be kept on life support if she's technically brain dead."

Skye nodded as the tears once again pooled into her eyes. "I don't blame her. I wouldn't want that either." She reached for Gage's hand as she struggled to swallow and then had to ask, "So what's the plan then? Is she technically brain dead? Are you going to pull the plugs?"

The bishop shook his head and reassured her, "Actually, there aren't really any plugs. She's not on a respirator or feeding tubes. She's getting an IV, but if she crashes again, we really shouldn't try to resuscitate her. There's no hurry, Skye. We'll give her a few days to see if there are any signs of brain activity, but yes, she's technically brain dead. The stroke was massive. I'm not here to tell you we're pulling the plug as you call it. I'm here mostly to check on you, but it's probably best that you know what she requested and know you're not the one who has to decide. That's not pressure you want to have right now, I assume."

Letting out a big breath, Skye assured him, "Right now or ever. I'm grateful you told me. I've been sick worrying about it." After a moment, she went on, "A few days will be good. Who knows? Maybe she'll snap out of this and we won't have to make that decision at all."

Her bishop looked at her sadly, but agreed, "Perhaps you're right. I hope you are. How are you feeling? Are you doing okay here? I know it's hard to leave when there's a chance she'd wake up."

Wondering what to say that would be honest, Skye looked at her bishop and then up at Gage and then settled for saying, "I'm doing okay, under the circumstances."

Both men watched her quietly for a second and then the bishop patted her hand and said, "I imagine you are, Skye, knowing you. You have a wonderful attitude about you. I wish everyone in the world could have such an attitude. What can I do to help you through all of this?"

Wiping at a stray tear, she assured him, "Nothing you're not already doing, Bishop, but thank you. Just keep praying for all of us and we'll be fine."

"I always pray for all of you, Skye. Rest assured. But is there anything else? Do you need some of us to help keep your shop going? We're not florists, but we could probably handle ringing up purchases."

Skye shook her head. "No, the shop will be fine, but thank you. Prayer is all we need. It's all anyone needs, isn't it?"

The bishop stood up and looked down at her. "No. Occasionally, we need the help God sends as answers to those prayers. That's the way He often works, you know. He sends someone to us on His errands. But prayer is definitely the most help of all. Please let me know if there is something we can do."

"I will, Bishop. Thank you for coming. You've been an immense relief."

He smiled at that and said, "To some people, I'm a relief when I come. To some I'm a relief when I go. Take care."

After he left, Skye was grateful for the smile he had brought her, no matter how brief. Whoever had figured out that smiling released good chemicals in your body had it right, for sure. And right now, she certainly needed those chemicals. Gage settled into the chair beside her and reached for her hand. Touch released those same good chemicals. Having Gage around during all of this had to be one of those answers to prayer the bishop had been talking about and she was incredibly glad to have him.

He was still watching her and she finally smiled sadly at him and said, "I'm not going to vaporize, or self-destruct, or whatever it is you're worried about, Gage. You can stop looking at me like that."

That didn't make him stop watching her, but he teased her anyway and said, "I'm just thinking that you're really beautiful when you're sad. I brought you some things from the cottage. And could I talk you into coming down to the cafeteria to eat with me?"

He handed her the bag he'd brought and she glanced through it, thinking that a shower and change of clothes sounded heavenly just now. "Do I have time to clean up before we eat? How starving are you?"

She got one of his heart stopping smiles as he said, "You know me. I'm always starving, but I'm fine to wait. Take your shower and I'll hold down the fort here for a few minutes."

Inside the bathroom, Skye was a little embarrassed that he'd brought her clean undies and a little surprised that he'd even known to grab her blow dryer and curling iron and cosmetics. He always said she was able to handle anything, but he was even more that way than she was. Nothing seemed to ruffle his feathers. At least nothing she'd ever seen. Well, she had to take that back. He'd been a little ruffled the morning he'd asked her to marry him. Under different circumstances, he'd have been pretty funny.

As she showered, she thought back to that first time he'd walked into her shop and she'd shot him with her water bottle. She shook her head and smiled, in spite of herself. She probably never should have done something like that, but he'd just laughed and then begun to pester her until she'd agreed to go out with him.

Since then she'd had more fun with him than she'd ever had in her life. That thought almost made her sad as she realized that as soon as Mama Woo passed away and was buried, Skye needed to finally leave for good. She'd hung around far too long already. And from what the bishop was saying this morning, Mama Woo could be gone in a mere matter of days. She turned her face into the spray to pretend she wasn't really crying over it all. Losing Mama Woo and Gage at the same time was going to kill her.

Skye couldn't see her watch in the dark, but she knew it was deep in the night at that time when even the machines in the hospital room seemed to be more hushed. As she came awake, she could occasionally hear the on duty staff as they worked around outside the room, but for the most part, the night was quiet and subdued and she wondered what had woken her. Then, as if by a prompting, warmth filled her heart and she sat up in the funny little bed and looked around the dimly lit room. At first she had no idea what she was being prompted to do, and then she realized she'd been prompted to simply wake up. It was time. She suddenly knew it and rose from the bed, amazed that the spirit that filled the room was of sweet, calming peace instead of the deep sadness she'd been expecting.

Stepping over next to Mama Woo, she reached to take the little, wrinkled hand that she'd held for a million hours these last few days. The tiny woman seemed to be resting comfortably and Skye wondered if she was mistaken and then she noticed the depth of Mama Woo's breathing. She breathed as one in the deepest of slumber except that the breaths were coming with far too long of breaks in between.

Skye looked up at the monitor above the bed, wondering why it wasn't beeping at the obvious respiratory failure, but the screen was blank and she understood that the nurses had known and had turned it all off. Innately, she also understood that it wasn't out of a lack of concern, but was out of respect and the wish that these last moments were filled with peace and not loud and troubling alarms. For that she would always be grateful.

She'd never been there when someone died, but she'd assumed it would be frightening and awful, but it wasn't. It was the most reassuring warmth and serenity Skye had ever experienced and she honestly found herself looking around the room for the spirits she felt had to be here, waiting to take Mama Woo with them to the other side. What else could explain the incredible tranquility that permeated the very air right now?

As she stood there, beside this dear friend, the breathing got more and more shallow, the breaths spaced further and further apart and almost inaudibly, Skye murmured, "Good bye, Mama Woo. I'm going to miss you. You've been such a blessing and inspiration to me. I love you."

At the end, several times Skye had thought she was gone and then several seconds later, she would take another small, incredibly shallow breath and then finally, the breathing stopped altogether. Still, Skye held the little hand, loathe to let either Mama Woo or this feeling of such peace end. Finally, she heard a sound and turned to the door where two nurses quietly stood and a single tear escaped her eye and trailed down her cheek as she whispered, "It's okay. She's gone. You can come in."

They came into the room and one of them gently put her arm around Skye's waist to give her a hug and said, "I'm so sorry, Skye."

Shaking her head, Skye inhaled to stop the tears as she replied, "No. She's finally with her own family. She would have wanted it this way. She was such a strong, sweet woman. It's sad, but she's gone on to a better place." Skye hugged the nurse back and went on, "Thank you for helping us through this. For helping her to die with dignity and for encouraging me through it." She tried to smile through her tears as she said in wonder, "I thought it would be frightening. But it really wasn't was it?" The nurse shook her head and Skye asked, "Is it always this way?"

Again, the nurse shook her head and said quietly, "Not always."

"Thank you for turning off the alarms."

With a last squeeze, the nurse said, "You're welcome. It's not much, but..." She walked to the bed and gently felt for a pulse and then touched Skye's hand as the two of them turned back toward the door and said, "Take as long as you like, Skye. We won't bother you."

It turned out that Skye didn't stay long at all. With Mama Woo gone, the sweet warmth in the room slowly dissipated and Skye had no doubt that the energetic little spirit that had filled that tiny body had gone on to more important things. She gathered up her few belongings and with one last sad look back, she walked out of the room and asked the policeman who was sitting outside to walk her down to the parking lot. She still had Gage's Jaguar and doubted Shane would be hanging around it at three-forty-one in the morning. After watching the parking lot for several minutes, they went out and she climbed into it, waved to the cop and drove back to the cottage in Snow Canyon. It would be several hours before she could touch base with either Gage or the bishop and as peaceful as Mama Woo's passing had been, it had taken the last vestige of energy out of her.

****

When Gage noticed the Jag gone from the place it had been parked in the hospital parking lot for the last few days, he got the strangest feeling down the back of his neck and picked up the pace into the hospital. When he walked into the hospital room to find it dark and empty, just for a moment, he almost panicked. After a very tired nurse explained what had happened in the night, but didn't know where Skye had gone, he wasn't sure whether to worry about Skye dealing with that alone or whether it was better that way. Surely death was the ultimate private occurrence, but he still wished he had been there.

He thanked the nurse and then stepped out the door into the hall and tried to call the new cell phone he'd given Skye. When she didn't answer that, he headed for his rental car on the run and tried her old phone number as well. It went straight to voice mail and it was all he could do not to sprint until he got into the car and sped away. He called the police and asked forLieutenantPederson and when he came on, Gage asked if they'd heard from her. When Pederson answered in the negative, Gage explained what was going on and then hung up, more worried than ever.

She wouldn't go back to her apartment. He was sure of that, and headed for Snow Canyon. Driving around to make sure he wasn't followed was incredibly frustrating and he had to caution himself not to take the curves in the canyon too fast.

As he pushed the button on the garage door opener and it slowly lifted to reveal the Jag, he felt the blood rush back into his chest as he pulled in. He tried to call again so he wouldn't scare Skye as he came into the house, but she still didn't answer and his heart began to race again as he fumbled with the key. Was she just upset about what had happened or had something even worse happened to her?

Nothing inside the house looked amiss except the blinds were all closed and the house was ominously silent for nine o'clock in the morning. Rushing through the house, he nearly ripped the door to Skye's bedroom open and couldn't begin to describe the feeling he felt when he saw her there in her bed. She was still dead to the world asleep and he hustled across the room and leaned down to make sure she was still breathing before softly saying her name as he began to gently rub her back. He should have just let her sleep, but he needed to make sure she was okay.

The sight of those mile deep baby blue eyes slowly opening was the most beautiful thing he'd ever seen and he was so relieved that he sat right down on her bed and hauled her into his arms almost roughly. Pulling her tight against him, he whispered her name against her hair, "Skye." Kissing the softness of it, he went on huskily, "You scared the tar out of me."

Still sleepy, she looked up at him in confusion and he didn't explain, just began to kiss her with all the rushing emotion he'd been feeling since seeing the car gone. The longer it had taken to find her, the more he'd become convinced Shane had finally gotten to her and it made his heart nearly convulse in his chest.

They'd both begun to breathe heavily when Skye let go of him and put both of her hands against his chest and gently pushed him away. Coming back to his senses, he pulled back and saw her hesitantly lick her lower lip and he realized he'd hurt her and felt terrible. "Oh, baby, I'm so sorry." He put up a finger and gently touched where she had and then leaned in and kissed it again gently. "I'm sorry."

Her eyes were huge and almost frightened and she pulled the blanket up over her pajama top. For the first time, he realized he was all but attacking her in her bed and he stood up and blew out a huge breath as he ran a frustrated hand through his hair. "Sorry." He looked up and then closed his eyes, took another deep breath and repeated, "Sorry, Skye. I didn't mean to burst in on you like this, but you were gone and then didn't answer your phone and…"

He sat back on her bed again and pulled her to him more gently this time and said softly, "I thought you were gone. I thought he'd found you." Kissing her hair again, he groaned and admitted tenderly, "You frightened me."

She hesitantly pushed him away again and he got up and headed for the door as he said, "I'm sorry I woke you. I just had to know for sure that you were okay." At that, he came back to the bed and looked down at her and asked gently, "Are you okay? After last night with Mama Woo?"

Still not saying anything, she simply nodded and pulled the covers up again and he sighed and asked, "Are you still tired? Or could you get dressed and come out and talk to me?"

She was obviously still tired, but she replied, "I'll get dressed. Go out and I'll be right there."

He took in her sleepy eyes and gorgeous tousled hair and skin still flushed from sleeping and glanced back over the length of her lying there and then back to her face and softly said, "You're beautiful in the morning, Skye."

His eyes dropped to her shoulder where the collar of her pajamas had begun to slip down and he looked back into her eyes that had gotten even bigger and he turned away with an inward groan. *Holy smokes, she was sexy in the morning.* He swallowed hard and walked resolutely to the door. He needed to get out of this bedroom and now! He'd seen a lot of pretty girls in his life, but nothing that moved him like seeing her there. He'd never dreamed he would be that tempted to go back in there with her. Walking out the door was almost painful.

Ten minutes later, she found him sitting on the back deck with a cold glass of juice, looking out over the expanse of red rock desert that flowed down the canyon. She was fully dressed and although she certainly remained a little sleepy, she looked more hesitant than tired as she approached him, still with big eyes. She wasn't saying much, and he continued to wonder how she was emotionally as he stood up to come to her. For several seconds they just stood there looking at each other and then he moved to wrap her in a tight hug and asked, "Are you okay, Skye?"

She nodded against his chest and then asked almost timidly, "Are you?"

The tone of her voice made him chuckle and then answer guiltily, "No. I'm not. Frankly, when I went into that room, I was worried about your safety from Shane, but after a couple of minutes, I was worried about your safety with me." He sighed and hugged her tighter. "Geez, you look hot in the morning, Skye." She didn't say anything and he finally pulled away enough to look into her eyes and asked, "Should I not have admitted that?"

She hadn't so much as thought about smiling and he began to wonder even more if she was okay as she slowly answered, "I don't know. I don't know what to think about you this morning. I've never seen you like this."

"Like what?"

Finally, there was the merest hint of a smile as she said, "Like... So guyish. I mean, you should have seen the way you were looking at me."

Gage smiled and let her go and took her hand to pull her back into the kitchen. "That would be because, deep down, I'm a guy. And you should have seen the way you looked in there. There should be a law against looking that good before you're even awake. Can I make you some breakfast?"

"Yeah, well, that look could have burned this cottage right down. That's what there should be a law against. Starting a house on fire. What are you making?"

"The combustibility was all your doing, so don't blame that on me, lady. I was an innocent bystander. I'll cook whatever you'd like."

"Innocent bystander? I woke up and you were sitting on my bed, kissing me senseless. How is that innocent? What are you in the mood for?"

They'd made it to the kitchen and he turned and raised an eyebrow as he looked at her with a grin. "I can't really answer that and you know it."

She folded her arms and gave him the look. "I was talking about breakfast, Gage."

"Oh." He leaned down and kissed her hard on the mouth. "Well, why didn't you say so?"

"For the first time, I can see that you really are related to Gabriel."

Gage grinned. "We're brothers, actually. I'm thinking ham."

"Oh, you're a ham all right."

He pulled her close and kissed her for a few minutes and then said, "I'm so glad you're joking with me. I've been so worried. I wasn't sure how you'd deal with all of this. Are you okay? Really?"

For the first time this morning, tears brightened her eyes and she looked down, but nodded. "It's weird. I thought I'd be devastated. And in a way, I am, but you should have been there, Gage. It was the most amazing experience. Something woke me and I realized she was fading and there was this most incredible, sweet peace in the room. I don't know how to explain it, but... For some reason, I've always thought that being there when someone died would somehow be gruesome or scary or something. In actuality, it was almost... Would it sound stupid if I said it was truly a spiritual experience?"

"No, honey, it wouldn't sound stupid. I've never experienced that, but I've heard others say they felt overwhelmingly close to the veil."

She nodded and then thought about it for a second. "That's exactly how it felt. I mean I honestly looked around that room to see if someone was there. Someone who had come for her. I know that sounds positively bizarre, but it's true. And it's actually been so comforting. I mean, I'm going to miss her desperately, but this morning took so much of the sadness out of her death. Not all of it, but somehow, I know she's back with her family and it's almost like passing the torch or something. I did my best to watch over her and now she's where she'll be taken good care of. Much better care than I could ever give her."

She paused and then finally started to cry in earnest and he wrapped her in another hug. When she could speak, she said, "I just wish it hadn't all been my fault. I'm sure worries over me and bringing her here and everything were what caused it. And even though she's in a better place, she could have still been here and healthy and..."

"Skye. Honey, don't do this to yourself. Don't put this all on your shoulders. Even if that were even a little bit true – which I don't believe, it would be Shane's fault and not yours. You've done the best you can under the circumstances. Let it go and be happy for her. I mean, we'll miss her, but be glad for her." He nuzzled her forehead. "They say that heaven is very nice."

She closed her eyes as he continued to kiss her head and her hair and asked, "Who's they?"

After a second he said, "I believe it was one of the prophets."

He moved to her mouth for a long kiss before she continued, "Then it must be true."

"It must. So be as happy for Mama Woo as you can. It's hard right now, but that's what she would want. I can just hear her saying –Life short. No worries." He stopped nuzzling her to smile down at her and add, "Let's try to remember the good things and not her death and then let's focus on the future. Let's look forward instead of back if we can."

He wasn't sure what he'd said, but Skye looked at him and he could almost see the distance seep into her eyes and she pulled away and turned toward the fridge and asked "What do you want with that ham you were talking about?"

He took her shoulder and turned her back around toward him. "Whoa, there Little Texas. What was that look and that tone? What just happened here? I thought we were happy in spite of losing Mama Woo. What gives?"

Skye looked up into his eyes with those clear baby blues and studied him for a minute and then sighed and turned back to the open fridge. "Nothing gives, Gage. I must just be tired. I guess I'm still a little too shell-shocked over it all to focus on the future yet. Eggs or pancakes?"

He moved around so he could look at her again and when he couldn't tell what the heck was going on, he finally gave up and said, "Eggs."

She went to reach into the fridge and he stopped her and added, "I love you, Skye. I love you, and I am looking forward to the future. I can't wait to stay at that little cottage on the beach at Roan Inish with you. And I don't need idealic. I'm good with going through all kinds of storms with you as long as you'll dance in the rain with me. I don't want to wait for everything to be perfect. I just want to enjoy the journey with a beautiful, up beat girl who chooses happy even if the rain hasn't stopped. Don't begrudge me that. I've looked for you for so long. Now that I've finally found you, let me be excited about it." She didn't say anything and he added, "Please?"

She finally nodded, but there was no joy in her eyes. If he was honest, there was actually more sadness than when she'd been talking about Mama Woo's death and it killed him, but he turned away to begin making breakfast anyway. She'd need some time. Time, and they still had to deal with the whole Shane issue. It was looming out there bigger than ever now that Mama Woo was gone.

Deciding to lighten things up, as he sliced ham, he said, "My mother has decided she adores Kitty. She said she didn't know there was dog in the whole world that was that well behaved."

Skye smiled and her mood did seem to pick up, but still, by the time Gage left early that afternoon, the smile had never truly reached her eyes.

Chapter 14

Shane smiled as the pop up appeared on the top of his computer screen announcing that the chiropractor was trying to call some one. After being bitterly disappointed to find that not only was the Jag gone from the parking lot, but the Woo woman had also died in the night and Skye had disappeared, Shane had consoled himself with the knowledge that this Woo would be having a funeral and very probably, Skye would attend it. That was where he would make his move. Everyone there would be distracted and he'd finally be able to talk to Skye and take her home.

Now as this guy tried to make a couple of phone calls, Shane didn't recognize the first number, but when it went unanswered, he immediately recognized the second one as the cell phone Skye had been using here before he came. That call didn't pick up either, but Shane smiled again to himself. He'd very probably just been handed the cell number he could reach Skye at.

She obviously wasn't answering right now, but he'd try the number later. Right now, he wished he knew where this Garrison pretty boy was, because he was probably going to go to where Skye was hiding since she wasn't answering her phone. The smile died out of his face as he once again felt that old familiar anger at knowing another man was spending time with her. It was going to be a huge relief to finally take her away from any other men for good.

****

Skye had just finished talking to her bishop about the funeral arrangements for Mama Woo when an unfamiliar number came up as an incoming call. Still focused on the simple graveside service set for the next morning that they'd decided on, she tiredly pushed send, expecting the bishop's voice to come on over the line again.

It wasn't the bishop at all, but Shane Cainan's low and suggestive voice silkily speaking her name and it instantly made the hair on the back of her neck begin to prickle. Stunned beyond answering, even if she'd wanted to, she hesitated for a minute and then quickly pushed end and put a hand to her beating heart. How had he gotten this number and how had she been foolish enough to even take a call that she didn't know who it was from?

She set the little phone down on the stone countertop like it was hot, wishing she understood more about how these things worked. Did this mean he could somehow find out where she was answering from? She'd seen a documentary on how cell phones could be traced like a GPS system, but at the time she'd thought someone had to have had actual physical access to the phone to plant something on it. How in the world had he gotten hold of this number?

Her heart began to race and her first gut reaction was to take her purse and literally flee. Struggling for composure, she tried to think this through. She had to leave. She needed to go now, before he found her or harmed anyone else who got in his way, but how and to where and what about Mama Woo's service? She shook her head and closed her eyes against the tears that began to fill her eyes. She couldn't face leaving without giving Mama Woo this very last goodbye. She couldn't. She just couldn't.

Deciding to stay until after the funeral, she began to try to brain storm about where she could go next and how to stay safe until she could leave. How to stay safe and keep everyone else that way as well. There would only be some of the members of their ward and a few from their neighborhood at the cemetery, but Skye would never forgive herself if someone was hurt because of her.

She desperately wanted to talk to Gage, but she knew that not only was it not safe, for either one of them, but it was also foolish, given the fact that within less than twenty-four hours she would be leaving him forever. The thought made pain literally rip through her heart, but she knew she had no choice. She loved Gage too much to ever put him at the risk that staying would. He was far too good of a man to take a chance on him being harmed in this crazy mess of her life.

Walking to the little kitchen desk of the cottage, she picked up the travel atlas she'd seen there and opened it to the map of the whole United States and tried to look at it objectively through her tears. She'd gone from Portland to Missouri the first time, and then to Florida and on to Minnesota before landing here on the border of Utah and Nevada. Where would be the least likely place Shane would expect her to go next? Where could she go and what could she do to make a living when she got there? She'd already done landscaping, gardening and built water gardens and now floral design. She was fast running out of things she knew how to do to make money.

She stared unseeing at the map for several minutes without figuring anything out except for the fact that she'd never cared about anyone the way she did about Gage. For the first time in this insane life of running, she wondered how in the world she was going to be able to do this. Not only did she care deeply for him, but she knew he was serious about wanting to marry her, in spite of this whole business with Shane.

She sighed in frustration. He was only serious because he didn't understand, but she still knew that getting him to agree to her leaving would never happen and more of the frustrating tears welled up as she realized she was going to have to leave him without even telling him goodbye. She was doing it for his own safety, but it would still be absolutely hurtful to do it. For both of them.

Wondering about maybe Montana this time, she made the decision to get into his car and go up and talk to her bishop. She didn't think Shane would be watching him and this way she could explain what was going on with Shane and try to keep the others at the funeral as safe as possible and get a message to Gage about Shane having her number at the same time.

It was just getting dark outside as she left the gated community and she was grateful for the poor lighting as she took a circuitous route to the bishop's house. On arriving there, she sat in the car for several minutes just watching and waiting for full dark and then she hurried to the door.

After telling him as briefly as possible about her situation, she asked him to tell Gage that somehow Shane had gotten her new phone number and that he probably had access to Gage's calls as well. As far as the service the next day, they agreed that she would come at the last minute by taxi, and then would leave before it was quite ended by slipping into the nearby grove of trees. After walking to the far side of the cemetery, she would leave in one of the bishop's cars that would be hidden across a fence behind a row of bushes along a ditch there. Later, she would leave the car in the parking lot of a large grocery store before she went back into hiding.

Her good bishop simply nodded after their plans were made and she knew he thought she would be going back to wherever it was she had been staying these last few days, but she had to do what she deemed best for everyone involved. That meant leaving the funeral and then immediately leaving the area for good and it brought overwhelming sadness as she got back into the Jag and started it up.

There was only one more thing that needed done. She needed to take the long detailed letter she'd written to the manager of her credit union and begin the process of getting the flower shop turned over so that when her father had time, he could eventually come to St. George and liquidate everything. With that goal in mind, she stopped into the credit union office just before it closed, left the letter and drained the account in big bills and a large certified check made to herself and then hurried back to Gage's car.

The sick, empty feeling in her gut as she drove back to the cottage was only augmented as she found that Shane had tried to call the new cell phone she'd left in the car at the bishop's and the bank. In fact, he'd tried to call her four different times and left messages every time and she turned the phone all the way off in complete discouragement. At least it appeared he didn't know where she was yet.

At the cottage, she methodically repacked the things Gage had brought her, wishing she could have gone back to her little apartment to get some of her most loved things and at least gotten something suitable to wear to a funeral, but it was completely out of the question. Even going out shopping for something wasn't worth the risk and she knew Mama Woo would understand.

As she straightened the beautiful cottage, and set everything back to the way she'd found it, she struggled to contain the tears that threatened to overwhelm her. She didn't doubt that Gage was going to show up here sometime tonight after he got the message from the bishop and she needed to keep up a positive game face until after he left. Then she could fall to pieces if she felt like it, but not before.

If she did, he'd figure out that something was going on and try to stop her and for both of their sakes, she had to leave tomorrow.

****

Still sitting at his desk in his office at eight-thirty that night, Gage was surprised when the night security guard called and asked if it was okay to let a Dr. Les Aiken in. Gage gave him an affirmative and then went down to meet them. What in the world was Skye's bishop doing coming to see him at his office at this hour of the night?

After a brief explanation, Gage saw him back out and then stood beside his desk, looking at his cell phone, wondering what to do about this Shane Cainan guy. It had now been exactly six and a half days since he'd shown up at Skye's shop and neither Gage's life nor Skye's had come out of the tailspin his appearance had caused yet. She hadn't even dared to go home and her shop had probably lost a ton of money, not to mention business from simply not being open for so long. She was basically in prison in a strange house without even her dog and tomorrow she was planning to bury her closest friend. What a mess!

In all this time, the police hadn't had so much as a glimpse of Shane and that was the most troubling part of it all. Not only was he still a threat, but if Gage knew Skye at all, she was nearing the point of calling the game and blowing this town. She knew exactly what Shane was capable of and she had this sense of protecting everyone that, while it was considerate of her, made Gage feel like he was living on a volcano that was building pressure and waiting to blow.

He tossed his pen onto the desk and shrugged into his suit coat. Without even bothering to pick up the questionable phone, he strode out of his office and to the rental car he was still driving. This was not a big town. How in heaven's name had the police not been able to find this guy?

After driving for a while to try to ascertain whether he was being tailed, Gage drove straight to the police station and then walked in and asked forLieutenantPederson again. Gage had gotten a little testy with him before and he appeared to be able to deal with it okay. Well, Gage was feeling way more than a little testy right now and he wanted some straight answers and hoped Pederson could give them to him.

After being shown in to a conference room, Gage waited until the young officer appeared and then he quickly outlined what had occurred in Skye's life in the last week and almost demanded to know what was being done about it. At least Pederson had the decency to look regretful as he admitted that Skye's case hadn't appeared to be overly urgent and that the chief hadn't felt justified in spending any more man hours than they already had on looking for a suspect who appeared to have left the state already.

Gage knew Shane hadn't left the state, and he suspected the officer in front of him believed that as well, but he had no way of proving that they needed to be far more diligent about this situation than they had been. In all honesty, Gage knew they didn't particularly care if his entire life was about to pick up and run to who knows where from him. They had far more pressing local crimes to deal with every second of every day.

Sighing in frustration, Gage got up to leave and Lieutenant Pederson stopped him and handed him another of his cards. This time he put his personal cell phone number on it and promised that if they had any trouble with Shane he'd make finding him his own personal priority. Gage thanked him, asked him to see to it that there was at the very least, a police presence at the service in the morning and stalked out the door. While he appreciated Pederson's offer, it was tantamount to saying Shane had to hurt Skye again before the police would do anything. Gage wanted to swear in frustration as he got back into the rental car. What was the world coming to that a sweet, kind, beautiful young woman had been effectively denied protection from the police in four different jurisdictions now?

He drove around again and when he was confident no one was following, he headed for Snow Canyon. He was irritable as a bear right now, but he needed to see Skye tonight. Both for his own peace of mind that she was okay, and because she was the one person on the planet who could iron out all of the wrinkles in his life by simply smiling. She'd made it infinitely easier for him to choose happy since he'd met her. She lived happy and spread happy.

The garage door had only just started to come back down behind his car when she poked her head out of the door from the house. She was smiling, but even from the car he could see that it still didn't really reach clear to her eyes.

When he walked in the door, he paused to really look at her and he'd been right. She wasn't happy. The sparkle he'd loved from that very first day was missing in action. He couldn't blame her after the week she'd had, but he still wished he could help her find it. He dearly loved her smile.

After searching her eyes, he took her hand and led her through to the living room, sat down on the couch and held a hand out for her to join him. Once she was settled comfortably beside him, he laid an arm along the back of the couch behind her and gently touched her hair and then pulled her head over to lean against his shoulder.

He didn't know what to say. He didn't think either one of them knew what to say, but at least the deep friendship was there in spite of the silence. Maybe even because of the silence. There was nothing he could say to fix everything, but she knew he was willing to stand beside her come what may and the comfortable silence only reinforced that.

Brushing the soft, shiny hair back from her forehead, he tenderly kissed her temple and she turned her face into his neck. Even the pressing issues dogging them right now appeared more handleable with her breath against his skin. He turned his face to hers and kissed her and felt more than heard the sigh of pleasure she released as he did so. She may not have been bursting with happiness, but his kiss could still evoke satisfied emotion in her.

Understanding that made him want to kiss all her struggles away and he put a hand up into her soft hair and pulled her so her face met his more surely and for a moment they were both lost in sweet kisses. The sadness and the distance and anything that tended to come between them faded behind this simple pleasure. This had to be the purest form of dancing in the rain in spite of the storms raging around them.

At length, he pulled back and she took a long shuddering breath as she settled snugly back against his chest again. They still hadn't said anything, but just that much basic intimacy had them truly back together as a couple at least for this night and this moment.

He wasn't even sure how long they'd been sitting there on that couch, sometimes kissing, sometimes just sitting snuggled together. But it was long enough that the subtle tension that had been there when he'd first arrived had dissipated into pure, honest companionship by the time he could tell she was getting sleepy on him again.

Feeling guilty for the way he'd woken her up after such a short night for her, and then feeling guilty for how much emotion accompanied that memory of how she'd looked and felt there in her bed, he hugged her tight one more time and stood up with a regretful sigh. "I should go, honey." He reached down to help her up and then pulled her back against him. "You're tired and tomorrow is probably going to be a long day, all day. Can I pick you up before the service?"

She shook her head without looking up and said, "No. Shane is bound to be around somewhere tomorrow. We need to be more careful than we've ever been. I'm sure of it. I'll just come at the last minute and see you there."

He wanted to talk her into changing her mind about that, but he could hear the fatigue in her voice and decided to just let it go. He would insist on taking her afterward instead. He'd take the afternoon off and maybe they could spend the whole weekend together. Maybe he'd even see if his parents would come and they could all stay here for a couple of days and never even have to leave and by Monday, hopefully some of this pressure and sadness would have let down some.

When she finally looked up at him, he leaned to kiss her one last time and simply said, "Lt. Pederson agreed to have the police at the service tomorrow, so at least you should be able to feel secure there. Go in to bed and I'll see myself out." She nodded and he softly said, "Goodnight, Skye Alexander. Sleep tight and dream about becoming Skye Garrison and the cottage on the Irish Sea."

Her eyes flew to his and he could swear that what he saw in hers was not the hope and happiness he'd wanted but pure, raw pain instead.

That pain haunted him as he drove home to his house and it was still haunting him as he tried to fall asleep later. It haunted his dreams and was still there foremost in his mind as he put on a black suit to head for the cemetery the next morning.

She had no intention at all of marrying him. That look had simply been the only outward sign that she planned to walk away from him without looking back and it was breaking her heart. And try as he might, he didn't know how to stop her. Finally, just before stepping out the door, he went back in and packed a bag and took it to the car with him. At the very least, he was going to go with her.

Chapter 15

Leaving the Jag parked in the garage of the cottage, Skye hefted her bag to her shoulder and walked to meet the taxi she had requested at the gated entrance. She was glad it was simply a gray sedan that sported a sign on the door instead of a regular glaring yellow cab that would have stood out like a sore thumb in this small city.

Trying to be utterly vigilant about what was going on around them as they drove, she had the driver take her to the waiting hidden car to stow her bag before dropping her near the cluster of people around the small casket in the cemetery.

She'd been planning to stay completely away from Gage in case Shane was somehow watching, but there wasn't another soul in sight of the service and there was a uniformed police officer standing a short distance away, so she decided she was going to be with Gage for this one last moment. It may have been foolish, but it was going to be hard enough to walk away without saying goodbye as it was. She desperately wanted to have his love and support beside her as she said her last goodbyes to Mama Woo. Her heart was in shreds as it was about leaving him, even though she knew she had to.

He'd been watching for her and as she quietly slipped in

beside him and took his hand, the intense look he gave her almost burned as she tried to meet his eyes and she wondered if he knew what her intentions were. He'd obviously had the same hellacious night she'd had.

She looked away, but still felt his eyes on her and she was almost grateful for the gravity of the situation. Burying Mama Woo was about the only thing in the universe that could begin to shift her focus from the thought of living without him. At least in this situation the tears that were fairly raging under the surface of her calm demeanor wouldn't seem out of place.

His large hand squeezed hers and then didn't let up as she fought to focus on what Bishop Aiken was saying. Even talk of Mama Woo made the memories of the times when the three of them had been together so happily sting. She'd never loved someone the way she loved Gage and the way he'd so readily embraced her tiny adopted grandmother had only added to that. And Mama Woo had loved him back; Skye had known it from the start. In some ways, Mama Woo had seemed almost relieved that Skye had become friends with Gage. That was a strange way to think about it just now, but it had been true.

A bird flew up and both Skye and Gage flinched and she realized he was every bit as tightly wound as she was and she looked all around again to make sure the cemetery was still secure as the service continued. She studied the grove of trees that extended almost right to Mama Woo's plot and felt incredibly guilty about what she was about to do.

At least the trees were there. In this desert landscape, a cemetery was one of the few places there actually were thick trees. Vegetation only thrived here where either someone tended them faithfully or there was a steady source of water, like the ditch that ran along the fence line across the way. The willows that lined it were thick enough that the bishop's car was completely hidden.

She realized that also meant the trees and ditch were the

only places that could be concealing Shane as well, but she doubted he would attempt anything without a sure way to get away afterward and that police officer standing there was marvelously reassuring during all of this.

Dragging her attention back to the eulogy being offered for Mama Woo, she glanced up at the incredibly handsome man standing beside her holding her hand so tightly and found him watching her intently. As she dropped her eyes, he leaned and whispered, "Don't you leave me, Skye."

Her eyes flew back up to meet his and the intensity of his gaze matched the intensity of his whisper. He knew. But that didn't change anything. It couldn't. She had to get away and protect him at the same time and she'd deny his most heart felt command to keep him safe. She knew that, even if he didn't. He had no idea what they were up against in Shane Cainan. Shane had been halfway civil to him so far. He'd been a lot more decent than that to Skye until she'd seen the savage come out in him. She still sported the scars that had left the knowledge of just how he could be burned into her brain forever.

She gave Gage the barest hint of a headshake and turned back toward the bishop. Reality wasn't warm and fuzzy, but it was what it was and she had to do what she knew she had to do, regardless of the raging blue eyes that were trying to speak to her very soul beside her. She glanced back up at Gage, wishing she could tell him all of the things in her heart before she did this. Looking away again, she understood that it was probably better that she couldn't. Moving on with their lives was going to be a miserably long road as it was–for both of them. She'd only known him for a few months, but long enough to know he was sincere to the core about how he felt about her.

She was trying to focus on the service again when he tugged at her hand. She looked back up at him and he whispered again almost fiercely, "No! Don't do it! We'll figure it out!"

The pain in her heart literally warred with the knowledge that made her barely shake her head just as fiercely as she whispered back, "Stop, Gage. Just stop. You don't understand." She turned back to the bishop and wiped angrily at the tears that began to pour out of her tired eyes. He just didn't understand. She prayed he never did. Hopefully, once she was gone from here, Shane would leave to try to find her at the next place and Gage would get over her and safely move on with his life without ever really experiencing what Shane Cainan was capable of.

She glanced down at her watch and back up at the bishop and knew the look he had just given her meant it was time. Gage was the one the bishop had asked to dedicate the grave and he must have known that as soon as he let go of Skye's hand and began the prayer that she was out of here, because he gave her a look that seared her to the bone before finally dropping her hand and stepping forward. She tried desperately to tell him with the look she gave him back. *I'm sorry, Gage. I'm so sorry.*

****

It took everything Gage had to make it through that prayer with any halfway decent focus on Mama Woo and protecting her gravesite through the eternities. He mentally apologized to the little Asian woman he'd grown to love as at length he opened his eyes and looked around frantically for Skye. He finally saw her there, slipping through the trees. At the same time, he saw a car speeding up the road and heading for the field on the other side of the cemetery. Officer Pederson realized at the same moment what was going on and the two of them broke from the cluster of people and headed at a sprint toward the fence across the way, scattering mourners in their wake.

Wanting to swear at her for what he was sure were her

good intentions to keep him and the others safe, he skirted the grove of trees, vaulted the fence and literally dove into the screen of thickly growing willows that bordered the ditch. When he'd finally forced his way through the dense brush, he could see Skye running toward a car that had been concealed on the other side of the saplings as Shane bore down on her at a speed that made the car he was in bounce and jar through the uneven field. Gage leapt the ditch running, wishing he'd exchanged the Italian leather dress shoes he was wearing for something with cleats. He swore under his breath, knowing he wasn't going to make it.

Shane must have finally seen him, because he sped up even more and Gage wondered what had happened to Officer Pederson as Skye neared the waiting car. Miraculously, Shane's vehicle hit what must have been a smaller intersecting ditch and bounced high into the air as it slid slightly sidewise with a loud thunk. For just a split second, his engine gutted as he tried to dig out of the rut and Gage finally felt a surge of hope that he'd make it in time.

He reached Shane's car as it slid sideways to a stop just as Skye ripped open the door of the other car. Shane jumped out of his and rammed Gage like a bull as Gage dove between the two cars, and Skye started the engine. She had the car moving before she'd even gotten the door closed. The force of Shane's momentum into him knocked the air out of Gage as he flew into Skye's vehicle and literally bounced off. Reeling from the impact and gasping to get a breath, Gage turned back to Shane and lunged to tackle him as he spun to go after Skye's car.

Gage only caught part of Shane's shirt and he heard it rip as the bigger man shoved him off and caught Skye's door handle. With everything he had, Gage lunged again and got a handful of fabric and hauled on it. Then, as he finally was able to breathe in the smallest, most painful breath, Shane lost his tenuous grip on Skye's car door and she pulled away.

Instantly, Shane turned on Gage in fury. He roared like a mad beast and before Gage could get set for it; Shane hit him with both fists, knocking the wind back out of him as he slammed backward into Shane's still rolling car. Lights exploded in Gage's head and he put up an arm, slugged Shane brutally in the face with the other and tensed for a second onslaught as he struggled desperately to take in air.

As Shane tore back into Gage, he glanced up. Whatever he saw brought him up short and instead of raging into Gage again, he spun and dove for the willows, disappearing into their tangled thickness.

Gage looked up to make sure Skye had made it out of the field, and that Pederson was after Shane, and then he doubled over gasping. Shane had just finished breaking the ribs Skye had cracked the other day, and Gage definitely didn't recommend swan diving into the side of a car head first and then being slammed into a car again. It took him a minute to even realize that his arm was pulsing in pain. Somehow that hadn't quite registered in the mix of things.

After a moment of trying to breathe, Gage turned and took off back down the ditch in the direction he thought Shane and Pederson had gone and when he finally heard scuffling, he turned into the tangle toward the sounds. He could hear the rustling of the brush and the grunts of a fight and then a solid thud and a crash and as he continued toward the sounds, he heard what could only have been one person moving quickly back in the direction they'd come.

Still struggling through the willow tangle, Gage almost stepped on Lieutenant Pederson before he saw him lying there, motionless and with a cut on his forehead streaming blood. Glancing toward where he could still hear the sounds of Shane getting away, Gage swore and then dropped to his knees beside the wounded officer to feel for a pulse.

On finding one, he wrestled the radio off the officer's

chest, thumbed the button and spoke into it. When a woman's voice replied, he explained what had happened and where they were and gave a description of Shane's car that he could hear starting up behind him and a description of the car Skye had taken. With help hopefully on the way, he dropped the radio and pulled off his now hopelessly tattered suit jacket and used it to put pressure on the fallen cop's head. Geez, they lived in the desert. How could these willows possibly be this thick? And how had his seemingly boring life dissolved into a mess like this?

As he pressed on the gushing cut, he wanted to swear in fear for Skye and in the fury that had his heart still pounding like a drum. Instead of swearing, he took a deep breath that hurt like the devil and began to pray for all he was worth. She'd only gotten a few minute's head start and he pleaded for divine help to make sure she'd gotten away. She had to get away. She had to.

After praying for a few minutes as he held pressure, he wanted to swear again, this time at Skye for running. Who was to say if she'd have been any safer there in the middle of all of those people, but at least he wouldn't be facing the fact that she had left him. She loved him dearly and he knew it, but she'd still looked him in the eye and taken off. At that, he did swear and then went back to praying again. He had to keep his head on straight here or he was really going to lose it.

He started to hear sounds coming from back down the ditch and for just a second, he wondered if Shane had come back to finish what he'd started. Then he heard Bishop Aiken calling his name. With a huge breath of relief, Gage answered back, knowing that a family practitioner would know what to do with this officer down.

Seconds later, when the willows parted to reveal the bishop's balding head, Gage almost got the gumption up to smile in spite of it all when he heard the bishop swear as he saw the bloody and unconscious officer just like he had. It was good to know that Gage wasn't the only cussing man among the fold today.

An hour later, with the wounded Pederson shipped off to be stitched up and the reports filed, Gage limped beside the bishop to their cars, wanting to swear once more after having just been told that yet again, the police had lost Shane Cainan. Gage looked at the bloody jacket he held and with the arm that wasn't so tender, lobbed it into the garbage can that was chained beside the fence in the parking area. Then he groaned from the resulting pain in his ribs. The bishop looked over at him and Gage shook his head and said, "I am definitely not supposed to be one of those macho, fist fighting types."

The older man chuckled and said, "Get in my car and I'll take you and have that arm ex-rayed. You shouldn't be driving with a brain concussion. We'll get someone to come back and get your car."

Gage sighed and got into the car as he was told. The man was right – Gage couldn't even see straight and the world kept tipping on him. He leaned back against the head rest with a sigh and wondered out loud where Skye had gotten the get away car. As he pulled away, the bishop cleared his throat and Gage looked over at him in disgusted disbelief. "You helped her? You? You helped her leave me? How could you do that?"

The older man shook his head. "She's not leaving you. She was just making sure she had a way to sneak in and out without him getting to her. She's gone back to wherever you were hiding her."

Gage shook his head and swore again under his breath, bitterly this time. "She's gone, Bishop. Long gone. And I don't have the stalking expertise Shane Cainan has to find her. She had no intention of ever going back to where we were hiding her." Gage looked up and then pinched the bridge of his nose and struggled to get control of his ballistic emotions as he repeated sadly, "She's gone. She did it to protect me. She thinks he'll come after both of us."

Looking across the car, the bishop calmly said, "He did. I'm sorry. I had no idea she was going to run away from you. I thought the two of you were going to settle down and get married."

Gage laughed a humorless laugh and swallowed the lump in his throat. "So did I, until last night."

When the ex-ray of his left forearm showed a hair line fracture, the bishop, who he was still frankly completely ticked off at for helping her leave him, casted it and handed him a prescription for pain medicine before loading him back in his car with an apology for not being able to do anything about the ribs and concussion.

When he asked Gage where he wanted him to take him, Gage hesitated. In all honesty he just wanted to go home and lick his wounds, but the smallest chance that she truly had gone back to the cottage had him asking to be dropped at his parents. He'd get his dad to run him back up to the cottage just to be sure. If she wasn't there, he'd have him take him home.

Gabriel was actually there at his parents' when Gage walked in completely thrashed and not necessarily able to walk a straight line between the brain concussion and pain medicine. Gabriel was thunderstruck enough that he still hadn't even said anything by the time their mother came around the corner with Kitty at her heels and gasped, "Gage! What in the world!"

She rushed up to him and he held up a tired hand. "No, Mother. Don't touch me. Everything I own hurts. Just tell me you would like to hug me and call it good. Is Dad around?"

She shook her head in shocked silence and he turned to

Gabriel. "Could I ask you a favor?"

The cottage was dark and silent, just like he'd known in his heart it would be. When they opened the garage, his beautiful car sat there like the final testament to her departure and Gage leaned his head back again and closed his eyes.

Gabriel pulled in and as they walked through the silent lonely rooms, neither one of them said anything. What could you say at a time like this?

In her bedroom, the tin soldier nutcracker standing stiffly on the nightstand beside the cell phone he'd given her was the last straw Gage could handle on this day and he silently picked them up, wishing he hadn't had to bring Gabriel to see him do this. He'd never dreamed that night those few months ago when he'd agreed to take care of Sophie and her ballet that he'd end up feeling like this. Honestly, he'd never dreamed in his entire life that his heart could hurt this badly. It was all he could do to paste on a placid face and walk back out to the car.

He had Gabriel take him to his own house. His mother was going to be offended, but he was honestly too hammered to care. He got out on his driveway, carrying the tin soldier and tiredly thanked Gabriel for taking him and then turned and went inside, not even noticing that for the first time in his entire life, Gabriel hadn't tried to tease him even once.

****

After jiggling it to get the key card to actually open the door to her room, Skye stepped inside, tossed her heavy bag onto the floor next to the little closet, and her old cell phone on the bed, and turned back around to shut the door behind her. She locked the dead bolt, turned up the air conditioner, and then peeled off her clothing as she headed for the shower. She wasn't really a headache kind of a girl, but her head was pounding.

She stood under the pelting spray, letting the water of the shower wash away the tears that she'd kept bottled up until she finally had the privacy to cry alone. The tears were pointless. She knew that, but as hard as she tried to choose happy, sometimes she couldn't help it and had to admit that she wasn't immune to caving in to the heartache this life tended to hand out occasionally. It would be just for a few minutes. She would wallow for a few minutes and then get some sleep and tomorrow she'd try to look at things more positively again.

It was probably just that she was having PMS, or maybe just that she hadn't gotten much sleep the last couple of days. She hoped it was that. She hoped she was tired enough to be able to climb into that bed and sleep for twenty hours straight so she wouldn't think about anything going on in her life right now.

Showering until she felt like a prune in the warm water, she finally shut it off and toweled dry and went back into the other room to put on clean clothes and get ready to go to bed. It was only mid afternoon, but she didn't care. Both her body and her spirit were exhausted.

She pulled on a pair of stretch exercise leggings and was just reaching for a t-shirt when her stomach growled painfully. Nothing really sounded great, but she'd better eat something today before she went back to bed.

Room service had put her on hold for a minute on the room line when she heard her cell phone buzz. She glanced at it in hopes it was the St. George police calling to tell her they'd caught Shane, but it was only him again. He'd called her almost hourly since he'd somehow obtained her phone number yesterday. She shook her head and hung up on room service, deciding that life was too short to be on hold for food she didn't want anyway.

Could it really have been only yesterday that Shane had

found her number? The last week of her life was so convoluted that she could hardly remember what day it was. All she knew was it was the day she'd had to walk away from Gage and that her heart had never been this sad in her life.

She got up and tried to close the curtain over the blind more tightly so she could shut out the strip of light and hopefully rest better. Sleeping was sometimes hard enough without knowing it was bright daylight for the rest of the world.

The room line rung and she picked it up and thanked room service for calling her back and then ordered a club sandwich. She ought to be able to force that down at least. Club sandwiches were usually her favorite. She sighed and laid down, thinking about how Gage had looked at her just before stepping forward to dedicate Mama Woo's grave. He'd been so incredibly intense as he'd tried to bend her will with only a look. And so handsome. She desperately wanted to call and find out if he was okay after seeing him slam into her car so forcefully. The police had assured her he was going to be all right, but it killed her not to be able to talk to him. There was no doubt that she would never have gotten safely away if Gage hadn't been there.

She shook her head and tried not to think about him. Instead, she wondered if she'd succeeded in throwing Shane off of her trail this afternoon. She'd taken the bishop's loaner car to the Smith's parking lot and then sat there, grateful for the tinted windows as she watched to see if Shane had been able to follow her get away path. When he hadn't shown in more than half an hour, she'd gotten out and gone toward the pay phone on the curb to call for another cab. As she'd passed a motor home where two retirees in shorts and funny socks were unloading a grocery cart, she'd paused and then on an impulse asked them if they happened to be heading for Las Vegas. They were and had gladly agreed to give her a ride and she'd settled onto the sofa behind their captain chairs, grateful that Shane would never be able to find a taxi driver who had driven her.

She'd even been grateful for the old folks' chattiness to her as they drove. It had given her a chance to somewhat decompress and not have to worry much about making small talk as toasted as she'd felt after all that had happened. Still, even with all of their friendly chit chat, she felt like her heart was going to implode. It was a good thing they hadn't known her to realize how much quieter she was than her usual self.

Vegas hadn't really been where she'd wanted to go, but it worked for now. It was actually a perfect place to buy a cheap car with cash, although Shane might suspect that she'd come here. Still, it was a big place and honestly, she was too tired to go further right now. Maybe in a day or two she'd feel like starting this huge project of relocating, just now, she wanted to crawl into a hole and feel sorry for herself.

Jaclyn M. Hawkes

Chapter 16

Gage heard his garage door start to go up and even as sore and groggy and drugged as he was, he was out of bed and grabbed the fireplace poker again and headed for his bedroom door. He could hear footsteps in his hall, but then there was something else. The sound of a dog walking on the hardwood and he lowered the poker in relief as his mother appeared in his bedroom door. "Gage, what in the world are you doing with the poker? And when did you get new French doors? They're beautiful."

Gage shook his head with a tired smile and turned back to his bed. "Honestly, Mother, you don't want to know the answer to either question. Just be glad that Kitty has good toenails."

She advanced into his room and put a gentle hand to his forehead. "So, I'm assuming you were in a car wreck. What happened?"

Chuckling humorlessly, he replied, "Oh, it was a car wreck all right. You should go, Mom. You're not safe here."

She looked at him in confusion and then asked, "Was your head hurt in the wreck? Why would I not be safe here?"

Not sure how to answer that, he picked up his phone instead and called Lieutenant Pederson's cell number off the back of his card. When he answered, he sounded as awful as Gage felt and after asking after him for a moment, Gage went on to ask, "Hey, could I ask you a favor? I need off-duty security again. This time at my house. And honestly, I'm too out of it to arrange it. Are you feeling good enough to touch base with whoever does that and have them put someone here 24/7 so I can be a zombie without worrying about being a dead one? Have them plan to come right inside. And have them do it right away; my mom just showed up. They can put it on the same card. Thanks man."

Pederson just replied, "Consider it done. Thanks for patching me up out there today."

"No problem. Just find him."

"The whole department's working on that right now."

"It's about time. See ya."

Gage closed his phone and his mom was staring at him wide eyed and said, "All right, young man. Out with it. What is going on?"

He laid back down and motioned her to the leather chair between his bed and fireplace and said, "Skye's been having a few issues. I told you she had to go stay with her friend at the hospital, but I didn't mention that she's been running for her life from a stalker. He's been after her for more than three years. He nearly killed her before she ran the first time. That's why she was even in St. George. She was basically hiding here. Well, he found her. Then he found me. He's the one who smashed the French doors. And that's why the poker. He was here the other night. He's around, but the police can't seem to catch him, bless their hearts." He couldn't help the disgust he could hear in his tone.

With another sigh, he continued, "Skye's little neighbor friend died day before yesterday and this morning was the funeral. Just a simple graveside service." He paused and closed his eyes and swallowed for a moment before he went on in a ragged voice, "I've known she was planning to leave, but I kept thinking if they could just catch him... Anyway, he tried to grab her at the cemetery. The officer who was there..." He opened his eyes and nodded at his phone. "He and I both tried to protect her and catch him. And Skye did get safely away." He didn't trust his voice for just a second. "At least I hope she did. The police aren't telling me anything. The officer was wounded and Shane got away. But before he did, he did a little bit of a number on me. He's big and angry and crazy."

Her eyes had gotten huge and she prodded him, "What's a number?"

He started to shake his head and then thought better of it. "Ah, I'm fine. I just need some time." He held up the cast. "A hair line fracture, broken ribs and a concussion." He tried to smile and said, "Never take a car to the head. They win every time."

Standing back up, she came over to the bed and touched his forehead gently. "Are you okay?"

He closed his eyes again so she couldn't see how he was really feeling and then said, "Body's fine. Heart's toasted." He'd been trying to sound flippant, but it ended up sounding incredibly tired.

He didn't open his eyes back up and after another minute she sat back down and asked, "So then, where is Skye?"

At first, he couldn't even answer her. At length, he simply said, "Gone."

"Gone where? She wouldn't just up and walk away from you, Gage."

When he could, he finally said, "That's what I thought, too."

His mother was silent for several seconds and then said positively, "No. No, I've seen the way that girl looks at you, Gage. She may have had to run, but she's not gone. Don't you give up on her. Especially not right now when she needs you the most. She's in trouble and she's bound to be heartbroken over her friend who passed away and now she's alone. You and I both know she was probably trying to protect you as well as herself. Don't you give up this easily. Yeah, you two are in a mess, but God is still in His heaven. Has the day of miracles ceased?"

Gage finally smiled to hear his mother ask the question she had asked him ten thousand times in his life. Before she could, he finished for her with the scripture from Moroni that she had so often used to encourage her children, "Behold, I say unto you, nay; for it is by faith that miracles are wrought; and it is by faith that angels appear and minister unto men."

"So then... Where is your faith? Straighten up and expect a miracle!" She laughed and patted his stomach and he groaned. That made her begin to apologize over and over and he reached and took her hand.

"Mom. It's okay. I'm fine. And you're right. You're exactly what I needed right now, even though I didn't realize it. I'm sorry I didn't come back to your house, but this guy really might follow me, and so you need to go. Being here could be dangerous."

"Oh, nonsense. The police will come and we've got Kitty. She's really quite an amazing watch dog. I don't know if you realized that. And I'll go out to my Escalade and bring in my little Sig Sauer and we'll be fine. You can rest and I'll deal with this big, angry, crazy stalker."

He sat right up in bed and looked at her. She'd lost her mind. "Mother, that's as nuts as he is. And what in the world is your little Sig Sauer?"

"The little twenty-two caliber pistol your dad gave me for Christmas the year he had that project over in Palm Desert."

"What?"

"Well, I didn't sleep so well when he was out of town.

He thought maybe it would make me feel more secure. And it worked beautifully. I liked it so much that he gave me another one for my car. I keep it under the driver's seat in case I ever get stranded somewhere late at night. It's very comforting. I'm quite a good shot, actually. Daddy calls me Annie when he takes me shooting. That's short for Annie Oakley, in case you don't get it."

Gage's mouth fell open and he couldn't even close it. He looked at her perfectly done hair and nails and the huge diamonds she wore on her finger and at her ears and was thunderstruck. His own mother! Packin' heat! She laughed at him again and said, "Oh, don't look so surprised, hon. This is Utah. Half the women in my ward's Relief Society have hand guns. That's why the crime rate is so low here. I'll bet Skye has her own hand gun too, if she's been through all of this."

Gage chuckled. "Yeah, but she carries a twenty-five caliber Glock."

"See. Go back to sleep, sweetie. We'll be fine. I've always wanted to shoot a Glock. When she comes back, I'm going to ask her to let me try it out."

He shook his head and rolled his eyes. "Mother, this guy tried to kill a cop yesterday. He's like six three and two forty and a drug addict. You are not going to hang out here and guard me while I sleep. Get back in your fancy little SUV and go home. But you can leave Kitty. She is a good watch dog. She's this funky German trained. Watch this."

He called the dog's name to get her attention and then said the words Skye had always said and the dog snapped to attention and began to look around alertly. It actually made Gage a little depressed again and he said sadly, "Skye really needs her right now. I did the best I could to stop him, but I just couldn't hang on to him. At least I think she got away. I knew she planned to go, but... And I know she hated the whole idea. She just didn't think she had any choice."

The doorbell rang and his mother patted his foot as she turned to walk toward the front door and said, "You just pray for her, Gage. Pray like her life depends on it. Rest up for a bit and then get up and begin to work toward your future together like you have some faith in God. I'm telling you. The day of miracles hasn't ceased."

As she went out the door, he called out after her, "Look through the peep hole first and if it's not a uniformed police officer who is *not* a blonde middle linebacker, don't you dare open it!"

****

Getting to sleep, even in the middle of the afternoon, hadn't been a problem. Waking up at two-thirty-one in the morning, alone and in a strange hotel room on the outskirts of the City of Sin was incredibly discouraging. Skye missed her home, she missed her dog, she missed Mama Woo, and she really, really missed Gage.

Not only did she miss him, but she felt like the biggest low life on the planet for basically ignoring his pleas to not go, then knowing he got hurt as he tried to protect her, and then leaving and not even checking back on him. It went against everything in her most basic character, but she didn't know what else to do. To try to contact him would possibly put both of them at risk.

Not only that, but as long as Shane wouldn't leave her alone, she couldn't be part of Gage's life anyway, so in all reality, walking away without looking back was the most kind thing for both of them. Not making a clean break was only prolonging the heartache.

She rolled over and gathered her pillow into her arms and tried to put him out of her mind. She needed to decide where she wanted to relocate to, and she needed to figure out how to make a living once the money she had right now ran out and she needed to do that without giving anyone any information that could be traced. She took a big breath and let it out with a sigh. This was such a huge undertaking every time. Trying to keep her head above water financially was hard enough without trying to keep from being killed put into the mix.

She turned back over and looked up at the dark hotel ceiling. She wished she could have brought her picture of Ireland with her. For all these years, when she got discouraged about living like this, she always thought about someday being able to go there and it had been a way to look forward with hope to that someday.

Thinking about Ireland automatically brought back thoughts of Gage again. He'd promised her a cottage on the beach. And the look in his eyes as he'd said it—holy moly, but he'd been tempting. If she let herself go there, she could see the two of them in the cottage. For that matter, she could see the two of them from the cottage, to parenting a whole troop of little Gages, to growing old together.

This was foolish and she had to stop! That was all in the past. In a really, really good dream that she'd been brutally woken up from and the harsh reality was that she needed to forget Gage and all of her life in St. George and work on moving on.

Tears welled into her eyes and she got up and went into the bathroom and turned on the shower. Bawling like this was certainly not choosing happy. At least crying under the warm spray didn't feel nearly as much like she was trapped focusing on the negative. She just needed some time.

****

Tuesday morning, Gage dragged into his office and when Sandy looked up at him and then got this look like she'd seen a monster in the closet, he smiled tiredly and said, "I know. I look like I've been driven over by a truck. And honestly, that's exactly how I feel, so let's don't even go there except for me to apologize in advance for being hopelessly irritable. I couldn't take anything very strong and be able to drive, and frankly, I'm sore as… I don't feel so good."

In her signature style, Sandy simply nodded and said with a cheery smile, "I just thought you'd been wrestling with Gabriel again and for once he got the better of you. Were you in a car wreck over the weekend?"

"No. Actually, I went to the funeral of a sweet, little Laotian woman and was attacked by Skye's stalker. We weren't going to go there, remember?"

Shocked, she nodded and then said just as cheerily, "Well, so all righty then." After a pause, she asked more seriously, "Skye looks better than you, I hope. Is she okay?"

Tiredly, he admitted, "I don't think so Sandy, but while I kept the stalker entertained, she ran and I haven't seen her. And honestly, if you keep asking me about her, I'm going to cry and embarrass us both. So… How was your weekend?"

She looked steadily at him for a couple of seconds and then switched into business mode. "Steiner won his malpractice suit, and Dr. Clements made a more than full price offer to counter the California guy. I tentatively told him you'd take it if he put five hundred thousand down and agreed to take over immediately, but he can't make any material changes until the deal is closed. Oh, and the clown fish died in the lobby aquarium. Deader than a doornail as I came in this morning. You have to fish him out. I hate that sort of thing."

"I'll fish out the dead clown fish. I asked about your weekend."

"Well, Stan had a cold, and you know how whiny men are, and then my grandson showed up for Sunday dinner with an earring. Frankly, I thought the dead clown fish and the five hundred grand were better news."

"Which grandson?"

"Parker."

Gage made a wincing face. "The perfect one?" She nodded. "Dang it. I thought he was going to be the only kid on the planet who made it all the way through adolescence without a bump. How did you react?"

"I hugged him and told him I'd made his favorite for dinner. How was I supposed to react? You can't lose a great kid over an earring."

Gage gave her a high five with his uncasted arm. "You passed the test then. If his parents did that well, the earring will probably be gone the next time you see him because no one came unglued over it. Clements will be perfect. It'll be good to know this place will be well run. Any word on selling the chiropractic practice?"

"Not yet." She gestured to his cast. "Should I call Aaron and schedule him indefinitely?" She paused and gave him a huge grin. "Or should I call Dr. Potawatame?" Gage did a double take and she went on, "Annalise Bowen came in and asked the receptionist about him. When Carol said that there wasn't a Potawatame on staff, Annalise was ticked. She said to tell you she didn't think your answering service was very funny. She said she wants the answering service woman's head on a platter and a private half hour session as an apology. Do we have a Dr. Potawatame on staff?"

Gage chuckled. "He's the shorter, heavy set one with the comb over. I believe Skye's exact words were." He tried to mimic her bored nasally voice. "He has a bit of a problem with halitosis, but I assure you, he's a wonderfully competent chiropractor." Sandy busted up and he explained, "Ms. Bowen called my cell phone on a Sunday evening and when I wasn't going to take the call, Skye picked up as an answering service. I almost blew it laughing in the background."

"Yeah, well, Carol did blow it, laughing in Ms. Bowen's front ground. It's probably a good thing you're out for a while. I'm just gonna guess that she can be feisty."

"Carol's always been feisty."

"I was talking about Annalise Bowen. What can I do to help you get everything done so you can go home and take your pain meds?"

Gage grinned. "There's a dead fish in the lobby aquarium that needs flushed." He laughed at her grimace and headed into his office. "Just keep making me laugh so I don't cry, Sandy, and I'll be fine."

He fished the dead clown fish out, thinking that he felt just the way that fish looked, and finally made it through a day that felt like two and then went home. There was a police car in front of his house when he arrived and it was incredibly comforting. He was going to take a pain pill and try to rest, in spite of the memories that were haunting him.

Gabriel and his dad had returned the rental and brought his car to him and as he pulled the Jag into his garage, the Journey song he'd slow danced to with Skye that night under the disco ball came on. His car even smelled like her. He sat and listened and then got out of the car feeling like his heart was as broken as the ribs that still made him wince when he tried to take a deep breath.

As he opened the door from the garage into the house, Kitty padded over to greet him, wagging her whole back end and he crouched down to pet her. She wagged even harder and licked his cheek and he wrapped a hand around her head and hugged her to him. "I miss her too, Kitty, Kitty. I miss her too."

His mother had left a plate of dinner when she'd dropped the dog and Gage picked it up, saying a silent prayer for his good mother who had somehow known he needed Kitty with him tonight. The plate was still warm, but he put it into the microwave to heat more, gingerly loosened his tie, waved to the officer who was reading in his living room and headed for his bedroom. He really wished he knew where Skye was tonight and if she was okay. After thinking for a couple of days about what his mom had said on Saturday, last night he'd called Skye's old cell phone number and left a message. He had no idea if she was even using that phone, but he had to believe they weren't just done. Otherwise he was going to lose it.

The pill helped him sleep for a while, but then in the wee hours of the morning, he woke up. He'd forgotten to pray as he'd gone down and right now, he could swear God was tapping him on the shoulder and saying, "Excuse me, but you didn't pray and we need to talk." There were times when he could fill the Spirit speaking to him like it was coming through a veritable conduit from heaven.

Skye was so on Gage's mind and his train of thought was so focused that he had to seriously believe this was the answer to his pretty much non-stop prayers for her these last several days. He'd thought seriously about what his mother had said about miracles, and his mother had been right about the way Skye looked at him. She did love him. He knew that without a doubt.

If there was any way possible, she would come back to him and he wasn't going to waste time waiting. She had to do what she had to do, but he did too and after laying awake and feeling thoughts and ideas literally pour into his brain, he knew just what he had to do. Even if it took a while, he was going to be working toward Skye coming home. He just hoped she was getting the same quiet impressions of hope he was. He got out of bed and started making a list of the things he needed to get started on. The first thing on his list was to find out where Hailee had gotten to.

****

Three days had gone by and she was still in her hotel in Vegas, ordering in room service and trying to stem the tide of her tears under the streaming water. She didn't know what was wrong with her. She'd never been like this. She'd cried enough that she didn't even dare go out to the swimming pool for fear she'd break down in front of other people like she had the two times she'd attempted it.

The garbage on TV held no appeal for her. Half of it here in the hotel was porn and the other half inane modern American society no-brainer stuff that was often crude and always pointless. When she realized how negative her attitude was, she felt guilty and dug for the Gideon Bible, but honestly, after three days it was getting old. She liked to read, and it did bring a better spirit, but some of these guys in the Old Testament weren't all that gripping. Even that attitude was negative and she lectured herself and went back to bed. She didn't even need to pull the drapes anymore. The darkness here inside this room fit her mood. At least she'd been safe here. That was a plus, even if she'd spent more of her days than not fighting tears.

Her phone buzzing woke her up and she glanced at it in hopes it was the police, but it was Shane again. It seemed like he'd called ten thousand times. Even Gage had tried to call her on the second day. He'd left a message, but she knew she shouldn't check it. She didn't either until in the middle of the fourth night. She'd been so miserably down and decided that as long as she didn't answer back, at least she'd only be causing herself more pain.

She pushed the okay button to play the message and his mellow, low voice was unbelievably comforting. All he said was, "Skye. I know you had to go. But please know that I love you and I miss you and I'm so looking forward to when you can finally come home. However long it takes, I'll be here waiting. I'm praying for you to be safe. I hope you're okay. In the mix of everything, don't forget to look forward with that perfect brightness of hope and know that our Heavenly Father is going to help us through this. Choose happy and if you ever can, call me. Goodbye."

Oh, Gage. She knew he'd been trying to help her, but it made her cry harder than ever. He was so sweet, even when she'd been such a jerk to him. That was like him to love her in spite of what she'd done to him. He shouldn't think she was ever coming back. As long as Shane was out there, she would never be able to go home to Gage, and it had been more than three years. It felt like forever and she'd about given up hope that it wouldn't always be like this.

Turning back over, she buried her head in her pillow, trying to make even herself believe she wasn't crying so bitterly about a future that was looking more like a life sentence than ever.

Although it was the wee hours of the morning, her phone buzzed again and she knew without even looking that it was Shane. It had to be. No one else would be hounding her at this hour. Sadder than she could ever imagine being, and tired to the bone, she had finally had enough and pushed send and put the phone to her ear and said through her tears, "Shane, leave me alone. Please, just leave me alone. I can't live like this."

She paused to swallow a sob and then continued, "I'm never coming back to you, Shane. I'm sorry, but I could never do that after what you did. I can't. Please..." She couldn't even speak through the depth of emotion that felt like it was burying her. Finally, she whispered, "Please. Please. Just leave me alone."

She knew he was there, even though he hadn't said a word and just when she was going to push end, he quietly asked in almost as sad a tone as she had been using, "You really fell for him, didn't you?"

His question made her worry about him going after Gage and she replied, "It wouldn't matter if I did fall for someone, Shane. I can never have a relationship because of you. I have to live my life alone and afraid and on the run because you keep trying to hurt me in the name of love." The tears overcame her again before she could go on. "That isn't love, Shane. That isn't love to ruin someone's life."

He sounded as if he thought he was being sincere as he replied, "I'm better, Skye. I'm almost completely better. This time I really am going to stay clean and sober and I've been reading so much about anger management. I'll take care of you. We'll be happy again like we were. I swear it, Skye."

In her room in the dark, she nodded and said, "I hope you do get better, Shane. I truly do hope that for you. But don't think I'll ever be a part of your life, whether you're clean or not. After what you've done to me, I never, ever want to see you again, Shane. Ever. It's bad enough to have to face the scars you gave me everyday of my life. I'm never going to be with you. I'm sorry, but I could never do that. It was too much. Far too much. So please, just forget about me. Find a new girl who doesn't know what fear and pain is like. Be clean and sober for her. And please..." She never did get control of the tears and finally had to just try to say it through her sobbing, "Please just leave me alone."

She pushed end and then collapsed onto her pillow in despair. The thought of this life forever hurt too much to even be able to handle and she cried until her pillow was soaked and her body finally gave into exhaustion and she fell into a brief respite of sleep.

****

After hearing Skye crying so hard on the other end of the line, Shane held the phone almost woodenly without even pushing the end button. What had happened to her? She wasn't like this. She was the happiest person he'd ever known. She didn't cry. She couldn't cry. Even when he'd hurt her so badly, she hadn't cried like that. Something was terribly wrong.

He tossed the phone and got up to pace the ratty carpet of the motel room he'd been living in. It must have been that pretty boy chiropractor. He'd done something to her to make her this sad. Anger flared in Shane and he thought about going after Garrison again, but something nagged at the back of his mind and made him pause in his pacing.

Skye was his life. She'd been his life ever since he'd first seen her there on the sidewalk in front of the environmental sciences building with the sunshine turning her hair to glistening gold. She'd looked like an angel walking there smiling even though no one was with her. A beautiful, tempting, happy angel. She had been happy. She'd always been happy.

Even when she'd tried to talk him into getting help for the pills she'd done it happily. Never once until that day she'd tried to leave him and he'd lost it completely and hurt her so badly had he ever seen her unhappy.

He looked at the phone in his hand and swallowed hard. What had he done? Guilt hit him like a sledge hammer and he sat down abruptly on the edge of the bed. What had he done to happy, beautiful, glowing Skye? He thought back to the way her chiropractor had fought to protect her and he had to face the fact that a man who would place himself in danger to protect her literally with his life hadn't been the one to make Skye cry like she just had.

That morning Shane had shown up in her flower shop, until she'd seen him, she'd looked more happy and beautiful than ever. Garrison hadn't done this. Garrison wanted her to be happy as well. Even as fierce, hot jealousy tore at his heart, Shane had to admit the other man had done a much better job of making Skye happy. Shane loved her. He loved her like life itself, but he'd hurt her and done something even worse. He'd stolen her light. That sparkle that made Skye the most marvelous creature on earth.

Facing that fact made him absolutely sick at heart and he kicked at a shoe lying in the middle of the floor and went back to pacing, hating the moody shadow that crept in and overpowered the almost heady sense of hope he'd been living on ever since he'd found the information in her dad's office about where she was. For the first time in more than three years, he honestly wondered if he needed to give up his dreams of possessing Skye Alexander. Even considering that thought made him overwrought and he fought the urge to become raving mad with every ounce of strength he had in his heart and mind.

She abhorred that anger. He can still remember the look she had given him when he'd first lost it that day. It had been shock and pain and then raw, unadulterated horror as he'd blown his fuse like never before and taken it out on precious, beautiful Skye. He let out a dry sob as he remembered that awful day. She'd said she was leaving him and his universe had quaked on its axis and he'd flipped.

Memories of the harm he'd done ripped through his gut and that now discouragingly familiar urgent need for the chemicals reared its ugly head, just like it did every time he faced an issue that tested his character strength. The self loathing he always felt when he admitted his crushing weakness rushed in behind the guilt and the overpowering need and they all congealed to make him a living, breathing, worthless swirl of hopelessness.

He couldn't win this. Oh he fought it. He'd been fighting it for these years now, but he'd never won. He'd been clean for weeks, even months at a time, but every single time, he'd eventually given in to what he'd come to find was the inevitable insatiable need for those cursed little white pills. He reached over and turned out the light over the bed and dropped onto it in abject defeat. Maybe if he went to sleep right this minute, he'd wake up and the over powering need would be gone and have taken this unendurable guilt over what he'd done to Skye with it.

Pulling the pillow over his head, he willed sleep to come and tried to focus on anything but the need. Usually he tried to think of Skye when this happened. Thoughts of her were the only thing that had been able to push these feelings of being pulled inexorably into the sucking whirlpool of addiction again, but tonight thoughts of Skye brought only the crushing reality that he'd heard in her voice on the phone.

He didn't have any pills with him. He'd been so sure he had a handle on it this time. Knowing he was going to come and get Skye and take her home and they'd be happy together had given him the confidence to turn his back on the pills and believe he'd never feel this vortex pulling on him again.

When the pillow over his head made him crave oxygen as well as narcotics, he turned over to look at the crack in the curtains that let in a sliver of light from the street lamp beyond and he wondered again like he had so many million times before if he was ever going to be able to lick this. Was he ever truly going to be free of this smothering craving, or was he going to be facing this hell forever? They all said it was a life long battle, but he had to believe otherwise or it would swallow him whole. He couldn't do this forever. He couldn't.

Once Skye had told him to pray. That God was the only one who could take this unbearable struggle and give him back the strength to fight it. And he so wanted to believe that, but he couldn't face God with weakness like this. He was too ashamed to admit he was no better than an animal that couldn't control its urges. Even her assuring him that God and Jesus loved him anyway hadn't been enough to be able to face them. He always told himself that as soon as he had some control, he'd go to them.

He'd tried everything else he could begin to think of. The counseling had helped at times, but he couldn't do that constantly forever. After a while he quit listening anyway, even if he could have found a way to afford it.

Laying there on his cheap motel bed, his mind went round and then around again with the thoughts of how facing this monster of addiction went, but when it finally came full circle, and he couldn't handle it anymore, he wearily rolled off the bed. Pulling the last of his cash from the pocket of his jeans, he counted it and ran a hand through his wildly messed hair and then in utter defeat, went three doors down and pounded on the door. He'd only talked to the guy staying there a couple of times, but it was enough to know he'd have what he needed.

Chapter 17

The high school principal had been a little skeptical about helping Gage talk to Hailee until Gage had explained everything in depth and then had asked for the football coach to verify that he was associated with Hailee's boss. Gage had had to get permission from Hailee's parents to even get to talk to her, which was fine with him. It was reassuring to know that the system was looking out for the youth like this.

When he finally got a chance to talk to her, she actually burst into tears and then he was a little embarrassed in front of the school office staff. He had never figured out what to do with bawling females.

He was hoping to talk her into helping him open Skye's shop back up. There was still a chance Shane was around, but Gage hoped Hailee would be safe enough if he was there with her so she was never alone, and he'd have the off-duty police security around as well. He figured if Hailee could handle the flower arranging end of things, he'd try to hold down the fort on the business end so that when Skye came back she wouldn't have lost her whole investment. Even if all they did was keep it viable until whatever arrangements Skye had made for it were transacted, at least it would still be worth more for her. And what he was really hoping for was that Skye would come home soon and run it herself until she settled down to focus on that family she'd spoken of wanting.

That afternoon after school, he and Hailee met a locksmith at the door to Skye's apartment and attempted to break in. Even with a professional, it was a project and Gage was again reminded that Shane had been able to get in here without even leaving a sign of forced entry. He needed to be careful to never underestimate what the guy was capable of. While the locksmith changed all the locks and worked on the big gate in the front, he and Hailee went on into the shop to take stock.

He was dismayed at the shape all of Skye's big pots of flowers were in. Every single one of them was flat and wilted against the dirt from the lack of Skye's tender loving care. He and Hailee had looked at each other as they surveyed the poor things and then Hailee had shrugged and said, "All we can do is try to save some of them. Grab a jug."

With everything watered as well as possible, they moved on to the cooler and the display cases and began the serious task of hauling out the dead and dying flowers and cleaning up the mess. It had been ten days since that fateful morning when Skye had had to flee.

The shop phone rang while they were working and Hailee gave Gage a thumbs up as she took their first new order for a bouquet. As soon as the worst of the clean up was done, Hailee began to work on a flower order and Gage tackled the huge pile of mail that had stacked up just inside the door under the mail slot. For the time being, he would have to pay the bills out of his pocket, but that was the very least he was willing to do for Skye Alexander.

By the time he locked the doors of her shop and went home that night, he was amazed to see that although a few of the huge pots of flowers were hopelessly dead, most of them had perked right back up with the water they'd been given. Almost all of the blooms were gone, but hopefully even they would be able to be coaxed back eventually.

Gage had taken the four flower arrangements out of the backseat of his car and put them back in the shop, but all the way home, he could still smell the unique blend of flowers and Eucalyptus and whatever else it was that made her shop smell like her shop. It had been good to work toward keeping things afloat for Skye, but in a way this day had been bitter sweet. He wanted to do this for her, but without her there, the shop had lost something precious and vibrant.

He'd been trying to do the most unpleasant things so Hailee didn't have to, but he asked Hailee to be the one to empty Skye's fridge. Facing her apartment more than just to walk through it to get into the shop the first time was too hard. Even that small glimpse of her home without her in it made his heart feel like it had been through a paper shredder.
.

He wanted to do this for Skye, but there were a couple of things he wanted to do for himself as well and the next day, when he unlocked the doors, he had two books of photos from Ireland. He spent part of the morning cutting pictures out and literally plastering the work areas of the shop with them. When Skye finally did come back, he wanted her to be thinking of that trip to the Emerald Isle they'd talked about — that he'd spent a ridiculous amount of time dreaming about. He truly was expecting a miracle, but he wanted to nudge it along a little as well.

Every once in a while, when he'd begin to wonder if he was acting crazy, he'd remember how he'd felt when he'd woken up and believed he was being prompted to do all this and try to refocus and have faith again. Then when Hailee came in, he had her order wildflowers. He couldn't go hand pick them right now with a double booked life and a cast, but he wanted there to be wildflowers here when Skye came home.

That night, he stopped at the grocery store and bought several packages of Hershey's kisses, in all different flavors.

As he piled them onto Skye's work table the next morning, he hoped it didn't take her forever to make it home as excited as he was to be fixing things up for her. The last thing he did was buy two first class ticket vouchers to Ireland with negotiable dates and pin them onto her photo of the Irish seashore that hung beside her work table. This was the craziest thing of all, but he was stepping out on faith. He had to expect a miracle. Otherwise, he was going to go nuts without her.

He'd been going into his clinic early and then bringing work with him to Skye's shop and working on his laptop and even taking work from both places home with him at night. The crazy pace of trying to keep up with the clinic and the shop did help keep him from being so lonely, but he still wondered where she was and if she was okay at least a thousand times a day.

There was that time at night between when he laid down and when he finally fell asleep that he'd begun to think of as the haunting time. There were times when he wondered if Shane hadn't gotten to her after all and sometimes he wondered if she was even alive. The police said she was, although that was all they would tell him about her. He even tried to make Lieutenant Pederson feel like he owed him for saving his life, but he still couldn't get anything more out of them. Maybe that was for the best.

Unless she came home to him because she wanted to, any efforts to force her would be just as wrong as what Shane was doing. He still hated the fact that she had been able to leave him, even though he knew she had probably done it partly for him.

It had only been twelve days since Mama Woo's funeral, but by that Saturday night, it felt like it had been a year.

****

244

Skye knew she was literally making herself sick staying here inside this dark hotel room, but she honestly didn't have what it took to leave it either. She was dealing with clinical depression now and she knew it, but she couldn't seem to make herself go buy that car and head for wherever it was she was going to relocate. She hadn't even decided that. It had been twelve days since Mama Woo's funeral and she was still having trouble leaving the room to go to the exercise room and the pool without the stupid tears that were plaguing her.

She'd bought a few clothes at the hotel gift shop, and she usually went down stairs to eat now, although she wasn't hungry much and typically only made it down there a couple of times a day, if that. Twice she'd been out for a long walk down the sunny Las Vegas street and on the way back in had bought a couple of books to try to occupy her mind. The books had helped, but in all honesty, there wasn't a thing that made her want to get up out of bed in the morning.

This morning, as she looked into the mirror and admitted she looked like she was the one strung out on drugs, she finally knew she had to make a decision and get moving on it. She was pale, except for the horrible circles under her eyes and she'd lost far too much weight in that short time. Even her hair had lost any luster or body. Time in the shower and then in the pool had nearly trashed it as much as the rest of her was. She sighed and got dressed and then began to pack her things into her duffle. Maybe she'd just get the car and then get on the road and see where she ended up. It wasn't like it mattered anyway.

She plugged her phone in to charge up the battery. It had been dead for almost a day now and she didn't even care. She'd given up hope that the St. George police had ever found Shane. He would have left there by now and started looking elsewhere for her anyway. At least he'd quit trying to reach her twenty times a day. Even he had quit calling her after the one time she answered in the middle of the night.

Gage had only called once. Just once. She'd listened to his message a dozen times and then stopped. It was scrambling her judgment and slowly making her too discouraged to be able to face living without him and she knew she couldn't do that anymore. She'd never erased it, but she'd finally found the strength to quit torturing herself with it.

She zipped her bag closed and put it on the luggage rack and then went to brush her teeth. She might as well get this car purchase over with. As she picked up her key card and pushed it into her purse, her phone buzzed and she glanced over at it and froze. The St. George police. Almost afraid to hope, she hesitantly picked it up and pushed send.

What the officer on the line had to tell her was the only thing in the world that could have been worse than telling her they hadn't found Shane. He told her they had found Shane's body. Beside a suicide note addressed to Skye Alexander. At least they thought it was Shane. There was no ID and to make things even worse, they wanted her to come back to St. George to positively identify him before they sent the body back to his family.

Skye began to cry uncontrollably as the officer tried to explain that it hadn't really been her fault. Shane had admitted to feeling like he could never get the drug monkey off of his back and had only written to Skye to tell her he loved her and hoped his death would help to bring her happiness and start to make up for the damage he had done.

She was crying so hard that the officer Pederson paused and asked if she was going to be okay. She slowly nodded her head and then when he asked again, she realized he couldn't see her nod and choked out a strangled, "Yes."

Finally, the officer asked, "Ms. Alexander, can I send someone to get you? Are you still in Las Vegas? That's only an hour and a half. I don't think you should drive as upset as you are." Again Skye nodded and managed to tell him yes

246

and where to find her. Then she hung up and collapsed onto the bed in abject misery. He had killed himself. She thought her heart was going to break in two.

****

After knocking on Skye Alexander's hotel room door and having her open it looking like a holocaust survivor, Lieutenant Pederson had been almost a little freaked out. This woman had been drop-dead, breath-takingly gorgeous just over a week ago. Even at her dear friend's funeral after a hellacious week of stress she'd been exquisite. Now she looked like a shell of that girl. Feeling as if it was somehow personally his fault for first not catching this Cainan guy and then for having to tell her about his death, when she went to the front desk to finish checking out, he called Gage Garrison back in St. George but couldn't get him to pick up. This girl needed some help and fast. She looked awful, and the next couple of hours were possibly going to be the worst of all. Identifying a body wasn't typically a good experience, even if they hadn't left you a suicide note.

****

Gage climbed into his car to head home from the title company after having closed on the sale of his clinic. It should have been a moment of celebration. It was what he'd wanted for a while and he'd made a fortune on the deal, but without Skye, it somehow felt empty. Without her in his life, he wasn't sure what he was going to do with himself now that he was essentially unemployed. He still had his chiropractic practice, but with one arm casted, he had hired another chiropractor to take over full time.

He was thinking of stopping at Francesca's and getting clam chowder to take home. That's probably how he and Skye would have celebrated. He could at least feed the guy guarding his house and give a bowl to the dog. Kitty would probably love it. He glanced at his watch. It was only two-thirty in the afternoon and he decided going to Francesca's would only fillet his heart. He wasn't hungry anyway.

Putting the key into the ignition, he settled on just going home. He was frankly thoroughly depressed, even after closing on his clinic and he was just going to try to sleep it off. As he walked into his house, Kitty came to him, wagging for all she was worth. He leaned to pet her as his phone buzzed and he looked at it absently and then froze as he recognized Officer Pederson's number on the screen. Gage didn't realize he had missed a couple of calls from him and pushed send to call him back.

As Pederson started to speak, Gage had to sit down. "Dr. Garrison, I'm probably not supposed to be telling you this, but I think you need to know. There's something wrong with Ms. Alexander. We finally located Shane Cainan. Well, we located his body. We believe he killed himself. He left a suicide note for Ms. Alexander saying he didn't think he could ever get clean from drugs and decided killing himself would try to make up to her for what he's done. When I called her and told her about the note, she pretty well came unglued."

Gage stood back up and ground out, "You told her about some note? After what she's been through? Of course she came unglued! What did you expect her to do? Why would you even mention something like that?" Gage clenched a fist, rolled his eyes and mumbled, "Unbelievable. You people are a piece of work. You know that? Where is she?"

"Now just hold on, Gage."

Gage only asked louder, "Where is she?"

On the other end of the line, Pederson said, "She's here in St. George. We needed her to come and identify the body, but she got so upset . . ."

At that, Gage nearly shouted, "You needed her to what? You didn't. No way. You didn't really ask her to do that."

For a moment, there was only the sound of Gage taking big deep breaths to try to calm himself and then finally, Pederson said, "Look, Dr. Garrison. It may not have been the most prudent policy. I was simply following orders. That's why I'm calling you. She sounded bad when I called her. Then when we picked her up, she . . . Uh. She's not well. She looks awful. She's sick or something. And she didn't stop crying the whole way here from Vegas."

Again, Gage asked, "Where is she now?"

"I shouldn't . . ."

"Where is she?"

"I had an officer drop her at her apartment behind her shop half an hour ago. I think you should check on her."

Still shaking his head, Gage said, "I guarantee you I will." Stiffly, he added, "Thank you for the call." He hung up the phone in complete disgust with the police department, but grateful that at least they'd called him. Geez, Skye would be toast.

But, she was home. His attitude surged upward even as he tried to think this through. She was home at least for the moment, and Shane was no longer an issue, as sad as that was turning out to be. Gage was almost sick about that. He'd prayed and prayed for a miracle, but this didn't feel like a miracle. It felt like a boot to the chest. To Skye it would be absolutely devastating. His heart went out to her even as he could feel the energy begin to flow steadily back into his life. Skye was here somewhere.

His gut reaction was to rush to his car and fly to her shop, but he made himself pause for a minute and think. He wished he'd have known so he could have been with her when she'd had to identify Shane's body. And if she'd been dropped at her apartment half an hour ago, she'd had more than enough chance to see what they'd done, and the photos, wildflowers, kisses and the plane tickets. But she hadn't called. Was that good? Or really bad? He picked his phone back up and dialed Hailee at the shop with the officer who was watching over it.

She answered with a pleasant, professional, "Miss Daisy's."

Gage hesitated and then asked, "Hailee, where's Skye? She's been there, hasn't she?"

The professional tone disappeared instantly as Hailee burst into the phone, "Oh my gosh, Gage! She's a complete mess! You wait 'til you see her! She's really sick and she started to cry when she saw the place and she never quit! I mean, we're talking rivers of tears! Oceans of tears!"

"Happy tears? Or sad tears?"

"I don't know. I don't think happy ones. She looked like she'd already been crying for a year before she even got here."

"Where is she?"

"I don't know that either. She took those plane tickets and the tin soldier and then hugged me for like forever and got in the van and just left. I didn't even ask where she was going. She was so in a fog anyway that I don't know if she would have even answered. Do you think she's okay? Do we need to call the police again? What if that guy finds her while she's this hammered?"

Gage's door bell rang and he couldn't help smiling at Hailee's theatrics, in spite of the anxiousness he was feeling in his gut. Walking toward the door, he said, "Look, Hai, I gotta go. Someone's at the door. If you see her again, call me. If I do, I'll call you."

"Do you think it could be her?"

"Gotta go, Hai. I'll let you know."

Kitty was standing in front of the door wagging herself nearly to death. She actually even let out a small bark, which he'd never seen her do before and it made Gage's heart skip a beat just for a second. He said a lightning fast silent prayer and then opened the door.

Chapter 18

Skye was standing there on the porch and she truly did look sick, but Gage had never seen such a beautiful sight in his life. For a moment he hesitated, not sure what to do and then Skye started to cry again. He stepped onto the porch and pulled her into the tightest, sweetest hug ever as Kitty stood almost on their feet trying to join in. Skye was home. Oh, but she felt like heaven.

He wasn't sure how long he'd been holding her, just letting her cry, but his shirt was plastered to him with tears and the lady across the street had come out to get her mail and was now peeking out of her front drapes at them. Stepping back, Gage kept an arm around Skye and shepherded her and Kitty into the house and to the great room where he pulled her onto his lap in a double recliner. For another several minutes, he simply held her and rubbed her back as she cried. When she finally looked up her eyes held unbearable heartache as she whispered, "He killed himself."

Nodding, Gage pulled her back in close. "I know, honey. I'm so sorry. I've been praying for a miracle, but I didn't want that. Anything but that."

She reached into her pocket and handed him a copy of the note as she added, "He said he did it for me."

Gage scanned the note and was once more disgusted with the local law enforcement. Why had they told her about this note? They could have left that detail out.

Trying for some damage control, he said, "Shane said he didn't ever think he could get out from under the drugs, Skye, so it wasn't all for you. And if he was willing to give his life to help you, he must have really, truly loved you. He just couldn't show it very well, honey"

He touched her cheek and continued softly, "Skye, listen. I know this is heart breaking. It's the worst. It is. And I'm so sorry. But try to remember he's in a better place now. Our Father in Heaven will take into account how sick he was. God understands how hard addictions are. And Shane is finally free of that struggle. It had to have been hell. He's finally free. And Shane knows how you're feeling. He must have loved you and just got a little twisted. He wanted to set you free and as sad as it is, he has helped you. He knew he was hurting you and did his best. It was a horrible way to help you, but it must have been the only thing he knew to do. In a way, it's the purest form of devotion. He loved you more than even life."

She nodded and he pulled her head to his chest and kept a gentle hand on her hair and let her cry again. After several more minutes, she began to wind down and he was amazed when he looked down and realized she had fallen asleep. Poor girl. The struggles in her life had gone from tough, to awful, to gut wrenching in the last weeks. He leaned his head back and pushed with a foot to gently rock the recliner. At least now, it was hopefully over for good and she could begin to heal her heart.

He glanced down and was appalled at the dark circles under her eyes. Pederson was right, she needed some care desperately. Well, he had forever to care for her. He snuggled her tighter and kissed her hair and smiled when Kitty climbed right into the recliner with them and then reached up and licked at the tears on Skye's cheeks. He carefully reached for his phone and texted Hailee and assured her Skye was with him and was going to be okay.

****

She could smell Gage and for the first time in what felt like years, she felt peace. It had been so long it was almost strange. Strange, but heavenly. She slowly opened her tired eyes and realized she really was snuggled with him in his great room. Her eyes widened as she realized Kitty was practically on his lap with her. Skye started to lift her head and also realized Gage had a cast on his arm. That must have registered when she first saw him, but apparently not very well. He truly had gotten hurt that day at the cemetery.

She put a gentle hand on the cast and snuggled closer under his neck, trying not to let knowing he'd been hurt because of her make her cry again as she murmured, "I'm so sorry you got hurt." That incessant need to cry had finally ebbed and she hoped she never shed another tear in her life.

With his chin on her hair, he only said, "No worries, Skye. I'm fine. Now."

Looking up, she found him watching her and she looked into his eyes, wishing she didn't look so thrashed. She was a wreck, but that wasn't changing the look she was seeing in his eyes. She tried to smile as she quietly accused, "You're letting my dog get on your furniture."

He simply watched her for another second and then said, "She's so happy to have you back that she needed to be as close as she could to you. Like me." He touched her cheekbone with a fingertip. "Welcome home."

Letting her head rest back on his chest again, she admitted softly, "I thought you'd be so mad at me for leaving and not even checking to see if you were okay, that you'd never want to see me again."

He pushed the recliner gently. "I hope you didn't really think that, Skye. I hope you know me well enough by now that you know you could never do anything that would make me never want to see you again."

She looked up into his eyes and said, "I have all this baggage, Gage. I mean, you know that, but..."

"Who doesn't have baggage, Skye?"

"But I . . . How can you . . . "

"And you never let it keep you from dancing in the rain."

He kissed her forehead and then glanced down at her mouth, and she said, "You're looking at me like that again."

"Like what?"

"Like a guy."

"Honey, I am a guy."

"I'm a little worried about that."

He grinned at her. "Nah, you can handle it."

She smiled hesitantly at him and then was thoughtful for a moment. Finally, she asked, "Does it rain much in Ireland?"

He leaned and kissed her tenderly on the mouth.

When he eventually pulled away, he said, "It rains a lot in Ireland. We're going to dance in it."

The End

About the author

Jaclyn M. Hawkes grew up with 6 sisters, 4 brothers and any number of pets. (It was never boring!) She got a bachelor's degree, had a career as a cartographer with the federal government, and traveled extensively before settling down to her life's work of being the mother of four magnificent and sometimes challenging children. She loves shellfish, Meat Lover's pizza, the out-of-doors, the youth, and hearing her children laugh. She and her extremely attractive husband, their younger children, and their happy dogs, now live in a mountain valley in northern Utah, where it smells like heaven and kids still move sprinkler pipe.

To learn more about Jaclyn, visit www.jaclynmhawkes.com.

Author's Note

I got perfect straight A's in college in my floral design classes. (Wait. Didn't I get straight A's in all my classes? Let me think. My memory dims. Ahem. I digress. Sorry.)

For a while there, I thought being a florist would be really fun. And it would be—most of the time. Then, I decided to actually try it out and worked as a temporary at a florist over Valentine's Day week.

Holy exhaustion! My fingers were all but bloody and even then, in my most buff and physically fit day, my lower back was toast.

Needless to say, my husband and I didn't have a very romantical Valentine's Day that year. Any need I had to switch careers and become a florist wilted with all the bouquets I put together that grueling week.

Since then, every once in a while I help out with the occasional wedding, and I love to arrange the flowers I grow, but I've never wanted to be a florist again. Still, that experience came in very handy in the writing of this book.

Mostly these days, I just thoroughly enjoy being blessed to be an at-home mom. It's been so much more rewarding than my "real career" was with the federal government. I give eternal thanks to my husband for always supporting and appreciating the decision to retire and come home.

As for the fruits of my labor, in spite of being raised by a lunatic mom, my kids are awesome! (Probably because of my secret weapon—their father!) They are marvelous! Way to be, guys!